Back in Black

Back in Black

An A-List Novel

by
Zoey Dean

LITTLE, BROWN AND COMPANY
New York ✢ Boston

Little, Brown and Company

Time Warner Book Group
1271 Avenue of the Americas, New York, NY 10020
Visit our Web site at www.lb-teens.com

First Edition: September 2005

 Produced by Alloy Entertainment
151 West 26th Street, New York, NY 10001

ISBN 0-316-01092-8

10 9 8 7 6 5 4 3 2 1

CWO

Printed in the United States of America

For Princess Roz and Princess Bella

The problem with people who have no vices is that generally you can be pretty sure they're going to have some pretty annoying virtues.

—Elizabeth Taylor

Glitterati

"**W**elcome to the Academy Awards," Samantha Sharpe told her friend Anna Percy. She gestured with a flourish toward the endless red carpet that led to the front of the palatial Kodak Theatre. "Or, as I like to call it, *The Young and the Desperate*."

"They don't look desperate," Anna observed, taking in the paparazzi snapping photos of the early arrivals, the reporters shoving microphones into the practiced smiles of perfectly coiffed celebrities. From bleachers on both sides of the carpet, fans who'd camped out for days to get seats waited with anticipation for their favorites.

"But they do look young, and most of them *so* aren't," Sam replied over the noise. "Thus proving that it's all smoke and mirrors."

"And plastic surgery," Anna added.

It seemed as if every other person Anna had met since she'd moved to Beverly Hills had had work done, including a lot of her classmates at Beverly Hills High School. None of them admitted it, of course. But show-

ing up after vacation with a different nose ("I had a
deviated septum; that's the only reason I did it"),
sudden cleavage ("I just developed late"), or newly
toned former thunder thighs ("I'm doing South Beach,
plus I found this amazing cream that melts cellulite")
was so commonplace as to be banal.

Anna had not been a part of this world for very long.
In some ways it was completely different from the tony
life on the Upper East Side of Manhattan into which
she'd been born and bred. And in other ways it was
nearly the same. Plastic surgery abounded on both
coasts, certainly: the pressure to look young and thin.
But what impressed people on one coast made those on
the other either yawn or roll their eyes. For example, in
Anna's former world, a gallery opening by an artist no
one had discovered yet, or a book reading by an author
who had been, say, a former political prisoner, was considered the height of hip. In this new world, such things
were barely comprehended. It was all about TV and
movies, glitter and glitz. And the pièce de résistance of
it all was the Academy Awards.

Sam shook her newly highlighted chestnut hair off
her shoulders. "Trust me, under the Botox and the
couture, they're sweating bullets—at least, they would
be if they hadn't had their armpits Botoxed, too."

Anna laughed. "No one really does that, do they?"

"You'd be surprised," Sam confided.

Anna had dined with royalty, but tonight she'd rub
elbows with royalty of an entirely different sort, thanks

to her friendship with Sam Sharpe. That was how she had come to be strolling the most famous red carpet in the world—the one laid down on Hollywood Boulevard in Los Angeles, the one that led directly into the Kodak Theatre—on Oscar night.

Well, Oscar afternoon. Sam had explained it all to Anna as they'd prepared for the event. In order to meet the requirements of international television—the world's most important motion-picture awards ceremony was seen by a worldwide audience that reputedly reached a billion—the preshow broadcasts kicked off while the sun was still high in the late winter sky.

That the event was called Oscar *night* was hardly the most dishonest thing about it. The intersection of Hollywood Boulevard and Highland Avenue, where the Kodak Theatre was located, was normally a very seedy place, but it had undergone a makeover for the television audience's viewing pleasure. The tarot card reader shops, tattoo parlors, fast-food joints, and Hollywood tchotchke storefronts had been wrapped in enough fresh cotton fabric to make Christo proud. Potted plants and shrubbery had been imported to line the red carpet, along with dozens of oversized replicas (hollow, of course—people had to lift the damn things, after all—but correctly proportioned) of the coveted Oscar statue itself. Once the celebrities stepped out of their limousines, they were inside an artificial Oscar world.

Anna gave her friend an encouraging smile. "Hey,

we're the observers, not the observed," she pointed out. "We can relax."

"Yeah, right, with all these photographers around?" Sam scoffed. "And I swear, if my father doesn't win this year, I'm gonna kill someone. That'll make a great picture for tomorrow's *Los Angeles Times*."

Anna nodded. She had conventional (albeit long-divorced) rich parents by East Coast standards—her father was an investment banker and adviser; her mother came from the oldest of old-money families and mostly spent her time getting to know intimately the young wunderkind artists whose work she loved to acquire. Sam, on the other hand, came from a Hollywood family. Her father was Jackson Sharpe, one of the most beloved movie stars in the world. An action hero in the mold of Harrison Ford but quite a bit younger, Jackson was pure box-office gold. Put him in one of those films where a lot of shit got blown up and the script didn't call for much character development, and a movie studio basically guaranteed itself a franchise.

"I should, you know," Sam argued. "This is his third nomination. It's getting worse than Martin Scorsese. Of course, the assholes in this town are probably rooting for him to lose."

"Sam, hi!" Sheryl called as she got out of her limo.

Sam waved. "My dad did a huge fund-raiser for cancer research with her," Sam explained to Anna. "Be right back."

As Sam went to chat with the singer, Anna peered

down the carpet toward the huge white theater—actually, a complex that housed the theater. The carpet itself covered the entire street and was divided down the center with a red velvet rope. An event security person was positioned every few feet. On either side of the walkways the event organizers had erected tiers of bleachers. The seats were already filled with photographers, studio employees, and obsessed movie fans who could both pass a background check and were willing to wait in line long enough to get an up-close-and-personal glimpse of their favorite stars. Sam had brought Anna reasonably early so that she could get the full gestalt of the event.

It had actually been tremendous fun, getting ready for the awards. The week before, Anna had purchased a new evening gown for the occasion—something she rarely did, because she preferred the vintage Chanels and Diors handed down from her maternal grandmother.

But Sam had insisted that they shop together. "Shopping" in this case had meant that a stylist had brought a selection of gowns over to the Sharpe compound, size four for Anna, size . . . well, larger than size four for Sam. When Anna had suggested that it might be easier to visit some of the boutiques on Rodeo Drive or Melrose Avenue, Sam had informed her that dresses for the Oscars definitely did not come off the rack.

Anna had ended up with a strapless white satin Vera Wang, with an elegantly simple neckline that was modest in the front but dipped down to just above her butt in the back. With it, she wore her maternal grand-mother's perfect pearls and the diamond stud earrings her paternal grandmother had given her on her six-teenth birthday. Her blond hair hung straight and shiny to her shoulders.

Sam, who always worried about her weight—by Beverly Hills standards, she was a long way from thin (read: she took a size ten or twelve)—had insisted on wearing black: an Oscar de la Renta with a low-cut neckline lined in lime chiffon. It matched her lime-and-black polka-dot Charles David pumps with black patent leather stiletto heels. She was dripping diamonds loaned to her by Harry Winston, as befitted the daughter of a famous star. The twenty-thousand-dollar diamond Cartier watch on her left wrist was her own. It was a gift from her father after the birth of his and Sam's new stepmother Poppy's baby, Ruby Hummingbird.

Oscar day—well, Oscar morning—had been a frenzy of preparation, Beverly Hills style. Anna and Sam had started at the Thibiant day spa on North Canon Drive, with contouring clay wraps, which included twenty-five-minute lymphatic-drainage massages followed by full-body clay masks to eliminate any surface toxins. These were followed by papaya-pineapple-enzyme exfoliations, which themselves were precursors to add-on collagen masks. Following longer massages, manicures, and pedi-cures, the pair had exited onto the sunny streets of Beverly Hills utterly transformed.

They hadn't been the only Oscar attendees in

Thibiant. Sam had pointed out Mena Suvari and Elisha Cuthbert and had even introduced Anna to Elise West, a major executive at one of the big movie studios.

After such pampering, Sam had insisted that lunch be pure and healthy. She'd taken them to dine at the Inn of the Seventh Ray up in Topanga Canyon. Located in a dell amid the Santa Monica mountains, the restaurant featured outdoor seating and a menu that included macrobiotic offerings. Sam had ordered a wholly vegetarian meal that had turned out to be remarkably delicious. Then they'd driven back to Beverly Hills, taken a quick swim in the Sharpe pool, and dressed for the Oscars.

"Oh my God, is that who I think it is?!"

The screeching voice was loud enough to stand out from the crowd, and it made Anna turn, only to realize that the young woman with the amazingly adenoidal vocal cords seemed to be looking directly at her.

Anna looked behind her, but no one stood there.

"It *is* her!" the screaming girl's friend cried, grabbing the first girl's arm in her excitement. Then she snapped Anna's picture. "Hey! Can we get your autograph?"

Anna had no idea what to say or do. But fortunately the crowd's attention, including that of her two admirers (mistaken as they might have been), shifted to the woman alighting from the latest limo.

"Sandra! Sandra! Over here!"

Anna turned to see a glowing brunette step out of a white limousine.

"Yves Saint Laurent," Sam decreed of Sandra's green

brocade halter-top gown as she returned to Anna's side. "Fifteen grand. Know why she's here now?"

"That's obvious, Sam: for the awards."

"Of course for the awards. But why would she get here at four o'clock when the show doesn't start until six? It's 'cause she's got a new movie that's opening in three weeks, and she wants E! to do a really long interview with her. If she arrives early, there's a better chance she won't be upstaged by someone like Nicole Kidman."

Anna was bemused. Who would have imagined putting so much thought into when you arrived at the Oscars? But Sam was evidently right, pointing out the arrivals of Penelope Ann Miller, Mischa Barton, and Carmen Electra in rapid succession. Anna, who spent more time with the poems of Elizabeth Barrett Browning than she did at her local Blockbuster, didn't recognize any of them.

"Ready for the show?" Sam asked.

Anna looked at her watch. The awards didn't start for another hour and forty-five minutes. Sam saw the baffled expression on her face.

"I mean the preshow show," Sam explained. "Let's get drinks and find a place to sit. I promise you that in sixty minutes, it's going to be more crowded on this red carpet than the subway in Manhattan at rush hour, everybody looking faaaabulous, darling. It'll be a hoot, you'll see."

An hour later, the red carpet was essentially impassable, a celebrity-strewn madhouse. Anna and Sam stood near the north-side bleachers, away from the late afternoon sun. As they took it all in, Sam provided the running fashion commentary.

"Julia! Who's home with the twins tonight?" a reporter yelled as Julia Roberts edged down the carpet. Her answer was nothing more than her famous wide smile, perfectly framed by a simple, understated black dress with a sheer bodice.

"Carolina Herrera," Sam discerned. "Designed for her."

To Anna's left, a TV producer was trying to lasso a pop star whom even Anna recognized for an interview.

"Britney! Come be interviewed by Melissa Rivers! Melissa would love an interview!"

Britney Spears and her escort moved toward the hostess, who was in the midst of an interview with an actor whom Sam told Anna was Antonio Banderas.

"It's like a shark tank," Anna observed, watching the insanity unfold.

"During a feeding frenzy," Sam added. "Celebrity heaven."

"Wait, that's what's-her-name!" a teenage girl with a mouthful of braces boomed to her friend. She thrust a finger in Anna's direction. "We love you!" she yelled.

"We totally love you!" her friend echoed.

Anna turned to Sam, slightly embarrassed. "I have no idea who they think I am."

Sam waved at the girls. "Me neither, so just smile and wave and they'll be on to the next."

Feeling ridiculous, Anna gave the girls a small wave,

which made them grab each other and squeal.

Sure enough, as Jennifer Aniston got out of her limo, the girls' focus shifted. After that, Sam ticked the names off of other arriving celebrities: Tom Hanks. Mena Suvari in Dolce & Gabbana. Julie Delpy in Dior.

"Wait, there's my dad." Sam jerked her chin toward a gold limo that had just pulled up to the carpet. "Which means that even now, the Stepmother from Hell is probably on her cell, cooing to her evil spawn."

"You can't hate a new baby, Sam," Anna chided.

"Wanna bet?"

Anna let it drop. Sam was just nervous on her father's behalf, she decided.

"My theory," Sam continued, "is that Poppy's we-need-our-own-limo thing happened after she found out I invited you. She figured that leggy-blond-patrician-beauty thing of yours would make her look like the overripe, undereducated melon ball she really is."

"That's kind of harsh, Sam. She just had a baby."

"Unwritten Hollywood rule: Stars don't come out in public until they've lost their baby weight. Every ounce. What do you think of the limo? The Pop-Tart insisted on gold. She had them paint it just for tonight so that it would match her gold satin-and-velvet Versace gown, designed to hide the extra fifteen pounds on her ass."

"Come on, Sam, give her a break."

Sam grinned wickedly. "Imagine Stepmommy Dearest's dilemma: Miss the Academy Awards where her husband might actually win, or show up looking like a cow. She chose the heifer look. Before you tell me to chill out, remember that Poppy said the best thing I could do for my father tonight was not show up."

Anna winced. "Ouch." She knew that Sam felt neglected by her father, especially now that Ruby Hummingbird was on the scene. Now she had to share him not only with his child bride but also with a new baby. But Anna stayed silent. Discretion, she knew, was the better part of most things, including friendship.

Since Anna had moved from New York to Beverly Hills on New Year's Eve, Sam was just about the only real friend she'd made. Here in the land of vipers masquerading as people, friendship was something that Anna knew should be guarded at all costs. Sometimes honesty was not at all the best policy.

Outside the Well-Bred-East-Coast-WASP Box

Each arriving celebrity had been greeted with Oscar-worthy accolades, but the reception for America's most beloved movie star, Jackson Sharpe, was what Anna had imagined would be reserved for conquering heroes returning from battle. The crowded bleachers erupted with cheers and applause. Every TV camera crew rushed to him. Even the other movie stars on the red carpet seemed to stop in their tracks to take in the image of the great one himself as the gold limousine pulled up at the edge of the red carpet. Jackson—tall, rangy, and with his colored-by-Raymond-but-nobody-had-any-idea chestnut brown hair swept straight back, wearing an Armani tuxedo with a quirky purple bow tie and cummerbund—stepped out, then helped his young wife from the limo.

Poppy took his arm. The fans screamed even louder.

"What do you think?" Sam asked Anna, making a face somewhere between a smile and a smirk.

"I wish my friend Cyn could see this," Anna told her.

In fact, Anna was tempted to open her Nokia cell phone right then and call her best friend from New York, Cynthia Baltres. She'd long ago decided that Sam would adore Cyn, who was an over-the-top kind of girl with a great sense of the absurd. Cyn loved wild and crazy antics at scenes like this one. In fact, conservative Anna had been known to live vicariously through Cyn, who was willing to test life's limits.

One of the many reasons that Anna had chosen to move to California and live with her father was to test some limits of her own. That had happened quicker than she'd ever imagined. On the plane from New York, she'd met the most fabulous guy, Ben Birnbaum. Theirs had been the kind of instant attraction that fueled the sentiments of so many of the pre-post-modern poems she loved. Ben had been her first . . . her first *everything*. But now Ben was back at Princeton, where he was a freshman. She was in California. And Anna didn't know what they were anymore, since they'd parted so badly.

She'd had other boyfriends since Ben. But somehow, she kept thinking about him, coming back to him. Maybe it was only because he'd been her first. Or maybe . . . well, maybe it was more.

Anna sighed. Here she and Sam were, standing at the edge of the red carpet at the Academy Awards, gazing at the world's biggest movie stars each taking their moment in the sun. Millions of people all over the world would have killed to switch places with her. And she was in overanalysis overdrive. *Stop*, she told herself. *Think later. Live in the moment. Enjoy this.*

"I can understand that you wish Cyn could see this," Sam agreed. "I wish Eduardo could, too."

Eduardo Munoz was Sam's boyfriend. He was tall, dark, handsome, rich, brilliant, and international. Shockingly—to Sam, anyway—he truly thought Sam was gorgeous. They had met at the Las Casitas resort in Mexico back in February. He'd taken her horseback riding on the beach and then to an open-air lunch on an island. He'd shown up in Los Angeles to see her instead of flying back to France for school and had sent her roses every Wednesday, to celebrate their having met on a Wednesday. But right now, Eduardo was studying international relations at a university in Paris, so he and Sam had a long-distance relationship.

"Have you talked to him?" Anna asked.

"All the time. By phone. But it leaves something to be desired. Actually, a lot to be desired. He's nine thousand miles away right now. Anyway, tell me the Popsicle doesn't look like a fat sausage in that dress," Sam chortled gleefully. Anna saw Poppy hanging on to Jackson, who'd stopped to sign some autographs for fans. "Star Jones will have a field day!"

"Be nice," Anna chided.

"Why be nice when someone could say the same thing about me?" Sam sucked in her gut and turned back to Anna. "I'm so freaking bloated. Why did I eat all that salted popcorn last night?"

"You look great," Anna assured her with complete sincerity. Sam's dress really was extremely flattering. In a place like New York City, where you didn't get points deducted for each ounce you were over the norm, Sam might even have been described this night as dazzling.

"You'd say I looked great even if my tits were shaking hands with my navel."

Anna laughed. "Gee, I think I'd offer more . . . *support* than that."

"Your problem is that you think good manners are more important than the truth." Sam bared her Chiclet-white, Rembrandt-enhanced veneers for Anna's inspection. "No lip gloss on my teeth?"

"Perfection."

"Liar." Sam pointed at Anna. "Now you, you bitch goddess, look like a young Grace Kelly. Which if you weren't my friend would make me hate the water you walk on."

Anna made a face. "I'm assuming that's a compliment?"

"You are so hopeless," Sam sighed. "You probably have no idea what Grace Kelly looked like."

Anna admitted that she did, but only because she'd been to Monaco for a state dinner at the palace where the classic American actress had once been a princess. She had never been big on movies, current or retro. Literature, yes—American, British, and French. But movies had never been that important to her. They'd always seemed somehow . . . disposable.

"Okay, you know Gwyneth Paltrow?" Sam asked.

"She's standing over to the left by those reporters. And you know Kate Hudson? She's with her mother, Goldie Hawn, about fifty feet to our right. Goldie's the one in the red dress. Check them out."

Anna did. "Okay."

"Cross them. That's you, with blonder hair." Sam gestured toward the crowd. "Those girls already thought you were someone-or-other. You have that look."

Before Anna could say that she seriously doubted that, Jackson Sharpe was in front of them. His smile was broad, but Anna thought he looked a little bit worried.

"Sam. Wow, sweetie, you look great." He kissed his daughter's cheek. "Hey, Anna, how's it going?"

"Fine," Anna replied. "This is fascinating."

"I hate wearing the damn tux, frankly," Jackson confided.

"Stop complaining, Dad," Sam instructed, then straightened the bow tie of his made-to-order Armani tux.

A few feet away, Poppy was engrossed in a conversation with a very pregnant, much older woman in black maternity clothes. Anna thought she recognized her as the mother of one of the students at her high school and wondered momentarily if the woman had taken fertility drugs.

"Nervous, Dad?"

Jackson gave them his best movie-star grin. "Razzle-dazzle 'em, babe. See you from the stage. Where are you sitting?"

"Second tier," Sam reported.

"Aww." Jackson's smile didn't budge. "If I win, next year I'll get you downstairs."

"When you win," she corrected him.

Jackson gave his daughter and Anna a big thumbs-up, then went to get Poppy. A moment later, Anna saw them both corralled by a reporter from the E! channel.

"Notice how Stepmommy Dearest is standing half behind my father to make her hips looks smaller on TV?" Sam pointed out. "What a hoot." She turned to Anna, frowning at the red carpet at the same time. During the last five minutes, it had grown noticeably more crowded. "Okay, this is the part I hate. We walk the plank. The media scrutinizes me. They all suck."

"Want me to hold your hand?" Anna teased.

Sam wagged a finger at Anna. "Just remember that someday when I'm a famous director and Sofia Coppola's Q rating is in the toilet and I've just come back from two weeks at Le Spa and I'm to-die-for skinny, they'll all be falling at my feet."

"I'll remember," Anna promised. She was a little nervous herself, having already been mistaken for a celebrity. She definitely didn't want to have her friends in New York calling to say that they'd seen her interviewed by Star Jones.

Sam took a deep breath and linked her arm through Anna's; they started down the red carpet in earnest. "I didn't think I'd be this freaked. Do you know how much fatter TV makes you look?"

"You look fantastic, Sam, honestly."

Sam squeezed Anna's arm with her own, in gratitude.

"Sam Sharpe!" someone yelled. "Marilyn Haskell, for *Inside Access*. "Sam has arrived with Hollywood's newest 'It' girl!"

"*It*" girl? Anna thought.

A young woman in her twenties made a beeline for them, a camera crew in tow. Her red hair had been flat-ironed into submission. As Sam steeled herself, Anna hung back. For one thing, she had zero interest in being interviewed, either as herself or as whoever it was people kept mistaking her for. For another, she didn't want to steal Sam's thunder.

"This is the daughter of Jackson Sharpe, the great one himself, who's been nominated once again for best actor," Marilyn gushed. "Sam, that dress is smokin'. Who is it?"

"De la Renta," Sam replied as the red light of the television camera glinted off her face. Anna watched her friend smile hugely. "What about you, Marilyn?"

"Bebe! And the bling was made by my younger sister in Oregon. Hey, it looks like you took off a few pounds since that *Vanity Fair* article a few months ago," Marilyn continued to gush in the same over-the-top tone. "That's fantastic." She looked over at Anna. "So I noticed you two were arm-in-arm on your way down the carpet." Marilyn poked her microphone toward Anna. "So are you two, like, *together*? Because you certainly look like you're *together*."

"I don't know," Anna responded innocently. "Are

you?" Anna looked back and forth between Marilyn and one of the cameramen.

Marilyn's smile grew forced. "You're the one being interviewed."

"Why do you say that? Are you embarrassed by the nature of your relationship?" Anna asked.

Marilyn frantically looked past Anna and bellowed, "Kirsten! Kirsten Dunst! Hey, over here, Kirsten! It's Marilyn Haskell, *Inside Access*!"

As the reporter scuttled away, Sam pulled Anna down the carpet, laughing so hard she had to gasp for breath. "That was priceless."

"My mother always told me that if someone asks you an incredibly rude question, instead of answering, ask them a question in return," Anna explained with a chuckle. "Remember that."

"I will." Sam chortled. "It rocks. Of course, it helps when it comes from the lips of a girl so cool she doesn't appear to have bodily functions. The new 'It' girl, no less."

Anna laughed. "Right. That's me."

They finally reached the security tent, stepped inside, and showed their credentials. They'd be sitting two levels up, near the front. With luck, they'd be able to see Jackson make his way to the stage. To her surprise, Anna felt her heart start to race with excitement. She hadn't figured that Oscar night—afternoon, evening, whatever—would have that kind of effect on her, but it was as if the crowd and the anticipation and even reporters like Marilyn Haskell had conspired to hijack her emotions. She grinned spontaneously, because she understood just what was going on.

She was having fun.

Make out in an airplane lavatory with a guy you just met on the airplane? Check.

Have sex for the first time? Check.

Attend the Academy Awards with the daughter of a superstar? Check.

Perhaps it wasn't quite as personally dazzling and life-altering as the have-sex-for-the-first-time thing, but Anna could not deny that attending the Oscars with the daughter of Jackson Sharpe was well outside the well-bred-East-Coast-WASP box. And outside that box was exactly where she wanted to be.

Crushed Velvet

"**S**am? Anna? Hey, how's it going?"

They were standing toward the back of the third level of the rapidly filling Kodak Theatre. Anna had been impressed when she came in—she'd been in many of the world's great performing spaces, but the enormous Kodak rivaled them all. The dominant color theme was red, and there was more crushed velvet than at a bad Italian wedding. There were three huge sections of red seats down below, while the tiers themselves swept around in a semicircle several hundred feet from the football-field-size stage. Everything still smelled new, since the theater was just a few years old.

Anna and Sam turned to see Parker Pinelli hustling down the aisle. With his dirty-blond hair, intense blue eyes, and cleft chin, Parker was a spectacular-looking guy and an aspiring actor. He was a friend from Beverly Hills High School, and Anna had learned through a number of conversations with him that his gifted appearance fronted a less-than-gifted intelligence. On the other hand, intelligence wasn't everything—Parker had always been very nice to her. He really seemed like a decent guy.

"Parker," Sam declared. "What are you doing here?"

"Seat-filler," he explained, with a grin almost as bright as Jackson Sharpe's. "Until I get my own nomination."

Anna regarded him blankly. "Seat-fill—"

"Seat-filler," Sam explained, waving her arms over the expanse of upholstered seats that spread out down to the main stage. "Basically, glorified props. Gil Cates—he's the producer of the show—hires people to fill the seats when actors or presenters have to go to the bathroom, or to do whatever, or when they're backstage. How would a bunch of empty seats look to the billion people watching on TV?"

Anna nodded, though she wondered why the television cameras just didn't focus on another part of the audience.

Parker smiled. "Last year I sat in for Ben Stiller for the last half hour. I heard a rumor he went to the Hollywood Coffee Bean and never came back. Renée Zellweger was in front of me, Angelina Jolie was behind me. How killer is that?" He smiled at the memory. "So, you guys up for Vegas?"

An announcement over the theater's speaker system reported that there were just twenty minutes until the show began; Anna wasn't sure she had heard Parker correctly over the noisy crowd and loud announcement. "What about Las Vegas?"

"Come on, Anna," Sam insisted. "I told you. The senior trip thingie."

Anna had heard about the senior trip. Later that week, the entire graduating class of Beverly Hills High—herself included—would be going to Washington, D.C., for several days. She'd already sent in her check for fifteen hundred dollars. Not that a trip to the nation's capital was a big deal. She'd been there at least a dozen times, including one time last year when she'd dined with Senators Clinton and Schumer and another time when she'd attended President Bush's first inauguration; her parents were smart enough to donate to both political parties.

"The senior trip is to Washington," Anna reminded them, though she was sure they needed no reminder. "I don't know anything about Las Vegas."

"You will." Parker took her arm lightly and edged her toward the seats so that the people in the aisle could pass more easily. Then he pointed across the theater. "See that skinny brunette standing near Charlize Theron? I auditioned with her once. Total space cadet."

Sam smiled. "I heard the brunette turned into this total coke 'ho. They had to replace her in *Grown-up*."

Anna tapped Sam on the shoulder. "Could you two please focus with me for just a moment? Isn't the senior trip to Washington?"

"Nope." Sam laughed lightly as the loudspeaker announced that there were just fifteen minutes to air time and that all Academy Awards personnel should be in their assigned positions. "I told you, we're going to Vegas. Vegas like you've never seen it before. Upscale Vegas."

"I've never been and no you didn't," Anna protested as once again she had to edge out of the way of people finding their way to their seats. The awards show had an orchestra in a pit below the stage, and it now started to play "There's No Business Like Show Business," which Anna recognized from the cartoons she'd sometimes watched as a child.

"Yes, I did. I'm sure of it. Hey, don't blame me if you didn't put it in your BlackBerry." Sam shrugged.

"I didn't put it in my BlackBerry because I don't *have* a BlackBerry. And you never said anything."

"Well, if I didn't, I meant to," Sam told her with a long-suffering sigh. "You try living with a father who's up for an Oscar and a stepmother from hell with a newborn spawn and see how perfect *your* memory is. Anyway, we're not going to Washington."

Parker shuddered. "Monuments, more monuments, Congress in action and all that shit. How boring would that be?"

Anna shook her head in disbelief. In her three and a half months on the West Coast, she'd discovered that Los Angeles was a different kind of place. But what kind of high school would change its itinerary at the last minute from Washington, D.C., to Sin City?

"Okay," she said evenly. "So we're all going to Las Vegas. Where does everyone stay?"

Parker and Sam looked at each other, then exploded in laughter.

"Anna, *everyone* doesn't go Las Vegas," Parker sputtered. "Just—"

"The cool kids." Sam grinned. "A few of the cool kids, really. It's tradition. Hey, check out the dress on Nipples over there. She's about ten rows from the front. Her dress is completely see-through."

Parker flashed his movie-star-wannabe grin. "Don't worry, Anna. It's a piece of cake. On Tuesday—that's when everyone is going—we call in to the school office with the stomach flu."

"The plane to Washington leaves without us, we hop on my father's jet, and we party," Sam went on, her eyes glued to the stage, where a couple of sound engineers were doing a final check. "An hour later we're in Sin City."

"Like Sam said, it's a tradition. Except for the jet, of course. Usually we drive over. It's a straight shot across the desert, and there aren't a lot of cops." The lights in the auditorium blinked on and off—an indication that it was just ten minutes to show time. "I gotta book." He leaned toward Anna and gazed soulfully into her eyes. "So, you *are* coming with us, right?"

"I'm not sure. . . ."

Parker put both hands directly over his heart, atop his single-breasted Ted Lapidus tux. Anna saw that it was slightly frayed at the cuffs. "You *have* to come, Anna. Really."

Odd. Parker had just shifted into obvious flirt mode. But their relationship lay in that vast gray area between friend and acquaintance. It wasn't like she'd ever had anything going on him. Then he gave her and Sam a thumbs-up before hurrying away to wherever the seat-fillers congregated.

Anna shook her head in disbelief as he departed. "Was Parker flirting with me just now?"

"Nah," Sam explained. "He told me he's up for a part in a couple of days on *Everwood*. They'll probably turn it into a U-five."

"What's a U-five?"

Sam laughed her patented Anna-you're-so-naive-it's-charming laugh. "Under five. If a script gives you under five lines, the producers don't have to pay you as much. Union rules. Anyway, he'd be this boy slut who uses fake sincerity to seduce every girl he sees. He was rehearsing."

Before Anna had a chance to respond, an older woman with perfectly coiffed silver hair stepped by them, nodding at Anna. "I loved you in that little independent film. So original. You've got a big future." She continued up the aisle.

Anna and Sam turned to each other and shrugged.

It was a long two and a half hours until they got to the Best Actor award; there were many times during the ceremony when Anna wished that she'd been watching at home. Up in the second tier of the theater—the third level, really—with the stage so far away that she needed binoculars (which neither she nor Sam had brought), she couldn't see very well at all. Evidently, nepotism was sufficient to get you a coveted seat at the Academy Awards, but it didn't mean you'd get a *good* seat.

Back in New York, Anna used to go to the annual Oscars party given by the parents of her classmate Olivia Macklow. The Macklows lived in a town house just a few doors away from the Percys; they were theater producers who'd compiled an enviable record in the last several years by producing a series of small-cast musicals about the sexual foibles of aging. The first show had been called *Forty-sex*, the second one *Fifty-sex*, and so on. The critics had hated these musicals— Anna remembered reading a scathing review in the *New York Times* of *Sixty-sex*,—but the public ate them up. Consequently, the Macklows had become filthy rich.

The feature of the evening was that Olivia gave every guest a supply of supple rubber bands before the broadcast began. The idea was that whoever fired a rubber band and scored a direct hit on the actress who showed the most cleavage went home with a bottle of Veuve-Clicquot from the Macklows' well-stocked wine cellar.

After another break for television commercials, it was finally time for the Best Actor award. Jackson had been nominated not for one of his summer tent-pole blockbusters but for a low-budget (read: under twenty million dollars) independent film he'd done as a favor for the Weinstein brothers. The picture was a tale of redemption called *Snow Job*, in which he'd played a disgraced-in-a-sex-scandal college basketball coach who took the only job offered him: coaching a tiny high school team in the Eskimo village of Ambler, Alaska, north of the Arctic Circle. The title was a pun on the location and on how Jackson's character was able to convince his group of misfit basketball players that their skills actually merited their participation in the sport.

Snow Job had garnered Jackson the best reviews of his career and won him his third Oscar nomination. But he was up against brutal competition: Leonardo DiCaprio, Sean Penn, Al Pacino, and a blind teenage British actor named Alan Bosworth, whose psychological thriller *Miracles* had been a dark-horse international hit. Sam had seen it and declared to Anna that it was a pretentious piece of shit. Objectively speaking, she'd said, her father deserved to win. But she'd offered Anna the caveat that in Hollywood, nothing was objective.

Meryl Streep and Danny DeVito were presenting the award. Sam grabbed Anna's hand as Streep tore open the envelope containing the name of the winner.

"And the award goes to . . ."

"Please, please, please," Sam chanted under her breath. "My father. But if not, anyone but the kid—"

"Alan Bosworth in *Miracles*!"

The crowd roared. Then, as Bosworth ascended the

stage, led by his German shepherd seeing-eye dog, everyone jumped to their feet for a standing ovation. It was so loud that Anna could barely make out the strains of the movie's theme, which had already won the award for Best Original Song.

Anna and Sam had no choice—they rose to their feet along with everyone else.

"Shit," Sam muttered. Anna could hear the sincere disappointment in her voice. It was touching. "I really thought this was my dad's year. Check him out, he's such a pro."

Anna craned her neck so that she could see Jackson, who was standing in the aisle, beaming and applauding as if the teen actor were his own child. Anna was touched, both by Jackson's magnanimous response and Sam's empathy for her dad. It wasn't like Jackson was a model father. Most of the time, Sam and her father weren't close. In fact, Jackson Sharpe pretty much ignored her—save for the one time several weeks earlier that he'd come to her rescue when she and Anna had gotten lost in the Mexican desert. Anna had hoped that incident would mark the start of a better relationship between Sam and Jackson. Sadly, it hadn't. They'd come home, and Jackson had reverted right back to his previous pattern of placing his daughter Sam as number eleven on a list of ten. He hadn't even come to school to see her student film when it was presented to her English class. And now that his new baby, Ruby Hummingbird Sharpe, had arrived, Jackson was more distracted than ever. Sam tried to act like she didn't care. But Anna could see how much it hurt her.

There was only one more award, for Best Picture. *Snow Job* had been nominated here, but Sam declared that it was a lost cause. She was right: It was the year of *Miracles*. Another mandatory standing ovation, and then the evening was over.

"What now?" Anna asked as the lights came up in the theater and people rushed for the exits.

"What now?" Sam repeated. "That's simple. Vodka."

Dr. Nose Job

The Governor's Ball was the traditional sit-down dinner and reception for the Oscar winners, nominees, and sixteen hundred of their best friends. Catered by the famous restaurateur Wolfgang Puck and held in a lavishly decorated exhibition hall housed in the same building as the Kodak Theatre itself, it was the first stop on what would be for many Oscar attendees a long night of parties. This year's theme was "Classic Hollywood," and as Sam and Anna followed the thick crowd toward the banquet room, they passed enormous movie posters of Oscar-winning films from thirty, forty, and even fifty years ago.

Sam had told Anna that everyone made an appearance at the Governor's Ball, even if half the room cleared out before dinner was served in order to attend one of the many hipper parties held at various clubs, restaurants, and private homes across the city, away from the watchful eye of the Los Angeles Police Department. Those parties didn't start until an hour or so after the ceremony, so the Governor's Ball was a good way to kill some time. Anna and Sam joined an endless line by one of the bars that was serving the evening's signature drink, a rum-and-grenadine concoction that had been hastily renamed the "Miracle."

"Fucking British wankers," a silver-haired man in front of Anna groused to his date—or maybe it was his wife—about the *Miracles* sweep. She was at least twenty years younger than he was, with a cascade of diamonds dripping into her saline-assisted cleavage. "I hate those sons of bitches. Americans still have an inferiority complex about that shit. Fucking members of the fucking Academy. In fact, what the hell are we doing at this party? Let's go home."

As the man dragged the woman away toward the main doors, Sam nodded knowingly. "That's Peter Marx. He wrote *A Heart Divided*."

Anna nodded. She recalled that *A Heart Divided*, taken from a young-adult novel about a Confederate flag controversy at a Southern high school, had lost out for Best Adapted Screenplay.

"Notice how he reeks of loser now," Sam observed as they watched Marx and the blonde depart, without a single other guest taking notice. "He's not going home; he knows he has to show his face tonight or some studio exec will mention it in an anonymous blog in the morning. He'll go to some after party and pretend to be thrilled to be nominated. Then he'll go home and post anonymously on some Web site about how he got robbed. Speaking of after parties, you still want to do Morton's?"

The Governor's Ball was the official Oscars after party—appearances were mandatory. But the *Vanity Fair* bash at Morton's restaurant on Melrose Avenue was the most exclusive of all the post-Oscar festivities—it was where the Hollywood A-list ended up after they'd hung out sufficiently at the Governor's Ball and at least made it through the coconut-shrimp appetizer. Sam and Anna had planned to go to Morton's, but that had been when Jackson was still an Oscar contender.

"I don't know. I don't suppose your father can be happy with the it-was-an-honor-just-to-be-nominated point of view?"

"Politically correct horseshit," Sam decreed as the drinks line edged forward. "No one really feels that way. My father and Poppy will stop there for like ten minutes so that he looks like a gracious loser; then they'll head home and cry into their low-carb beer."

Anna smiled. "You may be the last honest girl in Hollywood."

"Please. I'm only honest with you."

"Anna? Is that you?"

Anna swung around and recognized the slicked-back silver hair and chiseled features of Dr. Dan Birnbaum, Hollywood's most renowned cosmetic surgeon. Also, father to Ben Birnbaum. *Her* Ben. Well, at least he'd been her Ben for a while. Just thinking about him caused a pain in the area of her heart. She'd never, ever felt about a boy the way she'd felt about Ben. *Still* felt about Ben. Admitting that, if only to herself, caused the pain to deepen.

"Nice to see you again, Dr. Birnbaum," Anna said politely. She'd met him at the wedding where Jackson Sharpe had married Sam's stepmother, Poppy, and a few other times, too. He looked better now—his hair, which he'd allowed to gray perfectly at the temples, was neatly swept back, and he'd clearly been working out. Ben had told her that his father had nearly killed himself back in January due to gambling debts. She hoped that those problems were long over. But Ben had intimated that his father wasn't all that stable, so she was a bit wary. "This is my friend—"

"Sam Sharpe," Dr. Birnbaum filled in. "Come on, I've known Sam for years. She and my son grew up together."

Anna felt momentarily embarrassed, telling herself she should have remembered that.

He leaned over and kissed Sam's cheek. "Sorry your dad lost, Sam. I thought he was fantastic in that movie."

"Me too," Sam replied. "Thanks."

"Hey, what do those idiots know?" Dr. Birnbaum asked dismissively. "Every year I come to this thing to support my friends; every year some other guy wins. What can I say? I've got broad shoulders for them to cry on."

"Come on, Dr. Birnbaum," Sam chided. "The truth is, you did half the faces and boobs here, and you wanted to see how they look in comparison to one another."

Dr. Birnbaum wagged a finger at her. "I don't discuss my clientele."

"Please. They're all in the *Star*," Sam kidded. " 'Knife Styles of the Rich and Famous.' You ought to autograph your work. A little Dr. B tattoo on a well-lifted butt. Everyone will want one."

Dr. Birnbaum smiled at her. "Funny girl."

Sam peered around. "Where's your wife?"

"She never comes to these things." He touched Anna's arm. "Anna, dear, could I speak with you a moment? Privately?"

Anna was slightly taken aback. She'd never had a one-on-one with Ben's father before. What was this about?

"Uh, sure. Sam, you excuse us?"

"No problem," Sam nodded. "I'll go mingle. It'll take a half hour before we can get a cocktail, anyway." Anna watched as she moved off into the dense crowds gathered by the bars—she didn't get more than twenty feet before she was approached by a young man in a white Stetson and a jacket and string tie. The guy looked like he'd just stepped out of the O.K. Corral.

"You have good taste," Dr. Birnbaum observed to Anna. "Samantha Sharpe was always the brightest of my son's friends. I'm glad I ran into you. Ben sends his regards."

Anna was confused. "How did he know you'd run into me?"

Dr. Birnbaum smiled. "You're right. He didn't. But whenever we talk on the phone, he asks if I've seen you. The doctor waved to someone over Anna's shoulder.

"You look fabulous, Tom!" Then he turned back to Anna. "My son told me recently that he shared with you some of my past . . . challenges."

The gambling, Anna thought. And the lying. And Dr. Birnbaum's nearly killing himself in a hotel room because he was so deeply in debt.

"Yes," she admitted. "He did."

Dr. Birnbaum pursed his lips. "I'm glad he did, actually—much as it pains me to say so. I've been in Gamblers Anonymous for three months. I'm committed to a life of total honesty as discussed in what I like to call their Big Book."

Anna went for a polite smile. She was happy that Ben's father was getting his act together, but she didn't understand why a life of total honesty meant that he had to share this information with her. It wasn't like they were friends. And unfortunately, she was no longer involved with his son.

Anna's to-the-manor-born mother had a sort of mental Big Book of her own. Anna had mentally dubbed it the *This Is How We Do Things* Big Book (East Coast WASP edition). If that book had taught her anything, it was to keep skeletons in the palatial walk-in closet with the revolving shoe rack, where they belonged.

"You think this is oversharing, me telling you all this. Especially in public," Dr. Birnbaum observed. "I see it on your face. But the thing is . . ." He moved closer, his voice dropping. "Confidentially, I've never seen Ben as hung up on a girl as he is on you."

"*Was*," Anna corrected.

Dr. Birnbaum shook his head. "Still is, Anna. I know my kid."

Still? Anna's heart leapfrogged. Could that possibly be true? They'd parted badly when Ben had gone back to college at Princeton several weeks after they'd met. It had been very emotional then, and it felt the same way now. Anna was surprised that Ben would have shared those feelings with his father. In fact, Ben had once mentioned his father as an example of everything he did not want to be.

"We broke up, Dr. Birnbaum," Anna explained. "I'm sure he doesn't feel that way anymore."

"I believe he does," Ben's father insisted. "Look, Ben is doing great. Grades are top notch, varsity crew—it's all good."

"Except," Dr. Birnbaum continued, "that he's missing you. Look, I haven't always been there for my son in the past. Been too busy chasing the golden calf, you know? But I want to be there for him now. I know what he needs; I hear it in his voice every time he says your name. He needs you. Call him sometime." He put a hand on her arm. "Soon."

"He could call me." Anna paused, then gulped.

"Nah. He thinks he messed it up with you. Which means it's your move, if you want to make it." Dr. Birnbaum flashed a grin that could well have been the result of a dental-work-for-chin-implant swap. "My kid is the best, Anna, and he really misses you. That's for real, my hand to God." He held his palm up. "So do it, okay?"

"Yes, all right," Anna said nodding. She still wasn't sure what she would or should do. But she couldn't very well refuse. Not after Ben's father had bared his very soul to her.

"That's great, Anna. I won't mention this to Ben. I'll just let you take it from here. Have a terrific night. If you see Jackson Sharpe, tell him he got robbed, okay?"

As Dr. Birnbaum moved off into the crowd, Anna recalled the day she'd met Ben on the flight to Los Angeles, the day before New Year's Eve. Their romance had seemed magical at the time. They'd met on the plane, when Ben had saved her from the Seatmate from Hell by pretending to be a guy she knew and making the guy change seats with him. Ben was tall and broad-chested, with dark hair and the most amazing blue eyes.

She'd flirted with him—her, *flirting!*—something she'd always sworn she had no clue how to do! But up there flying high next to Ben, it had been so easy, so fun, romantic, sexy, exciting, like something out of her most girly fantasies.

Not long afterward, they were furiously making out in the plane's minuscule bathroom. She blushed just remembering it, amazed at her own daring. And yet, it had happened. She had done it.

When the plane had landed, the magic hadn't. Ben had invited her to be his date at Jackson Sharpe's wedding that night. Then there'd been the private midnight cruise on his father's yacht. A few weeks later, Anna had made love for the first time, with Ben. Looking back, that night seemed most magical of all.

Tears sprang to her eyes and she quickly brushed them away. Somehow after that, everything had gone wrong. They'd both been surprised by their feelings: Ben, that he'd fallen so hard for her, and Anna, that intimacy could be as scary as it was sweet. How could she be in this new Los Angeles life, where she wanted to experience everything, when she had so quickly become part of a couple? How could she want it yet not want it at the same time?

"Hey," Sam beckoned smoothly as she appeared in front of Anna holding two drinks. She gave one to Anna and tugged her out of the line. "Vodka tonics. Drink up. I've heard 'Your father got robbed' ten times in the past ten minutes. It's crap, though. This is a schadenfreude town. It's not enough that these people should succeed: Everyone else should fail. So what did Dr. Nose Job want?"

"He wants me to call Ben at Princeton." Anna took a sip of her cocktail. The conversation with Dr. Birnbaum had put her brain into overdrive. Again.

"Why doesn't Ben just call you?"

"That's exactly what I asked him."

"And?"

"And he said I needed to make the first move."

"Whatever," Sam responded dismissively. "The question is, do you want to call Ben or not?"

"I miss him," Anna confessed. "A lot."

"So take out your cell and call him! What's the BFD?"

Anna sighed. What *was* the BFD? "I just want to be sure," she finally said.

"Like that's ever gonna happen. You are the most look-before-you-leap chick I have ever known."

"I know. I hate that about myself. But what if his father is wrong? What if Ben has completely lost interest in me by now? What if I call and he feels pressured to—"

"What if you shut up?" Sam suggested with a smirk. "If you miss Ben, then *do* something about it."

Anna laughed. "You're right, I'll shut up."

Sam nodded. "Excellent." She looped her arm through Anna's. "Come on. Let's go to Morton's and see how many more people tell me my father got robbed and how many more people mistake you for a superstar."

Quite the Hot Couple

The scene on the street outside the Kodak Theatre was eerie. Four hours ago, the intersection of Highland and Hollywood had been blocked off to traffic for security reasons. Now, as Sam and Anna came outside to find their black stretch limo, it was almost as if nothing out of the ordinary had happened at all. While the ceremonies were going on, crews of workers had dissembled the bleachers and rolled up the red carpet—the fabric covering the seedy storefronts was gone, too. In fact, the only things that gave any clue that the night was special were the rows of remote-reporting television trucks lined up on both curbs and a long line of limousines awaiting their passengers.

Sam squinted up and down Highland, searching for her chauffeur and limo. As she did, she removed her lime-green-and-black pumps and hung them off her right index finger. "How can shoes this expensive kill my feet? And don't worry about my driver. He'll spot us."

Anna nodded.

"Still thinking about him?" Sam asked. But she

didn't even have to wait for an answer. "You know, if I didn't love you, I'd have to hate you," Sam decreed. "First, Ben Birnbaum, who is an eleven on your basic one-to-ten scale, falls at your feet. Then Adam Flood is ready to cut his heart out for you. Then there was that guy who coproduces *Hermosa Beach*—"

"Danny Bluestone," Anna filled in. "But we never got much beyond the friend stage."

"Then the edible surfing instructor down in Mexico. Just once in my life, I'd like to be the girl who can get any guy." Sam sighed.

"It's not about quantity, Sam."

"How about if I come to that conclusion after men fling themselves at my hurting feet?"

"Eduardo is *great*," Anna reminded Sam. Which was absolutely true. "You don't want to mess it up."

Sam looped some hair behind her ear as a limousine pulled up in front of them. But this one was purple— not theirs—and it moved off again into the night. "Like you messed up with Ben?"

Anna shrugged. "I don't know who messed up, really. Both of us, I guess."

Sam swung her shoes from her fingers. "So call him and tell him! Or call him and talk dirty to him. Or . . . oh hell, just call him. Ask him about Vegas. Even *he* went last year instead of going to Washington."

"He did?" Anna was surprised. Ben had once mentioned to her that he didn't like Las Vegas at all.

"Yep. We all did. I drove over with Cammie, even

though we were juniors. He and Cammie barely came out of his room at the Bellagio. The hotels in Vegas don't care who sleeps with who, though I don't think Ben and Cammie did a lot of sleeping. Where the hell is my driver? Wait here."

Sam slipped back into her shoes and started to march along the sidewalk, peering into each of the identical black limos. Meanwhile, Anna couldn't help thinking about Ben in bed with Cammie in a glitzy Vegas hotel suite. The notion turned her stomach. Cammie was one of Sam's lifelong friends. She was drop-dead gorgeous. She was also, in Anna's opinion, drop-dead evil. Evidently, Cammie and Ben had been quite the hot couple before Ben had broken it off. Now, it often seemed to Anna that Cammie would never forgive her for getting the boy she'd lost. It didn't matter that Ben and Anna were currently three thousand miles apart from each other. Anna had tried, on more than one occasion, to make nice with Cammie. It hadn't worked.

Sam came back, shaking her head angrily. "If you see our driver, tell him he's fired."

"Do you have his cell?"

"Programmed into my cell, which is in the black quilted Chanel pocketbook that's still on my nightstand. We'll probably run into him at Morton's."

Anna shook her head. "Your *chauffeur?*"

"He had a supporting role in *Miracles*. They shot it months ago and he hasn't worked since, so he's driving. Gimme your cell—I'll call a cab."

Anna handed over her phone.

Sam began furiously pressing the buttons. "Shit. Can you believe it? Arriving at Morton's in a taxicab on Oscar night. They probably won't let us in the door."

The Rock on Steroids

"You're kidding, right?" Sam asked the burly security guy outside Morton's on Melrose. Those who were on the list but not so famous that the doorman recognized them were waiting at the velvet rope to enter. Sam had been trying to skip the line. Across the street—one of the main shopping areas between the West Hollywood and Hancock Park sections, famous for its scores of exclusive boutiques, restaurants, bars, and clubs—dozens of movie fans who knew about the *Vanity Fair* bash were cordoned off behind police barricades, hoping to catch a glimpse of their favorite stars. A bevy of police officers made sure they stayed where they were supposed to be.

Sam had told Anna on the way over that just as many people had mistakenly showed up outside Morton's steakhouse on La Cienega, where absolutely nothing was happening. But the two restaurants had nothing to do with one another. Morton's on Melrose was happening. Morton's on La Cienega was nothing. That was just the way it was.

There were plenty of celebrities to keep the ravenous

fans happy. Sam and Anna had fallen in just behind Gwen Stefani, who wore a very short Jennifer Nicholson blue skirt held up by sapphire suspenders. But an asshole guard who looked like the Rock on steroids had stepped between them and the entrance.

"Need to see if your name's on the list," he grunted. Then he eased Sam out of the way to allow Courteney Cox-Arquette and Lisa Kudrow through the door. They were chattering happily to each other.

"Ever read *Vanity Fair*?" Sam snapped, once the two actresses were safely inside. "I was in it two months ago."

This was true. The magazine had done an Oscars preview story, and there'd been a family portrait of Jackson, Poppy, and Sam that accompanied the article. But the guard didn't look impressed. Sam realized that half the people inside Morton's at that very moment had also been in *Vanity Fair* in the last few months.

"Name?" the guy asked.

"Sam Sharpe," she sputtered through gritted teeth, then groaned as she spotted the E! television van roll to a stop in front of the restaurant. Sam knew she was about to be treated to another round of the ever-charming Marilyn Haskell.

The guard eyed Anna. "And you are?"

"She's Hollywood's hottest new young star," Sam answered for Anna, desperate to get inside before Marilyn cornered her again. "What difference does it make? Check your goddamn list. I'm plus one!"

The guard smiled mirthlessly at her. "Sharp. Is that with one *p* or two?"

"Sharpe," Sam snapped, with one eye on the E! van. Marilyn Haskell had just gotten out and was making a beeline to Morton's front door. "As in Jackson."

"Oh yeah, he lost." The guard scanned his clipboard. "Here you are. Samantha Sharpe plus one. Go on in."

"Thank God," Sam declared, stepping inside. As they did, the reporter from *Inside Access* shouted to her.

"Sam! How do you feel about your father's losing—"

Sam quickly closed the door behind her. "God, I can't stand Oscar night."

They made their way to the open bar through an intense crush of people. On any other night of the year, Morton's was merely another popular restaurant known as a good place for stargazing in a town filled with popular restaurants known as good places for stargazing. The interior lines were clean and elegant, the tables separated enough so that conversation was possible. But tonight the staff had cleared space to handle the crowd, and the classic rock and roll playing over the enhanced sound system was at earsplitting volume.

As Sam and Anna tried to get drinks, celebrity after celebrity—Nicolas Cage, Halle Berry, Kirsten Dunst, even Clint Eastwood—stopped Sam to offer their opinion: that she looked great in her dress and that her father had been robbed of the Oscar he so richly deserved.

A passing waiter carried a tray of champagne flutes.

Sam snared two of them and handed one to Anna. "Well, we're here." She touched her glass to Anna's in a toast. "Let's get drunk."

"Yes, let's," a voice behind them piped in. Sam and Anna turned—it was Cammie Sheppard herself. Sam took in how incredible Cammie looked: sooty eyelashes and MAC Pinkarat Lustreglass lip gloss on her pouty lips. A shrunken white tank top, 7 For All Mankind jeans, and lilac Judith Leiber pumps with a pointed toe.

Morton's was full of famous and gorgeous women. But by being underdressed, Cammie stood out. Damn. Somehow she always knew exactly what to do, exactly what to wear. Just standing next to Cammie made Sam feel fat, even in her carefully-purchased-to-conceal-pounds dress. Involuntarily, she immediately started to calculate how many calories she'd consumed in the last forty-eight hours.

"Hey, Sam, how's it going?" Cammie asked nonchalantly, as if running into her best friend at an Oscars party was an annual ritual. In a way, it was. "Hi, Anna."

"Hi. Were you there?" Anna asked politely.

Cammie shook her head, her perfect strawberry blond curls cascading to and fro as she did. "Nah. Been there, done that. Got tired of Hilary Swank. But I can see why you would want to be there, being new here and all. So how'd it go? Did your father win?"

Sam gulped down her hurt. She couldn't believe that Cammie hadn't bothered to find out if her dad had won. Jackson had been so good to Cammie over the years.

And he'd been good to Cammie's dad, too. Back when Clark Sheppard had been struggling as an agent—before he'd catapulted into the big time—Jackson had graciously steered some work in his direction. Cammie's attitude was so . . . ungrateful.

"He got robbed," Anna put in by way of an answer.

Sam smiled. Coming from Anna, the overused phrase had a certain wonderful irony.

"That sucks," Cammie replied, oozing sincerity. Sam couldn't decide if it was real or not. Cammie took a swig of the Corona beer she was holding. It was just like her. Everyone else was having a cocktail? She'd have a beer. And look great doing it, too.

"No Adam?" Anna asked her coolly.

"Nah," Cammie reported. "He has a cold. Before you jump to the conclusion that I couldn't have gotten him to come with me if I really wanted to, I decided to look out for his health."

"Hey, Sam." The famous magician David Copperfield waved to Sam as he edged by.

"I've got a great idea. When we're in Vegas, let's *not* see his show," Cammie suggested. She arched one of her perfect eyebrows at Anna. "You're not coming to Vegas, are you?"

"I haven't decided."

"Of course she's coming," Sam told Cammie. "You know, we thought about sharing the MTV suite at the Palms but thought you'd be happier in your own suite with Adam."

"How thoughtful," Cammie purred. "But the MTV suite has a pool table in the living room, doesn't it? I wonder if anyone has ever tried it out." Her wink made it clear that she wasn't discussing nine-ball.

"I'm pretty sure I've already seen you do the nasty on a pool table," Sam reminded Cammie, since she was feeling none too charitable toward her at the moment. "Last year, after Ben broke up with you, at Krishna's party, when you got drunk off your ass?"

Cammie shrugged nonchalantly. "Oh, right, that film major from UCLA. What was his name . . . Chuck or Buck, something like that. Not exactly memorable."

"I think Parker still has the photos he took, if you need any incriminating evidence," Sam reminded her through a smile she didn't feel. Sometimes Cammie was just too over-the-top.

Suddenly, the crowd around them parted like the Red Sea for Moses. But instead of Moses, Jackson Sharpe appeared. He strode over as soon as he saw his daughter.

"Hey, there's my girl and her best friends," Jackson declared as he approached. He put out his arms for a hug, and Sam embraced him. A *Vanity Fair* photographer snapped off a quick photo. Sam didn't even mind.

"You got robbed," Sam found herself saying. "And by the way, the whole town thinks so. Where's Poppy?"

"She wanted to get home to the baby."

Sam knew this was for the benefit of anyone within earshot, since she was well aware that Jackson and

Poppy had arranged for all-night child care for the damned baby. The only reason Poppy didn't want to come to the party was because her husband had failed to win his first Oscar. Again.

"When they announced the award, I threw something at the TV," Cammie declared. Which pissed Sam off all over again, since Cammie hadn't even known until Anna had told her. Cammie was supposed to be one of her best friends. Self-serving lies fell from Cammie's lips as easily as Paris Hilton's clothes fell from her bony-ass butt.

"Thanks, sweetie," Jackson replied humbly. "My actioners are too commercial and my low-budget ones too thoughtful. I swear, if they shut me out and then present me with a Lifetime Achievement award when I'm eighty, I'm giving it to Jim Carrey—they don't appreciate him, either. Anyway, I'm on my way out. Sam, you need a lift?"

"Yes, but not in the gold monstrosity."

Jackson laughed. "No worries. I had the driver take Poppy home in it and come back in the Beemer. Black. Very low key. We can drop Anna on the way."

"Excellent," Sam decided. "We're out of here."

Jackson took out his tiny platinum cell phone, punched in a few numbers, and then nodded. "Good enough. You know my new driver, Casey? He'll be at the side entrance. Don't want to face the hordes." He draped an arm around Sam. "Let's go home, make ice cream sundaes, and cry into the hot fudge."

At that moment, Sam loved her father so much. There was no Poppy, no drooling baby, no assistant directors calling him into the studio to reloop a scene, no locations for three weeks, nothing. Just a dad and his daughter.

"You're on," Sam agreed. "If Anna can join us?"

Anna smiled. "Lead me to the mint chocolate chip."

"You want a goody basket first?" Jackson asked them. He pointed to the far end of the restaurant. "I can get you one over there."

Sam thought for a moment. *Vanity Fair* always prepared giveaway baskets for all their party attendees. Last year's had contained a Dell portable jukebox, a bottle of Angel perfume by Thierry Mugler, and a PalmOne Treo 600 Smartphone. This year's was bound to be better. But then she shook her head. Stopping for a goody basket would ruin the moment and probably give Cammie time to figure out a way to horn in on the evening. Right now, she was enjoying a few moments of payback for Cammie's not having taken the time to watch the awards show. She'd probably catch hell for it later—Cammie was one of those girls who never forgot a snub—but right now it was well worth it.

No. She'd make do with her father's Oscar basket. Since he was a major award nominee, it would be a lot better than the one from *Vanity Fair,* anyway—an article she'd read in *Variety* had placed the value of this year's goody basket for actors at just south of ninety-five thousand dollars. Each basket was reported to contain gift certificates for cruises to Puerto Vallarta and Juneau, a spa weekend in Ojai, and a stay at the Carlyle Hotel in New York; plus a plasma television set (or rather, a certificate for one—you had to pick the set up at Circuit City), a box of Shu Uemura cosmetics for the actor's wife/girlfriend/lover of the moment, and a top-of-the-line Averatec computer. And that was just for starters. Sam reminded herself to grab the basket before the Pop-Tart got to it first.

" 'Bye, Cammie." She gaily bid her friend adieu. "Enjoy the party." It was fun to see Cammie left behind for once.

Seven Deadly Sins

"**G**ood morning, students! I just took my Fresno boobs for a walk on Rodeo Drive, and now it's my pleasure for us to welcome you to the Beverly Hills High School senior assembly!" Sam chirped to Anna, inventing a speech for their new principal, Charlotte Manning.

It was the morning after the Oscars, Monday, and the entire senior class was assembling in the luxurious Streisand Theater—donated by the famed singer/actress/director—for a group preview of the Washington trip, scheduled to depart on Tuesday afternoon. Built the same year as the Kodak Theatre, the Streisand Theater looked like the Kodak in miniature. Instead of several tiers of seats, there were only the orchestra level and a balcony, but the space still seated more than a thousand and had a lighting grid and sound system that would have been the envy of a top commercial performance venue. Streisand had paid for the entire million-dollar renovation.

Anna knew that Principal Manning had only been on

the job a few weeks and had, as Sam had intimated, come from a high school in Fresno. She'd replaced Principal Kwan, who'd been hired in midterm by Governor Schwarzenegger to head up the Office of Educational Diversity at the state capital in Sacramento. Most people found this hilarious, because, as Sam had told Anna, while Beverly Hills High School did have its share of nonwhite students, there was no economic diversity whatsoever. The average family income easily topped a quarter of a million dollars a year.

Everyone in the student body made fun of the new principal, known for her outsized breasts, her fondness for skintight cashmere sweaters, and her perk-perk-perky personality. As the fortyish woman stood at the podium and waited for her students to take their seats, Anna noted that today's cashmere was sapphire blue, with little fluffy pom-poms hanging from the cowl-neck collar. Which was a terrible thing to do to cashmere.

Dee Young—another of Sam's lifelong friends with whom Anna had become acquainted—slid into a seat next to Anna and Sam. She was petite, no taller than five feet, weighing no more than ninety pounds. With her wispy blond bangs that nearly touched her cornflower blue eyes, Dee seemed almost doll-like, except for her clothes, which were standard-issue Beverly Hills High School sexy without trying to be—blue Habitual jeans, a tiny white tank top by Emerge, and a plain white men's dress shirt from Brooks Brothers with only one button buttoned. The dress shirt was for the principal's benefit only.

"She really shouldn't wear blue," Dee mused, in her plaintive little-girl voice. "I mean, her aura is kind of puke green and it clashes. Do you think I should tell her, Anna?"

"I don't know, Dee," Anna replied, trying not to betray how increasingly odd she found Dee to be. "I can't see her aura."

"How about you, Sam?" Dee asked, wide-eyed.

"Definitely tell her," Sam instructed. "Right after the assembly."

"You're kidding me," Dee surmised.

"Gee, ya think?"

Cammie, who had just slipped into a seat in the row in front of them, craned around. "Dee?"

"Yuh?"

"After you talk to her about her aura, can you ask her for her opinion on the meaning of life? Because we're all just dying to know."

Dee scrunched up her precious little forehead; her cornflower blue eyes went dark. "I don't really need to. Last week at the Kabbalah Centre, a rabbi told a story about how the great sage Hillel was asked to explain the same thing. He said that what is hateful to you—"

"Stop." Cammie waved a hand, and Dee immediately shut up. "I can tell you what is hateful to me. What's hateful to me is that you actually wanted to answer my . . ."

Cammie's voice trailed off as Adam Flood made his way to the empty seat next to her. He moved with the rangy, athletic motion of the basketball point guard he was. Largely because of Adam's efforts on the hard court, the high school had posted its best record in years.

"What's hateful?" Adam asked.

Cammie grinned. "That we have to be here, instead of in my shower."

Adam plopped down in the seat. He'd recently cut his hair, so the small star tattoo behind his left ear was more noticeable than usual. "I'm with you," he agreed, and lightly kissed Cammie. He was wearing black jeans and a Beverly Hills High School basketball jersey.

"You know, Cammie, you're a much nicer person when Adam is around," Dee observed.

Parker, who was sitting to Dee's left, patted her thigh. "Don't let her get to you, Dee. Hey, so I got a callback for that gig on *Everwood*. If I get it, they're going to fly me to Salt Lake City, where they shoot."

"To play a boy slut, right?" Cammie asked. "Typecasting."

"Lighten up," Adam told her, giving her shoulders a squeeze.

"Sorry," Cammie said with a sigh. "I just hate wasting my time. Let's get out of here before the walking bad boob job starts her speech. I'm dying for a double espresso. How about the Coffee Bean?" She slid out of her seat and tugged Adam up with her.

"Later." Adam gave them a half salute as he followed Cammie away.

It was amazing to Anna that Cammie would say she

was sorry about anything. But if anyone could get her to say that magic word, it would be Adam. There'd been a time, not so very long ago, when Anna and Adam had been an almost-couple. But in the end, Anna had gone back to Ben, following her heart instead of her head. She'd never regretted that decision, but it had hurt Adam, and she was ashamed of herself for it. Adam Flood was perhaps the last of the truly good guys. Thoughtful, ethical, but not a helicopter guy who hovered over you all the time and swooped in when you wanted to be left alone. Too good a guy, in Anna's opinion, for Cammie. Still, they seemed happy together.

"Come on," Sam whispered to Anna as the principal tapped the microphone a few times, making sure that it was live. It wasn't, so she motioned to one of the school custodians to assist her. "Cammie's right. I can't sit through this shit, either. We're going to Vegas, not Washington. What do we need the travelogue for?"

"Well . . . I might go to Washington, actually," Anna began awkwardly. "I'm not sure I really want to spend any more time with Cam—"

"Shut *up*!" Parker exclaimed. "You can't!"

"Yes, actually, I can," Anna maintained.

Parker gazed into Anna's eyes. "I mean, I'd miss you."

"Why would you miss Anna?" Dee asked. "Are you two sleeping together?"

Anna sighed. "Dee, we're not dating. We're not even close to dating. Right, Parker?"

"Right," Sam answered for Parker. "Save it for your callback. Okay? Anna, you ready to book? We can go get a Robeks' juice and be back in time for second period."

"I think I'll stay."

"Suit yourself. I'll bring you back a smoothie." Sam edged out of her seat and headed for the rear doors of the theater.

As soon as Sam was gone, Parker switched seats to slide in between Dee and Anna. "I'll stay, too. I wouldn't want you to be here alone."

Dee pinched herself. "I'm real. As in, existing in this moment of time and space. I matter." She shook her head. "I mean, I *am* matter."

Fortunately, Principal Manning began her spiel about the Washington trip, sparing Anna any more conversation with Dee and Parker. The presentation was high-tech and included a professional-quality film that spotlighted all the trip's key destinations. Anna noticed that Dee was taking notes, in her very tiny, very precise handwriting. When the assembly broke up, Anna was no clearer on where she wanted to go the next afternoon. To Vegas, where she'd never been? She was definitely inclined to experience it, but—and a major peach-shaped butt it was—it meant days in close proximity to Cammie Sheppard. On the other hand, there was Washington, D.C.—minus Sam, her one real friend in Beverly Hills. Who would she hang with if she went to Washington? Her mother had gone to boarding school with the wife of a senator from Virginia; Anna could look her up. On second thought, she'd met the woman—a right-wing conservative who broke into Latin now and then simply to prove that she could speak it.

Cammie Sheppard was looking better by the nanosecond.

"I'm sorry I can't be your roommate on the Washington trip, Anna," Dee chirped as she and Parker walked with Anna across the central quad, heading for their second-period American history class. "I can't go. And I'm not going to Vegas, either."

"Really," Anna told her. She'd been sure that Dee would be part of the Las Vegas contingent. "How come? And why were you taking such careful notes in there if you weren't going?"

Dee tore the pages out of a zebra-striped spiral note-book and handed them to Anna. "I did it for you."

"Wow, talk about thoughtful." Parker wrapped an arm around Dee's slender shoulders.

"I'm not really into having sex right now, Parker," Dee warned him. "My body is a temple."

Parker removed his arm and looked confused. "Who said anything about sex?"

"You put your arm around me. That means you entered my personal space," Dee explained. "Right now, I'm at a celibate life stage. Sort of like the Essenes around the time of Hillel. Do you know anything about the Dead Sea Scrolls?"

Parker stopped and peered at her. "Are you, like, *medicated?*"

"No," Dee replied. "All illness is in the brain. We create our own reality. I have chosen to create perfect health. Oh, and virginity. Excuse me."

She drifted off, leaving Anna with Parker in the center of the courtyard. Anna realized that she'd never gotten an answer as to why Dee wasn't going on either of the two trips. Maybe part of her new celibacy meant that she wasn't allowing herself to get anywhere near a hotel room?

Parker shook his head as Dee departed. "Okay, I agree—she's really out there." Then he tapped the notebook pages still in Anna's hand. "You're not really thinking about going to Washington, are you?"

"I'm not sure."

Parker casually touched a stray hair that had fallen out of Anna's messy ponytail.

"I'd really love it if you'd come with me," Parker confided.

"We're just *friends,* Parker," Anna told him. Didn't this guy ever get a clue?

"But we could be friends with *benefits.* I've had my eye on you for a long time. You're special. Really special."

What the hell was he talking about?

"Parker?"

"Yeah?"

"Tell me something. Are those lines from your audition?"

"Busted." Parker sagged visibly. "How'd I do?"

"Very . . . convincing," Anna reported. Then her cell rang. She extracted it from her purse and checked the number. It was Cyn, calling from New York. "I've got to take this, Parker. Excuse me."

"Sure. But it would be great if you came to Vegas. You'll love it there."

"I'll definitely think about it." He moved away as Anna raised her cell phone to her ear. "Hello?"

"Bitch!"

Anna laughed. She and Cyn had been inseparable in Manhattan, ever since the day when they were both in preschool and Cyn had peed on Anna's mother expensive Hermès handbag.

As they'd grown up, Cyn had turned into the sexy daring one, Anna into the proverbial good girl. Cyn was the one who had introduced Anna to the joys of a perfect margarita. She had gotten Anna to stay out all night at after-hours clubs in the East Village and brought her to see bands she'd never heard of. Anna had liked all these experiences—some more than others, of course. It was an unlikely friendship in many ways. But overall, she couldn't have asked for a better friend than Cyn. And Cyn loved Anna just as much— she claimed that Anna was smarter and more insightful than pretty much anyone she'd ever met.

Anna's life would probably have continued on that way if Cyn hadn't hooked up with the boy on whom Anna had been crushing forever, Scott Spencer. Seeing them together, hearing about how sexy Scott was, what the two of them did, in excruciating detail—it had gotten painful.

Before Cyn and Scott were a couple, Anna had played it close to the vest, never admitting to her friend how she felt about him. Now that he and Cyn had become a couple, she never would. Though she didn't know him well, Anna knew that Scott was so obviously not like other guys from her world as to be from another galaxy. His family had plenty of money, but that was the only similarity. He'd been raised in Boston, not New York City, and had moved to New York only couple of years ago, after his parents' divorce. His father wasn't in high finance or an industrialist but was a distinguished professor of government at Harvard who'd been lured to NYU with a named chair. Scholarship was a big part of the Spencer family tradition. Scott's mother was an editor at a highbrow literary magazine. Anna had never seen Scott without either a hardcover novel or a humor magazine under his arm. He reeked of smart. She found that endlessly fascinating.

His taste in girlfriends had gone similarly against the grain. Before Cyn, Scott's girlfriends had tended toward the exotic: Ethiopian, Indonesian, Moroccan. Rarely had he dated anyone from the northern hemisphere, until he'd met Cyn.

Even his looks were personal and distinctive. He was just over six feet, just under a hundred and seventy-five or so. His hair color shifted with the seasons—darker in winter, dirty blond in the summer. He tended toward a day or so of stubble and had welcoming green eyes and the complexion of a guy who loved to be outside. He was a jock intellectual, and Anna found him incredibly attractive.

When Anna had decided to spend the second half of her senior year in California, she'd been sad to leave Cyn behind. But it hadn't hurt at all to get three thousand miles away from the evidently blissful Cyn and Scott.

Anna didn't have the kind of friendship she had with Cyn with anyone in Los Angeles—Sam Sharpe was her closest friend, but they didn't have the same history that Cyn and Anna shared. But Anna realized her instincts had been correct: She found herself thinking about Cyn and Scott a lot less now that she was in California.

"I love you, too," Anna replied with a laugh into her cell phone. "What's up?"

"You were supposed to call me last night, remember?" Cyn asked.

Anna took two steps over to one of the benches that lined the paths of the courtyard and sat down. She knew she might be late to American history, but she hadn't gotten less than an A on any test or paper, plus she'd already been accepted early decision to Yale. She was reasonably confident that her teacher would cut her a little slack.

"You're right," she told Cyn. "Sorry. But I went to the Academy Awards."

"The Academy Awards?" Cyn echoed incredulously. "You're kidding. I'd do anything to go sometime. You didn't invite me? What were you, a seat-filler?"

"I went with Sam Sharpe, actually."

"Jackson's daughter. He was robbed, you know. So what was it like?"

"It was amazing."

"Tell me everything," Cyn commanded. So for the next ten minutes, with her best friend prompting her, Anna told her the whole story, from how designers had brought dresses over to Sam's for the two girls to try on, to her experience on the red carpet, right through to the ice cream sundaes with Sam and Jackson at their kitchen table. As she did, Anna relived the moments, feeling the thrill and the excitement all over again.

"Damn," Cyn uttered when Anna had finished. "Last night we went to see some performance artist friend of Scott's roll around naked in crushed fruit— somehow I think you had a better time. I'm moving to Los Angeles. Does your dad have a guest room for us?"

Us. Meaning her and Scott. It was no surprise to hear that Scott had a friend who was a performance artist. He hung with everyone—uptown, downtown, no town.

"How is he, anyway?" Anna tried to sound casual.

"Oh, you know," Cyn responded vaguely. "Hey, listen, girl, I'm proud of you."

"Why?"

"Because you did something that's interesting and fun, instead of the same old shit. I don't suppose you made out with any superstars in the lobby?"

Anna laughed. "That would be you, not me."

"God, you're just so hard to corrupt! So what other cool West Coast shit are you up to?"

Anna grinned. Cyn was calling *her* cool.

"Like what's the most decadent thing you've done so far?" Cyn prompted.

Nothing truly decadent came to Anna's mind. She did, however, want to impress Cyn. So she opened her mouth and words came out. "I'm going to Las Vegas, where I plan to indulge in many of the seven deadly sins."

"Sweet!" Cyn cried. "When?"

"Tomorrow."

"With who?"

"Friends. Sam, some others," Anna tried to sound nonchalant but realized how tightly she was grasping the phone. This was so unlike her—to decide something on the spur of the moment. "We're leaving tomorrow."

"You have to stay at the Palms," Cyn decreed. "It's where they film all those poker shows on TV."

"I don't play poker."

Anna heard the bell ring. Second period had started.

She knew she'd be late, which was fine. But she didn't want to be ridiculously late.

"It doesn't matter. All the stars stay at the Palms. It rocks."

"When were you in Vegas?"

"An overnight thing with a wild Spanish guy I met in San Francisco," Cyn explained breezily. "We only stayed long enough for his thousand-dollar-a-chip craps game. Damn, you're going to Vegas and I go to some crappy art opening at Ivan Karp's gallery in SoHo. Erich Ommerle's cousin from Boston. Know how Georgia O'Keeffe painted flowers to look like giant vulvas? This woman paints vulvas to look like giant flowers. But Jeff Koons is supposed to be there, and I want to meet him. And—"

Anna waited for Cyn to finish her sentence and then realized the line was dead. She checked out her cell. No juice. Well, she'd just call Cyn later and apologize. At least her mind was made up about where she'd go. Viva Las Vegas. Seven deadly sins.

It could work.

Four-inch Red Heels

Lime green Bebe capris with a powder blue camisole lined in lime green velvet and grosgrain ribbon. Black-and-white Stella McCartney pin-striped trousers that barely cleared the zone where her pubic hair would be if she hadn't just gotten a Brazilian wax at Pink Cheeks. She'd wear the pants with a shrunken white six-ply cashmere sweater by Isaac Mizrahi, with diamond buttons added at Nobex Custom Tailor on Santa Monica Boulevard. Three pairs of basic pants; one Chanel, one Miu Miu, and one DKNY (with Lycra, for those bloated-fat-girl moments). Various tops—white silk Valentino, off-the-shoulder pink Vera Wang, and a red chiffon with lace overlay by Badgley Mischka. Two blazers—the very fitted black velvet Dolce & Gabbana and the more forgiving dove gray raw silk Matthew Williamson.

Sam gazed at the pile of clothes on her new queen-size bed with the twenty-thousand-dollar Hastens mattress imported from Sweden. These were the items that she had laid out for Vegas. She chucked the low-slung lime green capris. Like she would ever wear those in public—her thighs would look as if they were entering the room three minutes before she did. She knew they'd been a stupid purchase—she'd fallen for them on a Barneys shopping spree after a three-day wheat-grass-juice fast. That she had imagined her hips in these trousers without imagining two green warthogs that wrestled each other every time she took a step—she must have been hallucinating from the lack of solid food.

She sighed. It was too late to return them, so she'd have to give them to one of the maids. Whatever. She replaced the capris with a pair of black Mavi jeans hand embroidered by Willow, a blind artist who lived on Venice Beach and claimed she could "feel" each color she was embroidering. Pants she'd embroidered went for anywhere between five hundred and five thousand a pop. Willow's pants were the "It" thing of the moment. In a week or a month, her embroidered pants would be toast. The new look would be Parisian frills or monk-like simplicity. Whatever. Sam knew the secondhand stores in the valley would end up with a ton of Willow's embroidered pants. No one who knew anything would wear them anymore, of course. But then, the valley was another planet.

Sam threw her new oversize Tuff Betty carpetbag on the bed, then went into her palatial bathroom suite to arrange her toiletries. This part was easy, since she had Louisa the maid keep one set of all her faves in a Brontibay Paris travel case—Crème de la Mer, Z. Bigatti, plus her RéVive Glow Serum that sold for six hundred dollars an ounce at Neiman Marcus but which was hardly ever in stock. She'd been delighted to find a jar in her father's Academy Awards goody bag.

Shoes. She peered down at the new pink-and-white Swiss Masai athletic shoes with the two-inch rocking soles. The manufacturer swore that just walking around in them melted cellulite; they'd sent her a pair in hopes that Sam would be ground zero for a Swiss Masai athletic shoe buying spree by all her friends and classmates. But she'd never worn them, since they were so ugly. Hmm. Should she take them to Vegas? Melt some cellulite there? There certainly were some thigh dimples she wouldn't mind getting rid of during a stroll on the Strip. Or should she switch to the new Christian Louboutin black patent leather ankle boots with the four-inch red heels?

No contest. She tossed the athletic shoes back into the closet and zipped on the boots. With ankles like hers, form definitely won out over function.

Okay. That was that. Anything else she needed—or wanted—she'd simply buy in Vegas.

Funny, she wasn't all that into going on this trip. Probably because Eduardo wouldn't be there to enjoy it with her. Eduardo. Her boyfriend. She loved the sound of that.

Back in Las Casitas, Mexico, where she'd first encountered Eduardo, the fact that he'd fallen hard for her had made zero sense to Sam. Because shit like that never happened to her. To Anna—oh yeah. Anna was some kind of a low-key guy magnet. Cammie—five times a day. Even Dee Young got her share of lust at first sight—there were plenty of guys who liked the cosmic-waif thing. But even with all the money she'd spent on her appearance—the clothes, the hair, the spa days—Sam didn't measure up to her friends. Which, on a day-to-day basis, was one of those things that sucked hard, but there was nothing she could do about it. Of course, that didn't mean she shouldn't try. What kind of girl would she be if she didn't make an effort?

And yet here she was with a fantastic boyfriend who thought her pear-shaped self was perfect. Go figure. The only problem was, it was an LDR—a long-distance romance. Eduardo didn't mind flying—he'd already come to Los Angeles twice to visit her. And he was making noises about a summer position at the Peruvian consulate, which would mean he'd be around all summer.

Sam's heart soared when she even thought about Eduardo. What was amazing was that they hadn't made love. They'd kissed, yes. Those kisses had left her breathless. But when she'd intimated on the day before he had to depart for Paris that she was more than willing to come to his suite at his hotel, he'd declined with a graciousness that Sam had never before seen in a guy. He didn't want hit-and-run sex, he'd said. Did she understand? She had. She'd reveled in his touch. She was in love.

Well, maybe. When it came to matters of the heart, Sam Sharpe was jaded beyond the usual jadedness of

Beverly Hills kids, which was to say eleven on a scale of ten. It wasn't like she had a role model for romance. Her famous father always fell into bed with the ingenues on his movie sets. When the shoot ended, he was always careful to let them down gently and carefully. With, say, a piece of Harry Winston jewelry in the mid-five-figure range as a parting gift.

That was all Poppy Sinclair ever should have been. Sam would have forgiven him Poppy. Instead, though, he'd knocked her up. Instead of upping the jewelry to mid–six figures and sending Poppy on her way, Jackson had done the stand-up thing: He married her. Which was why Sam now had a six-week-old half-sister down the hall named Ruby Hummingbird, aka the Hummer. If the Hummer wasn't down the hall, she was in the kitchen. Or the living room. Or the bathroom. Or swaddled and at Poppy's breast in some inappropriate location. Sam couldn't understand how, on an estate the size of Aaron Spelling's, the little brat couldn't get lost, hopefully forever.

But no. The Hummer was everywhere. At age six weeks, she already had an entourage. A day nurse. A night nurse. A wet nurse. And all the Baby Einstein CDs that a six-week-old could handle. Plus the media, which had discovered that America and the world had an insatiable appetite for stories about the older action-movie star, his child bride, and their baby with the cute name. Suffice it to say that every coo, gurgle, and crappy diaper produced by the Hummer had been broadcast 24/7 on *Inside Access* and chronicled in *People* since she had arrived courtesy of the Cedars-Sinai maternity ward and a midwife flown in from the Farm, a commune in Summertown, Tennessee.

Sam hoisted her Tuff Betty bag and headed for the circular stairway. It was only ten o'clock, but the minor chords and lilting clarinet of klezmer-style music hit her before she reached step three.

Shit. Dee was at it again.

"Oh, Miss Sam?" Svetlana, who was Sam's favorite out of all the household help and had recently come to America from one of the western republics of the former Soviet Union (Sam couldn't remember whether it was Moldova or Belarus), was waiting for her at the base of the stairs. She'd been trained as a medical doctor in her home country but had chosen to emigrate to America to seek a better life for her children. She and Sam sometimes had long discussions over tea about Russian literature and the merits of capitalism and socialism. "Mrs. Sharpe would like you to join her in family room."

"Thanks, Sveta," Sam told her. "Who's visiting us today?"

"American fashion magazine," the white-uniformed maid reported, then pushed some brown curls off her forehead. "I think *InStyle*. I return to kitchen now."

The klezmer music got louder as Sam passed through the enormous white-tiled foyer on her way to the living room. She dropped her travel bags on the floor—she'd get them later, when she left for the plane—wondering what the theme of the *InStyle* shoot would be. Then she remembered: There was going to be a special Hollywood baby section in an upcoming issue, and Poppy's new-mother meditation group was going to be prominently featured.

Fine. She didn't have to be a part of it, since she didn't have a kid and wasn't pregnant. She'd peek in, say hello to her father and Poppy, wave at the photographer, and then go the Beverly Hills Coffee Bean for some serious caffeine stimulation. In just a few hours, she'd be in Las Vegas and forget that she'd even had the experience.

Sam went into the living room, which had recently been redecorated after Jackson had gone to a dinner party at Simon Cowell's house in the Hollywood Hills and been smitten by the layout. The only difference was, Jackson's living room was six times the size of Simon's. But after Jackson had gotten Poppy's approval, out had gone the old and in had come the new: There were four beige overstuffed Italian couches covered with white goose-down pillows from Slovenia and a handwoven rug from Istanbul, beige with red stripes. All the artwork had been consigned and replaced with photo-realistic paintings of rural Ireland. The fireplace had been completely redone so that it could burn real wood. Though it was now April, a blaze roared away. Sam liked the redecoration but wondered if it had been necessary, since the living room had been completely made over not eighteen months before in an Art Deco style she'd adored.

The room was crowded with coiffed mothers, all of them young, beautiful and skinny—or at least their perfectly applied cosmetics and professional plastic surgery made them look that way. All wore some variation on the upscale hip yoga-wear look du jour: Zen Nation black or gray pants and plain white T-shirts over sports bras. Sam found the whole thing kind of . . . well, she knew that Svetlana would describe the uniformity of uniform as unintentionally Bolshevik.

The couches had been moved so the six new mothers could sit in the lotus position on their rattan yoga mats on the floor. Surrounding them were bright photographer's lights and the *InStyle* camera crew. A thirtyish producer in a black-and-white pin-striped Armani pantsuit issued directions to her crew in hushed tones. Beyond her, a posse of young makeup artists and hair stylists stood at the ready—the only difference in appearance between these assistants and the moms was that the assistants weren't in yoga uniform. Sam saw that they were armed with Chantecaille Future Skin, whose light diffusers made it appear as if each new mom had perfect skin; Laura Mercier Lip Glaces, for shiny, pouty, "natural" lips; and HairfixTotal Detox spray, in case a single glossy hair should pop out of place.

From somewhere in the distance—the gym off the family room, maybe?—Sam heard the collective wailing of babies. Certainly, they were not unattended. Most likely, each woman had brought her own day nurse.

Suddenly, the klezmer music stopped. Well, thank God for small favors. At least Dee Young wouldn't . . .

"Hi, Sam."

Sam turned. There was Dee, wearing one of the same Zen Nation black pants/plain white T-shirt combinations as the new mothers. Dee had met Sam's step-mother at the Kabbalah Centre in February. They'd become good friends, and then Poppy had asked Dee to stay with the Sharpes while Dee's parents were on a business trip back east. Dees's father was a famous music producer; her mother had accompanied him to try to head off one of the business-trip liaisons that she feared was threatening their marriage. That business trip had extended and extended and extended, and Dee had never gone back home. In fact, Dee's parents were now in Europe. Meanwhile, Dee and Poppy were now bonded like sisters, though Sam sometimes wondered whether her friend was getting more attached to the new baby than to her mother.

Sometimes it was fun to have Dee around. They were both only children—well, Sam had been until the arrival of the Hummer—and they'd been best friends forever. But Dee seemed to get wackier on a daily basis—she'd taken her study of Jewish mysticism to new heights (she was now attending Shabbat services at Chabad of Beverly Hills on a regular basis, though her record producer father was an avowed atheist and her mother raised a Lutheran), and somehow melded it with her own peculiar brand of New Age spiritual thinking. Half the time, Sam had to admit that she had no clue what her longtime friend was talking about. Nor did Poppy or Dee make any effort to invite her into their troika with the new baby. Sam felt left out. And sometimes it hurt.

"I'm leading the mothers' meditation," Dee reported. "Poppy insisted." She motioned to the floor. "There's room between Felicity and Francesca. Would you like to join us?"

Felicity and Francesca—one blond, the other red-haired, both wearing identical yoga uniforms—motioned with big smiles and waves for Sam to slide in.

"I don't think so," Sam demurred. "I don't really love the smell of yoga in the morning."

Dee shrugged. "Suit yourself. If you change your mind, there's lots of room."

There was an open mat to Francesca's left, and Dee went to it. As Sam stared in disbelief, she assumed the lotus position, closed her eyes, and, after explaining to the yoga moms that the tune they were about to hear was a famous Hasidic melody, began to hum. The tune's lack of lyrics was deliberate—the notes were designed to bring those chanting it closer to the Eyn Sof, the highest degree of God in kabbalistic terms.

As the lithe *InStyle* photographer sprang into action, the meditation circle picked up the chant, which continued for a few minutes, waxing and waning in intensity. In a certain way, Sam found it soothing and beautiful. In every other way, she found it absolutely bizarre. That her friend Dee should be leading it—the only one in the circle who didn't have a child—was most bizarre of all. Yet the mothers seemed to have no objection. On the contrary, they were getting into it.

Then Dee spoke, her eyes still closed. "I am eternal bliss, I am eternal happiness."

"I am eternal bliss, I am eternal happiness," the women echoed, their eyes closed as well.

"I am at one with my baby. We are at peace together," Dee chanted.

"I am at one with my baby. We are at peace together," the women responded.

Sam rolled her eyes at this picture of Dee leading a meditation circle. Dee honestly probably couldn't even *spell* meditation. Then she mentally relented. Her friendship with Dee had never been based on the intellectual. She had other friends, like Anna, for that. Instead—at least before she'd become the poster girl for Jewish mysticism—Dee was sincere. Sweet. Loyal. She'd stood by Sam through thick and . . . well, thicker (Sam had never come within striking distance of *thin*).

Sam saw one of Poppy's eyes pop open.

"Sam!" her stepmother wheedled. "Come join us!" Then she quickly scanned the room for the lead photographer, making sure that her right profile, which was her best side, faced him.

"I'll pass," Sam grumbled as she checked her new

Patek Philippe watch, uncertain how long the meditation circle was planning to continue. "Dee, are you packed? We're leaving for Vegas really soon."

She knew she was exaggerating for effect, but she also knew that Dee was one of the world's great procrastinators. That she had gotten her friend to change her mind about the Vegas trip had been a minor miracle in and of itself.

Dee fixed her cornflower blue eyes on her dear friend. "I don't need clothes. What I'm wearing is fine."

"For four days?"

"I'll wash my things out and hang them over the tub," Dee replied, a serene expression on her face. "When there is inner peace, the outer trappings are so unimportant." She turned and smiled at the camera.

Gawd. Dee was actually playing to the camera. How nauseating. "Dee, this is Vegas we're talking about." Sam tried to keep her voice even. "It's *all* about the outer trappings."

"For you, maybe." Dee held her palms up to Sam. "Wherever you go, Sam, there you are."

"What does that even *mean*, Dee?" Sam demanded.

"Do you mind, Sam? You're upsetting the *chi* in here," one of the new mothers with a punk platinum blond hairdo blurted out. She seemed to want to raise her eyebrows with indignation, but since her face had been Botoxed into submission, it was difficult to tell.

"Well, *chi* wiz," Sam quipped.

"Don't worry about it, Sam—this is great stuff!" the

InStyle producer chortled. "I love that natural family vibe! Do you mind if we get a few shots of you?"

"Yep, I sure do mind." Sam slapped a perky smile on her face. "Dee, if you don't mind, could I speak to you and your *chi* in the study?"

Without waiting for an answer, Sam turned around and headed for her father's study—actually an ornate library done in nineteenth-century British style. Bookcases lined three of the walls from floor to ceiling; four plush leather chairs faced one another at right angles, each with its own Tiffany reading lamp. There were two rolling ladders to reach books on the highest levels and a huge picture window that looked out on the only weeping willow tree Sam knew about in Bel Air.

All the world's greatest literature was on those shelves, bound in leather. Sam was the only one in the household who actually ever read any of it. While waiting for Dee, she pretended to busy herself with a first edition of Herman Wouk's *Youngblood Hawke*—a novel about an aspiring writer that Sam had always thought was a masterpiece of storytelling. She heard rather than saw Dee pad into the room.

"What is it?" Dee asked, blowing her wispy bangs off her forehead. Evidently, meditating had caused her to work up a sweat.

Sam wasn't exactly sure how to approach what she wanted to say. So she lifted one of the priceless gold Fabergé eggs that decorated some of the small bookstands around the library, then absentmindedly tossed it from one hand to the other. "You know how much I want you on this Vegas trip. I mean, we've been planning it forever."

"Careful with that egg," Dee cautioned. "It's worth about a million dollars."

"Two million." Sam set the egg down. She didn't want to hurt Dee's feelings, she really didn't. But her loony spiritual bullshit could ruin the entire Vegas trip. "Anyway," she continued, "I'm not sure that you're in the right frame of mind these days to really enjoy Vegas." She hoped she sounded sincere. "What I was thinking was, your parents are still out of town. This seems like the perfect time for you to go home and embrace the quiet. For your spiritual growth, of course. Without any of us around to distract you. Think what a pleasure that would be."

Dee's lower lip trembled. "You don't want me to come?"

"Of course I want you to come!" Sam insisted, perhaps a shade too enthusiastically. She tempered her pitch for the sake of covering over her bald-faced lie and bought a moment's breathing room by putting *Youngblood Hawke* back on its shelf. "But seriously, Dee—look at yourself. You're a changed person. You don't drink anymore. You've become a vegan. You don't have sex. You don't gamble. I admire you for it, I really do. But why would you even *want* to go to Las Vegas?"

"Oh, see, that's the beautiful part." Dee's face lit up.

"People in Vegas are so lost, you know? I really think I could help them."

Sam felt like heaving into the nearest planter. "You're going to Vegas to help the sinners?"

"I'm doing so much healing work now, Sam," Dee explained earnestly. "It's so life-affirming, you know? It's God-realization. A kind of tikkun olam, a repairing of the world, a regathering of the divine sparks that were lost at the moment of creation. If you would come with me to the Kabbalah Centre just once, you'd see exactly what I mean. Ultimately, work on the self and work on others is the same thing."

I have no fucking idea what she's talking about, Sam thought. She didn't want to say that, though. Hurting Dee's feelings was easily accomplished. But unlike Cammie, who seemed to get perverse joy out of cutting Dee to shreds, Sam remembered that the essential core of Dee was good, even if she got a little—okay, a lot— flaky around the edges.

"All righty, then," Sam chirped. She had no clue what they were going to do in Las Vegas if Dee was serious about changing the souls of its inhabitants. But there was always the chance that the change in scenery would help bring her friend back to a clearer sense of reality. "Well . . . cool. So meet me and the others out front in an hour, okay? That'll give you time to do . . . whatever you need to do. Take whatever you want. Or don't want."

"Sure." Dee put a minuscule hand on Sam's arm. "And Sam . . . it will be fine. Really."

Yuh. Whatever.

An hour later, having rewatched the opening reel of *Apocalypse Now* in her father's screening room, Sam meandered back to the front hall, where Svetlana had just let Cammie and Adam inside. Adam had on faded no-name jeans and a plain red T-shirt—his usual understated look. Cammie wore a beige Sass & Bide silk camisole under a beige Michael Kors fitted suede jacket, and a paler beige Calvin Klein beaded silk skirt, with French Mephisto walking sneakers. She'd kept her lips glossy and pale, her eyeliner smudgy, and her hair wild.

In comparison, in her own travel outfit of a black Armani T-shirt under a red leather J. Crew blazer, and Seven jeans with black satin peep-toe Stuart Weitzman pumps, Sam felt like a dump truck.

"Sorry we're late. Adam would not let me out of bed," Cammie reported.

Adam winked at his friends. "Don't let her fool you. We just grabbed a burger at Tommy's near the Westside Pavilion."

Cammie smiled and stood on her toes to kiss him. "I know. But before that." The kiss turned into something more passionate, which made Sam recoil from the public display of affection. It was annoying, like a ninth grader showing off that she was hot enough to kiss a guy in public. But Cammie wasn't in ninth grade, for God's sake. She was a senior. Eduardo would never have done anything like that. He was far too cultured, too civilized. For a fleeting moment, Sam was tempted to go join the meditation circle in the living room, but the sound of laughter and the photographers packing up meant the shoot was over.

Four days in Vegas. Gawd. Cammie and Adam would have their tongues down each other's throats the whole time. Dee would be converting sinners. Parker wasn't exactly stimulating company. Her friends Krishna and Blue had copped out at the last moment because Krishna's parents were in a vicious custody battle and Krishna had to testify. Blue was hanging out with Krishna to offer amoral support.

If Anna wasn't going on this trip, I swear I'd bag the whole thing, Sam thought.

As if on cue, the front doorbell—a renovated antique French one that had been programmed to play the first five notes of the theme from *Snow Job*—sounded. Sam opened the door to find Anna. "Hi. I'm not late, I hope."

"Nope, right on time. If we can pry Dee loose from the young mothers' brigade in the family room, we might be able to get out of here early. Parker's meeting us at the Van Nuys Airport after his callback for *Everwood*. It's at the WB studio in Burbank."

Anna looked great—pulled together as always, in a vintage Chanel tweed blazer over a simple white tee and no-name black trousers from some bygone era. She wasn't even wearing heels; instead, she had on black Ferragamo ballet flats. She carried a Maschera Italian pink woven tote bag over her shoulder that could only have carried half the gear that Sam had chosen to bring along.

"He won't get it," Cammie decreed. "A client of my father already has first refusal."

"So why do they bother giving him a callback?" Anna wondered aloud. "He'll get his hopes up for nothing. That's just mean."

"Aren't you sweet to care," Cammie cooed, in a way that made it perfectly clear how much she *didn't*. "I'm sure Parker will let you kiss it and make it all better."

"Meow," Sam said. She picked her stuff up, thinking it was time for them to get going.

"You really need to be declawed," Adam told Cammie, but he put his arm around her anyway.

"Not while I'm in heat, sweetheart," Cammie purred. "Because you know how much you love it when I scratch."

Sam sighed. It was going to be a very long four days.

A Deep Thinker

Parker Pinelli was a man with a plan: Get in with the innest of the Beverly Hills High hip crowd. Use protective coloration—that would be his six-foot-tall-with-a-six-pack, James Dean–esque good looks—to swim with the sharks. And ride the wave all the way to superstardom on the silver screen.

The problem was, Parker came from a long line of bottom-feeders.

His mother, Patti, who'd had no education and had come from even less money, had been an exotic dancer while waiting for her "big break." It had come in the form of Bruno Pinelli, owner of the Jet Strip club in North Hollywood where Patti danced. Bruno had used his "connections" to get her cast in an R-rated straight-to-video piece called *Posers*, in which her major responsibility had been to take off whatever top she was wearing at regular intervals. That had been the beginning and end of Patti's big career as an actress.

Four years and two sons later, Patti divorced Bruno—or, as she so fondly called him, "that son of a bitch"—and moved on. "On" had meant scraping by as a dancer—the older she got, the further the clubs were from home—or a waitress and renting whatever crappy makeshift apartment she could afford that put her sons on the tattered edges of the 90210 zip code. Her sons would go to school in Beverly Hills and hobnob with the best, Patti had stubbornly decided. They'd have access. Access would lead to success. Her ex— who'd told her once when he was drunk that she had a saggy ass—could kiss her tush and rot in hell. Her big dream was to be Parker's escort to the Oscars—to walk the red carpet with the whole world watching. And especially with Bruno watching. She repeated this dream often to her son, the way other parents repeated the Golden Rule.

Now, Parker sat alone on Jackson Sharpe's glorious private jet, which had departed from the Van Nuys airport just a half hour before, feeling his mother would be very proud of him. The others were watching *Hooligans*, starring Elijah Wood, on the new plasma TV. That was fine. He was content to stare out the window and feel good about where he was in his life.

Parker had been on the plane once or twice before, but that didn't mean it didn't impress him. It was a fifteen-seat Gulfstream that Jackson had acquired from John Travolta when John decided to upgrade. The Gulfstream could fly as fast as many commercial airliners, and the group was already halfway to Sin City. The plane had been redecorated since the last time Parker had flown in it. There were new leather seats and a custom-made sleeper couch in the deepest shades of brown; the entertainment center was brand-new, with a fifty-inch high-definition plasma television and state-of-the-art sound system; and Jackson had recently added a small games area, with foosball, table hockey, and a poker pit.

That was nice. But the important thing was, the members of the Beverly Hills High School A-list were on that plane, and Parker was firmly part of that group. It wasn't a big crew. Sam Sharpe and Cammie Sheppard and that gorgeous new girl, Anna Percy. Dee Young. Cammie's boyfriend, Adam Flood.

It didn't hurt to be the only unattached guy on this outing. Vegas meant gambling and drinking. Gambling and drinking meant lowered inhibitions. With lowered inhibitions, who knew what could happen? It wasn't that he was necessarily interested in sex, though he certainly wasn't morally opposed. But two of those four babes had fabulous industry connections, and Anna Percy had to know a ton of people too. And connections, after all, were what it was all about.

Normally, Parker would even have made something of the opportunity of the flight. Sam had told him that the pilot had written a pretty good screenplay about an Air Force officer who blew the whistle on wrongdoing at the Pentagon that her father had actually optioned. One charming conversation with the guy, and Parker figured at the very least he'd be able to snag an audition. And if the pilot were gay . . . well, Parker wasn't morally opposed to that either.

He closed his eyes. Parker was sure that no one would suspect that he was deep in thought. Doubtful any of them would even consider the possibility, since none of them considered him a deep thinker. They all saw him as Richard Gere in *American Gigolo*, when he knew he was actually Richard Gere in *An Officer and a Gentleman*. Of course, that was if they'd seen those pictures. Parker was reasonably confident that Sam had, since she was obviously the smartest of the bunch except for the chick from New York. As for the others, who knew?

He thought for a moment about Richard Gere's dad in *An Officer and a Gentleman*. Man, was he messed up. Parker could relate. His mother was equally messed up, diagnosed as manic-depressive years ago. When she took her clozapine, she was on the fringe of functional. When she didn't, she was a wreck; it was everything he and his younger brother, Monty, could do to keep her out of either jail or a mental institution.

But things were looking up. For the last month, Mrs. Pinelli had been part of a clinical trial at the UCLA Psychiatric Institute, where a new drug was being tried out—a drug so new that it didn't yet have a name, just a number. The good news was that the drug worked much better for her than any of the previous drugs. Parker's mom was calmer, more functional, sometimes even funny. He hadn't come out of his room in the middle of the night to find her scrubbing the kitchen floor on her hands and knees with a tiny sponge since she'd started taking the drug. Plus it only had to be taken once a week, thereby increasing the odds that his mother would actually ingest it on a regular basis.

The bad news: QVC.

The new drug gave his mother insomnia. Chronic insomnia. One particular night when she couldn't sleep, she'd discovered the joys of shopping via TV. Now it was a nightly ritual. She'd get home from her cocktail waitress job at the Sheraton by the airport and turn on the television, chain smoking and watching until three or four in the morning. It wasn't a rare thing for Parker to awaken for school and find his mother snoring on their threadbare Sears tan-and-black tweed couch, the remote still in hand, the plastic hotel ashtray she'd pilfered brimming with Merit Ultra Light cigarette butts.

And the things she bought! She kept a messy hand-scrawled list on the battered coffee table: European-inspired Amadeus fine linens, Tiffany-inspired limited-edition lamps, Polish-inspired functional ceramic cookware, even though she didn't cook and the family lived largely on deli-counter takeout from Ralph's supermarket. How she could afford all this stuff, he wasn't sure. But the boxes arrived by UPS, sometimes on a daily basis. And the goods stacked up in her closet, even squeezing out her limited wardrobe. Once or twice Parker and Monty had tried to talk to their mother about her QVC habit. The conversations had been futile.

"Hey, what's up?"

Parker looked up to see Sam plop down beside him. He recognized her outfit, the black Armani T-shirt under a red leather J. Crew blazer, and Seven jeans with black satin peep-toe Stuart Weitzman pumps. He remembered that she'd worn a variation on it to school a few weeks ago. Parker knew fashion—it was part of the image he wished to maintain, although his own outfits were usually purchased on the sly at one of the many upscale used-clothing boutiques found in the San Fernando Valley, that vast wasteland of suburbia over the hill from Beverly Hills and Westwood. He understood how shocked many in flyover country would be to know how many of their favorite stars lived such lavish life styles that they were reduced to selling off their wardrobes when they were "between deals." He'd run into some of them at the consignment places in the valley where he liked to shop.

Now Parker flashed Sam what he knew to be his killer smile and made sure his tone came off casual, easy. "Not much."

"Hey, I heard about the *Everwood* thing, that bites."

Parker shrugged. "What can you do? Cammie's father is a great agent; mine can't compete with him."

Sam nodded. "Good attitude."

"Doesn't do any good to complain. Maybe one day Clark Sheppard will take me on."

"So anyway, Vegas will help you forget all about it, right? No worries? And make me forget about Eduardo for a few days. Maybe."

"For sure," he agreed.

There was one thing, though, that Parker was worried about: money. He'd planned to be part of the cool kids' alternative senior trip ever since he'd first heard about it his freshman year. Of course, in his fantasies, he'd already have been a star at that point, throwing cash around like water. Reality was more than slightly different. As in, he had ninety-three bucks on him, and only that much because he'd recently filmed a local advertisement for a really bad mattress company that would be shown in movie theaters before the trailers started. If Parker didn't win a bunch of money quickly, he knew he'd have to do his usual hustle to cover his costs on the trip.

He wasn't *that* worried, though—he'd been in situations like this before and had always come out okay. Life wasn't fair, and it was a tribute to his acting skills that he'd this far been able to fool everyone into thinking that he was one of them.

"Mr. Pinelli?" The flight attendant, a tall guy in his twenties with closely cropped red hair, held out a tray with steaming hot washcloths.

Parker knew from past experience on the Sharpe jet that the flight attendant always knew everyone's name ahead of time. He took a washcloth. "Thanks."

The flight attendant moved on to offer hot wash-cloths to Cammie and Dee. Parker turned to peer at the girls. They'd given up on the movie and were deep in conversation about something or other. And at Anna, who was reading a thick hardcover novel, probably by some dead writer from England or France whom he'd never heard of. No, life was not fair. But he was sick of being the poor kid pretending to be rich. Look at them! Cammie, so hot it was painful, and so rich that she never wore the same things twice. Her father made a fortune as an agent—she was almost as rich as Sam. Dee, with her lost-little-girl thing, spent more on clothes in one month than his mother made in a year. And Anna . . . well, there was the very distinct possibility that she was the richest of them all.

The flight attendant came around again holding out his empty tray for the used washcloths. Parker deposited his. The attendant moved on to Adam.

Parker really liked Adam Flood. He was the epitome of a stand-up guy—laid-back and genuine. He might not have the deep pockets of the others, but his parents were both lawyers, which meant they had to do mid-to-high six figures, easy. He was certainly well-heeled enough to hook up with the Princess of Heat, Cammie Sheppard. In fact, right now she was all over him.

Parker made a mental note to pay extra attention to Adam. The guy was such a study in contrasts. He'd seen Adam on the basketball court, and the guy was a warrior. Once, when he'd thought one of his teammates had been fouled too roughly, he'd gotten right in the face of the aggressor, a guy ten inches taller and sixty pounds heavier than he was. The refs had had to keep the two players apart. But at other times, Adam seemed mild-mannered and laid-back. Who was he, really?

"Miss Sharpe, the champagne you requested?" The flight attendant had just wheeled in a magnum of Veuve-Clicquot in a silver bucket, buried to the hilt in ice chips. After Sam approved the bottle, he handed everyone champagne flutes. That everyone on the plane was underage was not an issue. Jackson Sharpe had given instructions that the pilot and flight attendant were to treat the passengers as if they were adults. The only thing that wouldn't be tolerated would be felonious substance abuse.

"Who wants to pop the cherry?" Sam sang out, holding the bottle aloft as her friends gathered around her and Parker.

"I'd be honored," Parker volunteered. "And I'll try to make it good for you, sweetheart."

"What a guy." Sam ceremoniously handed him the champagne bottle, which the flight attendant had wrapped in a white towel monogrammed with Jackson's initials.

"Better you than me," Cammie cracked.

Whatever. Parker didn't rise to the bait. He knew most things that a boy who faked being rich in Beverly Hills should know, including how to remove the cork from a bottle of champagne that cost more than all the cash in his wallet. Undo the cage—there were always six half turns, no matter how expensive or cheap the brand. Hold the cork in one hand, twist the bottle with the other. When you felt the cork start to release, you had to press down on it, so that it released with absolutely zero spillage. (Parker couldn't believe that Alexander Payne had given this last tip away in his screenplay for *Sideways*.)

Whoosh! The cork ejected with absolutely zero spillage or foaming, earning Parker some minor accolades. Then he himself poured everyone a tall glassful before handing the bottle back to the flight attendant.

Sam hoisted her glass in the air. "Here's to wild and crazy us in wild and crazy Vegas," she pronounced. "Sex, drugs, and rock and roll! If only Eduardo could be here."

"To Eduardo!" Anna chimed in.

Everyone clinked glasses—Parker was quick to notice that Cammie touched her glass to everyone's but Anna's. So. Cammie was still holding a grudge because of how her old boyfriend, Ben, had hooked up with Anna. It was time she got over it. Parker knew both these guys, and Adam Flood was way cooler than Ben Birnbaum any day of the week. But trust these girls to continue their ongoing Catfights of the Rich and Famous. It wasn't like they had anything else to worry about.

Parker drank. Whoa. Tasty. He loved good champagne; it flowed down his throat like honey. One of the problems of pretending to be rich was having developed the tastes of the rich. It was hard to go back to Korbel after enjoying the stuff on the top shelf.

The flight attendant touched his right ear, where he had an earphone that connected to the cockpit. "Please take your seats and buckle up, everyone. We're starting our descent into Las Vegas. We'll be on the ground in twenty minutes."

Sam handed her champagne flute to Parker. "I'm going back to my seat. Drink up. You look like you could use it."

He grinned. Fair enough. It was good champagne. He should have swallowed his distaste and tried to try to hook up with Sam long ago. With her on his arm, he'd have had access to everything. And she wasn't all that bad looking, either. But now she had some South American boyfriend whom she talked about in every third sentence.

Well, Parker knew Beverly Hills relationships just as well as he knew fashion: Today's in-love couple was only one step away from their big breakup. It was only a matter of time.

"So, what did Ben *say*?"

Anna looked up—she'd been lost in *Vanity Fair*— the Thackeray novel, not the magazine. For some reason, she found it calming to lose herself in another era, and when she read she felt as if she were actually there. But she forced her mind forward from the last century to this one. She was in an airplane—Sam's father's jet.

The lights of Las Vegas were off in the distance—they could only be minutes from landing.

"Ben?" Sam prompted. "On the phone?" She fiddled with one aqua quartz earring that had gotten tangled in her hair.

Anna flushed. "I didn't exactly call."

"Because . . . ?"

Excellent question. Anna had stared at the phone, nearly dialing Ben's number a dozen times. She didn't know what she'd say to him. Also, she didn't know what he'd say to her. What if he said, "Look, Anna, could you please not call me anymore. We're history, my father was delusional?" Possibly. If there was anyone in the world who could make her lose her carefully nurtured sense of control, it was Ben.

Sam leaned against the back of her seat. "You wussed out."

"If I just knew how he felt, maybe I'd—"

Before Anna could finish her sentence, Sam was waving her own cell phone in Anna's face.

"I can't call from an airplane, it'll mess up the pilot—"

"Please. That's total bullshit," Sam scoffed. "We do it all the time. Just press send. I already dialed his number."

"Why did you—?"

"I might not have known you very long, Anna, but I do know you very well." Sam smiled smugly.

"And you knew I wouldn't call him."

"I'm so brilliant I scare myself. Now go to the back of the plane. And call."

Sam hadn't left her much of an option. And there was no evil commercial airline flight attendant to turn her over to the federal marshals for leaving her seat while the FASTEN SEAT BELT sign was illuminated. So Anna went to the back of the plane. Sat down. Pressed send. Prayed to the gods to spare her from her fate.

The gods were with her. Voice mail.

Her heart felt as if it were jumping around inside, and she could barely catch her breath. "Hi, it's me. Anna." She kept her voice low, not wanting anyone to overhear her. Then she realized that the noise of the Gulfstream's engines made that impossible. In fact, she'd better speak up or she'd be completely drowned out.

"I'm calling you from Sam's father's jet." Anna winced. Great. Now she sounded like she was booming over a public address system. She made another vocal adjustment. "We're on our way to Las Vegas. It's the senior class trip." Then she remembered that of course he knew that; he'd gone the year before. Dumb. But too late now. She plunged on. "Umm . . . I saw your father at the Academy Awards. He looked really good. And . . . he said that you were doing well. I'm happy about that, and . . ."

Her voice trailed off. What did she want to say, really? "I'll be in Las Vegas until Friday. Maybe we can talk when I get home."

Should she add, I think about you a lot? Or how about, Come to Vegas and ravish me. But then she remembered yet another lesson that had been imparted early and often by the one and only Jane Percy: You rarely get into trouble for the things you don't say.

So all she finished with was, "I guess I'll see you later."

Nothin' but Lobster

"How tacky is this?" Cammie rolled her eyes as the group strode through McCarron Airport in Las Vegas. They had to dodge around every type of tourist—from old ladies with walkers to cheap-T-shirt-clad middle-agers from flyover states.

"No shit," Parker agreed. Plus the noise was overwhelming. A row of slot machines lined the hallway they were traipsing through on their way out of the airport. Men in business suits, couples, and a set of what looked to be fortyish triplets in matching gingham shirts played the machines with utter concentration.

Cammie shook her hair off her face. "God, it reeks of desperation."

"The odds must suck," Adam added.

Parker wasn't so sure. A guy he'd met at a Chippendale's audition (they'd been more than willing to hire him, but he hadn't had a fake ID at the time and he'd been just sixteen) had said he'd won five grand in the Reno airport on the slots while he was killing time before a gig at Harveys Lake Tahoe. All it had taken was a buck and a press of the button on the machine.

The chump change Parker had in his pocket wasn't even going to buy a round of drinks at Rain, the night-club at the Palms Hotel, where they'd all be staying. Five grand sounded good right now. Really good.

"Hey, what the hell, I'm a lucky guy," Parker offered casually. "Hold up, you guys."

"Parker, if you want to lose your money, why don't you give it to a worthy cause?" Dee rushed to suggest, righting her carry-on as it nearly fell over. "If you give it to me, I'll be sure it gets into the right hands."

"Sorry, Dee." Parker was careful to keep his tone light as he fished a tenner out of his pocket and fed it into the bill receiver of a slot machine—he couldn't risk having any of them guess how badly he needed to win. "But this money *is* going to a good cause right now. Me."

He scanned the rules of the slot machine. A buck a bet. Three of the same symbol on the same line and he'd win five bucks on his dollar bet. Four of the same symbol and he'd win fifty bucks. Five of the same: plums, cherries, orange slices, and he'd win five thousand bucks. The big money was five dollar signs in a row. If that came up, he'd win twenty thousand dollars.

Sweet.

Parker blew on his fingers for luck, then wiggled them in the air. He hit the game button and got only two matches.

"Tough luck, dude," Adam consoled him, as the others gathered around to watch.

He tried again. Two matches. Again. No matches.

"Come on," Adam suggested. "Press the refund button and get the rest of your money back.

"Nah," Parker was stubborn. "This is my machine. I can feel it."

Whether he could feel it or not, the machine was eating his money as fast as other machines were eating the money of gamblers to his left and right. In two quick minutes, the ten dollars were gone.

"Sucker!" Cammie cooed cheerfully. "I could have bought half a fill for that at a manicure mill in Studio City."

But Parker knew that Cammie didn't do manicure mills in Studio City. She went to Elle on Beverly Boulevard, where the mani-pedi combo ran a hundred and twenty-five dollars. That was where all the girls went; they had weekly standing appointments.

"I'm not ready to quit."

He pulled a crisp twenty from his pocket, smoothed it out, and fed it into the machine, knowing all the while that if he lost it, he'd be down approximately thirty percent of his total stake for the trip. This time, he asked Cammie to hit the play button. Then Anna. Then Sam. Then Dee. She refused. So he pressed it himself. Nothing. Shit.

"It's probably rigged so that it never hits, man," Adam sympathized. "You really should just cash out."

But Parker was too far in it now. He hit the play button, and finally, up came three cherries. The machine registered that he had five dollars, and a sign lit up asking him if he wanted to cash out.

"Take the money and run." Sam leaned against the wall. "Let's go to the hotel."

Parker rubbed his hands together. "I'm just warming up, darlin'." He played on. And lost. Over and over and over. It felt personal now. He was not going to let this machine take advantage of him. It felt too much like his life—a have-not trying to get something from the haves. Oh, sure, he knew full well that was the whole point—for the machine to take advantage of him. If the machine didn't take advantage of him, there'd be no machine. There'd be no Las Vegas, for chrissake.

But he fed the machine another twenty.

"Can we just go?" Cammie asked irritably. Adam started rubbing the back of her neck. She leaned into him.

The twenty disappeared as quickly as did the rest of his money, with a few five dollars hits along the way to tease him.

He took out his last ten, feeling sick to his stomach. But he kept a cool smile on his face.

"Really, Parker." Sam sounded annoyed. "Let's go!"

Maybe he really should. Parker hesitated—he knew he'd be living off his friends' largesse for the rest of the week. Those friends were urging him to quit, too, even if they were nice about it. They had no idea how much winning would mean to him. They all thought he was just like them.

Yeah, right. He wasn't even sure his home phone would be working when he got back, because his mother only had part of the money for the phone bill.

But hell if he'd ever let on to any of them. Parker summoned every last ounce of dignity he had left and smiled at Anna. "Hit play for me?"

"On your ten dollar bill?" Anna asked.

"Hey, go for it." Parker put his hands behind his head, a man without a care in the world.

Anna leaned over and hit play.

A dollar sign came up.

Then another. And another. And another.

And . . . *yes.*

A red light atop the machine began to blink on and off; bells went off and sirens wailed. A fire-engine light whirled on top of the machine, flashing crazily. From all over the betting area—from all over the terminal!— people were running toward Parker to see what he'd won.

Parker couldn't help it. He leaped into the air. "Holy shit! I just won twenty thousand dollars!" He grabbed Anna and gave her an exuberant kiss.

"Congratulations, guy," Cammie smirked. "You're buying dinner tonight."

"Lobster, baby, nothin' but lobster," Parker declared. "So how do I collect?"

An overweight woman in an I WENT TO VEGAS AND ALL I'VE GOT LEFT IS THIS STUPID T-SHIRT! T-shirt sidled up and pointed to the sign above the machine. It read, ATTENDANT PAYS ALL WINS OVER $500.

"You wait for the guy to pay," she told him, her accent thick and Southern. "Dang, I've never seen anyone win that much before!"

Parker craned around, looking for the attendant. Meanwhile, the crowd of travelers edged closer to him, peering at the machine, marveling at his good fortune.

A gaunt older woman with an unfortunate bulbous nose in a gray uniform lumbered over to him. Her name tag identified her as Arlene Spector. She peered at the five-dollar-sign screen in real amazement, then inserted a key into the machine that turned off the bells and whistles.

"Wow, sir. You really hit it."

"You're the attendant?" Parker asked.

She nodded. "Damn, I been working here for six months and I never seen anyone hit it before."

Parker threw his hands in the air. "Must be my lucky day!"

"You can say that again," Arlene agreed as she took out a form and wrote some codes from the winning machine on it. Then she propped an OUT OF ORDER sign on the machine and shut off the bells and whistles. "Come with me, sweetheart," she told Parker. "We're going to the office so you can collect."

"Can we come with him?" Adam asked.

"You'd better," Arlene bantered easily, "if you want him to buy you dinner before he escapes into the night."

The crowd of tourists around them laughed heartily, then parted so that the slots attendant could lead newly

famous Parker and the others deep into the bowels of
the airport. They trekked through a red high-security
door marked NO ADMITTANCE! and then down a
narrow corridor.

"Surreal," Parker muttered.

Finally, they came to a utilitarian room with two
desks, some computer equipment, and a row of wooden
chairs against the wall. Behind one of the desks sat a
late thirties-ish gaunt-faced blonde with serious roots
in a gray uniform. Her face was spackled with makeup,
her lips outlined in an entirely different color than her
lipstick.

"Who's the lucky winner?" she asked as Arlene led
the kids into the room.

"That'd be me," Parker declared, oozing cool.

Man, this was so amazing. Screw *Everwood*. All he
could have gotten for the gig would have been scale—
the Screen Actors Guild minimum—plus ten percent. It
would have only come to a small fraction of his win.

"Name, Mr. Winner?"

"Parker Pinelli."

"Parker 'The *Man*' Pinelli," Adam teased. The others
chuckled and gathered around.

The woman fixed her a steady gaze on Parker, her
face impassive. "I'll need to see some identification, Mr.
Pinelli."

Parker flashed his perfect smile again. The signs
posted by the slot machines very clearly stated that you
had to be twenty-one to gamble. He had this covered.

Even as he felt his friends' eyes on him, he opened his wallet. Removed a perfect falsified California driver's license he'd had made after his minor humiliation at Chippendales. Took three steps toward the desk and tossed it to her.

"Here ya go."

The woman studied it—it identified him as Parker Pinelli of Beverly Hills, California, but gave his age as twenty-two. Then she looked up at Parker, who was deliberately rubbing his hands together. He thought that was probably what some guy who was just about to collect twenty grand might do.

She shook her head. "Sorry."

Parker didn't understand. "What does that mean?"

She held the driver's license out to him. "Your ID is fraudulent, young man."

"No, it's not," Parker blustered. "Ask my friends."

"He's totally twenty-one," Sam insisted, shoving in next to Parker.

"Uh huh," Cammie agreed mindlessly, flipping through a copy of *Vegas Today* magazine that had been on the counter. Anna had taken one of the orange plastic seats near the door. Adam and Dee sat with her.

"According to Nevada gaming law, unless you can produce genuine identification attesting to your age, it is my obligation to deny you your payout," the official droned. "Violation is a potential felony. For me. Not that you ever gave that a second thought."

"But it's legit," Parker insisted. He managed to keep

his voice even, even though his insides were tied in knots. This bitch *was* going to pay him.

The woman motioned Parker closer. She flipped over the ID and pointed to a thin black strip on the back. "Let's find out."

Shit.

She slid the ID through something like a credit card reader on her desk. "This talks to the DMV in Sacramento. They'll confirm all the information on your license electronically, and if the license is good, this light will flash green. If it's not good, it'll flash—"

The light blinked bright red.

"Ooh, that's gotta hurt," Cammie quipped.

"Been here, seen that." The woman handed Parker back his ID. "Why you kids keep trying to get away with this is beyond me." She scribbled something on an official-looking pad, ripped off the top sheet, and handed him that too.

He peered at it. "You're giving me a *ticket*?"

"Pay the fine within sixty days. By certified check or money order."

Shit, shit, *shit*!

Parker slinked out of the office, his friends in his wake. Did he have the worst luck in the world or what? If one of his friends who *really* had money had managed to win twenty thou, no doubt they would have figured out a way to actually collect it.

"Sucks, man." Adam punched Parker lightly in the bicep.

"Tell me about it," Parker muttered. He was already starting to think about having to do his Las Vegas hustle. It wasn't much different from the Hollywood hustle. Find a female who looked rich, lonely, and insecure. Lavish her with attention. "Discover" that he had forgotten his wallet or his credit card or whatever so that she'd pay. Then make her so happy that she really didn't care that she never got paid back.

Dee reached up and put a tiny arm around his shoulder. "Wow, Parker, I'm so sorry that happened to you."

"Me, too," Anna agreed.

They turned a corner, heading for the glass doors that led outside. Dee frowned. "Have you been putting out bad karma, Parker? Because you know, whatever you put out into the universe is returned to you tenfold."

"Come on, Dee," Anna chided, shifting the strap of her vintage Louis Vuitton overnight bag to the other shoulder. "Sometimes good people have bad luck."

Dee shrugged, unconvinced.

"Hey, whatever." Parker stuffed his fake ID and his ticket into his back right pocket. He didn't dare say more. Truth was, he was close as he'd ever been to crying in public.

Cammie slipped on her new pink Bebe studded sunglasses. "At least it was only twenty thousand," she said philosophically. "I mean, it's not like you won really big money. Now can we get out of this damn airport?"

As Cammie led the group to where their hired limo was waiting, Parker tried to process the insane events of the last fifteen minutes. He'd won, and then lost, *twenty thousand dollars.* He had a couple of crumpled dollar bills left in his wallet, a hundred-dollar ticket for illegal gambling in his pocket, and a pricey week ahead with no way to pay for it.

The whole situation could be summed up in four words: He was so fucked.

All Tease and No Please

Cammie Sheppard switched to her silver cat-shaped Foster Grant sunglasses—she was already bored with the pink Bebe glasses, but fortunately, she always traveled with two pairs. The late afternoon sun was glaring off the road as the black stretch limo cruised from McCarron Airport to the world-famous Las Vegas Strip. And then, beyond it, to the Palms Hotel. She couldn't help thinking that this ride in from the airport did not offer a favorable first impression of Sin City. Lining the boulevard were cheap motels, cheaper places to eat, the same kind of tchotchke stores that you'd find in Hollywood, only with a Vegas theme instead of Tinseltown. Billboards—dozens of them—advertised big hotels and the various over-the-hill stars playing off their name recognition there, just to have a steady gig. Also touted were the extravaganzas that only tourists from Des Moines would actually pay to see: the Folies Bergere at the Tropicana, the Cirque du Soleil at the MGM, and their pathetic moral equivalents at the

Luxor and the Rio. Skimpy costumes, big breasts, long legs, all tease and no please.

And who could forget the headliners? Cher, who kept promising to retire but couldn't keep her butt off a stage—Cammie was ready to *pay* the woman to pack it in. Tom Jones? Engelbert Humperdinck? Puh-leeze. They'd been washed up even when her father and his high school friends had come out to Vegas.

Still, Cammie knew that Vegas had always been happening for Hollywood's young and hip, who skipped all the over-the-top tacky cheesy tourist shit. Or else reveled in the joy of mocking the tourists, an art form unto itself. They were all about private parties at VIP locales, special unadvertised after-hours shows that you had to know about, things like that.

The limo was a stretch job. The buttery leather seats were arranged facing one another. In between, a bar was tucked into one side and a digital sound system connected to a library of thousands of MP3s into the other. Cammie had been in dozens of limos just like it—but not with Adam. Now they sat next to each other, her body fitting easily against his.

"Ready for a great time?" he asked softly.

Cammie nodded and smiled up at him. He smiled back, leaned in, and tenderly kissed her forehead. Nice.

Only one problem. "Nice" and "Cammie Sheppard" weren't often used in the same sentence. She liked Adam. Maybe even loved Adam. But lately she'd begun to feel like she was in sugar shock. There was no doubt that in Cammie's long career with the opposite sex, no boy had ever been so wonderful to her. True, some might have been better in bed (Adam had been a virgin until Cammie had relieved him of that burden), or richer, or all-around sexier. But none of them had had his genuine character, his depth, his sensitivity.

Character? Depth? Sensitivity? Gawd. She wanted to gag all over again. Adam was the definitive good guy; she was the proverbial bad girl. And the truth was, bad boys were just so much . . . juicier.

But. The "but" was a killer. Any time she gave even a passing thought to the notion of breaking up with him, she felt sick to her stomach. Anxious, stressed, and so alone. He was inside her skin. She needed him the way she needed to breathe, needed someone to see the best in her. Even when she couldn't see it herself.

One of the reasons she'd been psyched about this trip with Adam was to see if she could bring out his naughtier side. If Adam could be just a little bad, maybe she could appreciate that he was usually a lot good.

Or maybe he could even just play at being bad. Fun and games. She glanced up at him and he smiled. No, he would never pull it off. Her cutthroat über-agent father was fond of saying that character was destiny, and bad-boyness just wasn't in Adam's character. Anyway, he'd never know about any of the thoughts she'd been having recently. It wasn't like she was about to tell him the truth. He'd be hurt. He might even dump her. She'd lose him. No. The truth was definitely not an option.

The limo driver made a right turn.

"Welcome to the Strip," Cammie overheard Sam tell Anna. "Where America runs away from its Puritan roots."

The lights of the Las Vegas strip—the miles-long main street of hotels, restaurants, casinos, and attractions that made Las Vegas so famous—blazed so bright Cammie could feel them glint off her face. She leaned forward and brought one of the limousine windows down. She loved the energy of this place—the decadence and the insanity, where the poorest tour-bus octogenarian lady and the richest sultan from the Persian Gulf could both escape . . . well, whatever it was they were running from. The famed hotels—the Mirage, the Venetian, the Luxor, the Bellagio, and a dozen others—all had an otherworldly quality, illuminated against a sky that was not quite day and not quite night.

"This has to be the most intense place on the planet," Sam observed, peering out the window. "It's over the top for the sake of being over the top."

Dee, who sat opposite Sam, nodded solemnly. " 'Sound and furry, signifying nothing,' " she quoted.

Cammie shot Dee a withering look. "*Furry?*"

Dee nodded. "Shakespeare."

"I *know* that, Dee," Cammie told her, speaking slowly, as if to a child. "But it's 'fury,' not 'furry.' "

Dee blushed the same shade of salmon as her Sass & Bide silk camisole. "Oh. Well, it could have been *furry*. Like how rich women here wear slaughtered animals' pelts on their backs. All in the name of fashion."

Cammie bit back a blistering comment and leaned back into Adam's arms. It was hard work for her to restrain herself with Dee. The retorts were right there for her to fire back at her friend, and part of her longed to let them fly. Something like, "Dee, if I were you, I'd stick to quoting Dr. Seuss."

"Oh, I love him!" Dee would probably squeal.

Cammie forced herself to keep her mouth shut. Why? Because of Adam, that was why. Adam wanted Cammie to be nice. There it was again. Nice.

"Whoa, check her out." Parker pointed out the window to the crosswalk that led to the Aladdin Hotel. Cammie had stayed there once—it had a desert theme, and its Elemis spa featured treatments influenced by ten different ancient cultures. An apple-cheeked young woman with her platinum blond hair in a high, tight ponytail waited for the light to change so she could cross the street. She looked like she was sporting at least three sets of false eyelashes and wore the shortest of short red Daisy Dukes with black fishnet hose and black boots. Above the waist, a purple faux fur shrug hung over a purple bra top. Her implants—so artificial they made the new BHH principal's boobs look natural—threatened to trigger an avalanche at any moment. Still, all around her, tourists with cameras slung around their necks gawked to see if perhaps she actually was *someone*.

"Damn. I was going to wear that today," Sam joked.

The light changed and the limo turned left. It was

just a mile or so to the Palms, a place too hip to be located on the Strip itself. Instead, it was to the north of the freeway, along with the Rio Hotel.

Seeing the tricked-out showgirl wannabe gave Cammie an idea. Her lips curled into a wicked smile.

"It's perfect," she announced. "Absolutely and hilariously perfect."

Anna turned away from the window. "What?"

Cammie took a moment to study Anna, who was sitting next to Dee and across from Cammie. Her hair was pulled into a loose ponytail at the nape of her neck and tied with a black ribbon. She wore very little makeup. Damn her to hell, she looked just about perfect. Not only that, but even though Cammie knew that Anna hated her, Anna had listened to her. Damn it to hell, that was *nice*.

Cammie clenched her teeth. Anna Percy brought out the very worst in her, the part of her that always made Adam cringe. It had all started at Jackson's wedding to Poppy, when Anna had shown up on the arm of Ben Birnbaum. Cammie and Ben had been an item the year before. The sex had been sizzling. Cammie had actually thought it was more than that—Ben was the first guy she'd actually given a shit about. When he'd broken up with her, she'd felt confident that he'd come crawling back. After all, she was irresistible, wasn't she? Everyone said so. But he hadn't come back. And seeing him with Anna at the wedding . . . well, Cammie had seethed at the attention that Ben was paying to a girl he'd met on an airplane just a few hours before, a kind of total attention that he had never really paid to Cammie. At least with Adam, she knew she'd never have to deal with getting dumped.

Then she felt Adam give her a little squeeze. Cammie exhaled. This was definitely no time to scratch Anna's eyes out, much as she might want to do just that. She'd have to resort to plan B.

"Here's what I was thinking," Cammie told Anna as Sam and Dee listened in. "We should have a tacky Vegas fashion contest. You up for it?" She raised one golden eyebrow that had been arched to perfection at Valerie's on Rodeo Drive.

Ha. Take that, she thought. Let's see if Miss East Coast Big Inheritance bows out on the grounds that it's beneath her station or something.

"Count me in," Anna said easily.

This was the thing about Anna that bit Cammie's peach-shaped butt. Just when Cammie was most confident, Anna would slide right off whatever little psychological hook Cammie was trying to impale her on.

Bitch.

Adam waved a hand. "Count me out."

"I'm with you, my man." Parker gave Adam a fist bump.

"I was thinking females only," Cammie clarified. "The sight of you two in leather corsets is deeply scary. Dee?"

"Tacky Vegas clothes? I don't think my rabbi would want me to wear stuff like that."

"Your rabbi isn't here, Dee," Cammie pointed out.

"Oh, he knows everything—he doesn't have to physically be there. Also, I read in this brochure that there's a past-life-regression yoga class at the Venetian that I'd like to check out."

Cammie waved a hand in the air. "Check away, Dee. You're on your own. If you think your rabbi would approve."

As far as Cammie was concerned, Dee was getting loonier by the nanosecond. Better for her not to participate.

Parker grinned. "Hey, here's an idea. The guys should pick the winner."

"Oh, yeah," Adam agreed. "*And* the prize."

"As long as the prize isn't either one of you," Sam joked.

Dee nodded earnestly. "Because that would mean you weren't being true to Eduardo. I guess you could just not tell him. Do you think it's cheating if you do something and the other person doesn't know you did it?" Dee mused. "I still think it's cheating."

Cammie narrowed her eyes at her. "How many little Dees are in there having a conversation with you right now?"

"She's shining you on, Dee," Adam assured Dee, who still had a quizzical look on her face. "We'll just have to come up with some deeply diabolical prize."

The limo crossed a bridge over Interstate 15, the main route between Los Angeles and Las Vegas. The Palms was just a quarter mile or so ahead, on the left-hand side.

"Do your worst, gentlemen," Anna challenged.

Anna's voice grated on Cammie's ears. It sounded so Old Hollywood, like from those black-and-white 1930s and 1940s movies her dad used to make her watch with him when she was a kid, under the guise of preparing her for the business that he wanted her to enter. Greer Garson in *Mrs. Miniver*. Kate Hepburn in *The African Queen*, back before she'd turned into a vibrating old prune. Cammie had no intention of following in her father's footsteps, but those actresses and movies had stayed with her forever. Not that she had a clue as to what she *did* want to do with her life. She just couldn't abide the notion that she would follow her father and loathed stepmother, Patrice, a well-known actress, into the family business.

"We can go clothes shopping together right after we check in," Sam suggested to Anna. "We just have to find the tackiest place in town."

"Want to come with us, Cammie?" Anna asked.

Double bitch. Like Anna really wanted Cammie to come along.

"Oh, I'll just cruise on my own," Cammie replied, as if it were exactly what she wanted to do. "May the best woman win."

That was *so* going to be her.

She'd have to do it quickly, though. Because now that she'd arrived in Sin City, there was something else on her mind. Make that *someone* else.

Male. And his name wasn't Adam.

Voodoo Economics

The Palms Hotel and Casino, also known as Hollywood in the desert. Even now, a few years after it had opened with much fanfare and hype, the Palms was still *the* Las Vegas home-away-from-home for the movie and TV industry glitterati. At least, the on-camera glitterati. Producers and writers (who could afford it) tended to favor the Bellagio—there were times when the Prime Steakhouse restaurant there was as jammed with producers and scribes as the *Desperate Housewives* writers' room after a profanity-laced phone call from some ABC network executive deep-sixing an episode outline. But most actors and actresses preferred the Palms. They thrived on attention and knew there'd be plenty of people to stare at them.

The limo pulled into the wide circular driveway and came to a halt in front of a long row of glass doors. As it did, Sam read the large marquee behind her:

FRIDAY NIGHT AT RAIN: LENNY KRAVITZ

Rain was the Palms' post-trendy nightclub. Sam had no intention of going to see Lenny with the masses, even if the place *was* supposed to be happening. She'd seen him last year with Dee (courtesy of Dee's record producer dad) at an industry showcase at the House of Blues. There had been an audience of maybe a hundred, plus a killer buffet of mini saffroned scampi crepes and twenty different types of imported caviar with various toppings—sour cream, capers, minced red onions, crushed egg. They'd been invited to Lenny's private party afterward, of course. At Rain there would be an audience of a couple thousand tourists killing themselves not to look like tourists. Not Sam's idea of a good time. She found herself wondering if Eduardo had ever been to Las Vegas. She made a mental note to ask him.

The limo driver opened the doors for his passengers. Sam noted his perfect silver hair and the perennial tan and chiseled profile of a former somebody reduced to a current nobody. She made another mental note: He'd be a good character for some future movie—a one-hit wonder who had faded into oblivion and fallen on hard times, reduced to chauffeuring around the kind of people who used to ask for his autograph. Maybe he'd been a professional boxer. Lots of them tended to settle here in Vegas, where all the championship bouts took place.

"Miss Sharpe?"

Sam realized she'd been staring. "Oh, thanks." She smiled at him as she stepped out into the warm night air.

"You're welcome, Miss Sharpe."

He popped the trunk; an insufferably hip valet in knife-creased black pants, white shirt, and black sports jacket extracted a mountain of luggage from it. His thick glasses and black hair made him look like Elvis Costello. Sam suspected that he encouraged the comparison.

The driver handed Sam his card; Sam said she'd call when they needed him. Then she pressed a twenty-dollar tip into his hand—a reasonable amount of money, but not so much that Mr. Now-Nobody would turn into a fawning sycophant. There were enough of those hanging around her father . . . and, by consequence, her. She and the others followed the valet and their luggage through the front doors.

The Palms had no lobby per se. Just the expanse of the casino—slot machines, blackjack and craps tables, bars, and noise. The registration area was over to the left—a long and narrow counter with just enough room for the young, brown-uniformed desk clerks to check them in. Sam understood full well why the area was so cramped. Every square foot of casino space was precious. Lobbies and registration desks didn't generate cash 24/7 the way slot machines and table games did. In Vegas, it was all about the chip.

The hotel was surprisingly crowded for an ordinary Tuesday in April. Old ladies wheeling portable oxygen tanks mixed with young couples; the well-dressed skirted the tacky as if the tack would rub off on them; the desperate and the thrilled and the burnouts and the superstars mixed in a mosh pit of money, a certain percentage of it lost every day to the house. It was an equal-opportunity wasteland of voodoo economics.

But the Palms sold something else besides Hollywood glitz to the eager consumer: sex. Behind the reception wonks were a row of about twenty video screens showing a loop of Rain on a hot night—mostly videotape of scantily clad girls in their twenties dancing as sexily as they could without being arrested for public lewdness. Ditto video from Skin, the outdoor poolside club, which featured the same girls in white string bikinis. Intercut with these were clips of the Palms Girls, the hotel's resident babes-of-the-year. The six Palms Girls even had their own Web site. New Palms Girls were selected annually at a poolside competition every June that coincided with the owner's birthday. It was your basic *Playboy/Penthouse*–type sex-bomb contest: If you looked the part and were willing to publicly shake your parts, you might be in. When the Palms had sent Jackson Sharpe a gift basket for his Oscar nomination, on top of a thousand dollars in poker chips and a bottle of Cristal champagne had been a Palms Girls calendar.

"Hey, Sam, check it out." Parker touched her arm as they approached a long line snaking back from the reception desk. "Is that Ben Affleck?" He nodded his head toward a dark-haired guy who was threading his way through a bank of slot machines with what looked like a Budweiser in each hand. He was gone before they could decide for sure.

"Hmm. Imagine the possibilities," Sam grinned.

"Hey, you're already taken," Adam joked.

"Let's see," Cammie teased. "You or the male star of *Jersey Girl*. Who to pick?"

A sign on an easel at the reception desk welcomed Magic Johnson Enterprises to the Palms for the company's annual retreat. Sam considered the delay, then crooked her index finger at a bellboy—young, tennis-player buff, with long blond pin-straight hair—and beckoned to him. He reminded her of photos she'd seen of Andre Agassi from back when Andre had hair. And hadn't Agassi been from Las Vegas?

"Yes?" he asked.

Huh. Maybe this guy was his doppelgänger. Sam handed the bellboy a hundred-dollar bill. "Be a sweetheart and register for us, okay? We're the—"

"Sharpe party! They told us you were coming. I saw that piece in *Vanity Fair* a couple of months ago. Your father got robbed the other night, by the way."

Sam sighed. "Yeah, thanks. Anyway, we'll stop back in twenty minutes."

"Cool. Make it fifteen. If you'd like to run into Justin and Cameron, may I suggest you visit our—"

Sam cut off faux Andre with a curt shake of her head. If she wanted to hang with singers and actresses she knew, there were a hundred places in Los Angeles she could go. She suggested to her friends that they take a stroll around the Palms while the bellboy was getting them registered. Even this early in the evening, there was already a lot of action. The main casino was dominated by slot machines and table games. Cocktail waitresses in black bustiers, black pleather miniskirts, fishnets, and black boots wended their way among the guests, taking drink orders.

The casino was as loud as it was glitzy. Rock and roll piped in over the sound system mixed with the *whir-jangle-whir* of the slot machines, the shouts of the winners, and the groans of the losers. The air—despite the best ventilation that money could buy—still stank of cigarettes. Sam was momentarily nostalgic for the laws in California that prevented people from smoking in restaurants and bars.

Off to the sides of the casino were smaller, heavily monitored rooms reserved for high rollers. These were people who were willing to gamble thousands, or even tens of thousands, on a single turn of the cards or roll of the dice. These people didn't have to pay for anything—not their rooms or their meals or their drinks. And why should they, when they were capable of losing the median income of the state of Minnesota in the time it took to down a Sex on the Beach? Those rooms were already semibusy, the clientele mostly wealthy Asian men in their twenties and thirties. Sam idly wondered where they got their money. Everyone she knew who was rich was either in show business or connected to show business.

They checked out Rain. It wasn't open yet. Neither was Little Buddha, the chichi Chinese restaurant. Most people seemed to be eating at either the Mexican joint, the coffee shop, or at the ubiquitous buffet. Sam shuddered. Who knew how long that curried shrimp had been dying a slow death on the buffet steam table?

Directly across from the eating areas were a bank of small boutiques that opened directly into the lobby.

The biggest one was called Stuff; one window mannequin wore a flouncy black lace miniskirt lined with
pink tulle, and a black T-shirt that read, I DON'T DO
ROADIES. Another mannequin had on a minuscule piece
of black leather that was masquerading as a dress.

Yuh. Like I could ever get my ass into either of those,
Sam thought.

There were also a tattoo parlor and a jewelry shop;
they passed both of these. Then Adam nudged Parker
and pointed into the casino. "Hey, check it out: a James
Dean slot machine."

They drifted over to the machine, which featured an
airbrushed photograph of the 1950s actor from his
most famous film, *Rebel Without a Cause*. Sam knew—
hell, everyone knew—that James Dean was Parker's
patron saint, and not just because Parker looked an
awful lot like him.

"That's so you, Parker," Sam observed.

"You should try, Parker," Dee urged. "Maybe James
Dean wants you to win!"

"Um, Dee? No gambling?" Cammie reminded her in
a long-suffering voice. "The age thing? Parker's ticket?"

"Oh. Right," Dee agreed. "But I just thought since
it's James Dean . . . Hey, I've got a great idea. We can
set up a séance, and you can ask James Dean when the
security guards won't check. Then you can come down
and play and probably win big."

Sam was more than a little afraid that Dee wasn't
kidding.

"Don't worry, guys. I know a place that allows

underage gambling," Cammie announced. "We'll go later. Maybe Parker can win back his twenty thou."

"Sweet," Parker proclaimed. "Where is it and how fast can we get there?"

"Later," she promised.

Sam saw faux Andre the bellboy waving to get her attention, so they headed back toward the reception area. "I booked three suites, by the way. Cammie and Adam, me and Anna, Dee and Parker. Unless you two don't want to share?"

"If it wouldn't hurt your feelings, Parker," Dee told her friend, "I think I'd prefer my own space."

"Oh, sure," Parker agreed. "Totally."

"You put this on your credit card?" Anna asked.

"Guaranteed it," Sam reported. "We'll figure it all out later or whatever."

Faux Andre hustled over to them even before they reached the registration desk, waving three envelopes with their key cards. "Your suites, Ms. Sharpe."

"We'll need one more," Sam instructed him, thinking of Dee.

"Right away, Ms. Sharpe, anything you ask. I'll have it for you in two minutes." He hustled away.

Sam smiled. Sometimes it was really was good to be the daughter of the king.

Hey, Baby

"What's the address?" Sam asked Anna as the limo drove them back toward the Strip. They'd passed various massive hotels and the ubiquitous tourists, plus a billboard for Siegfried & Roy that still hadn't been taken down.

Anna looked at the advertisement she'd torn out of *Las Vegas Weekly*, the Sin City equivalent of NYC's *Village Voice*. "Two-ten Flamingo Road. Feelings USA."

"Let me see the ad again."

Anna handed it over. Feelings USA featured a line of clothing called Hey, Baby—the blond Hey, Baby model in the ad had a Barbie-doll body clad in an ultracheesy tiger-print bra-and-thong combo. She was on all fours, with a faux-sexy do-me look on her face.

Sam frowned, then leaned forward and pressed a button on the stereo. A female voice that Anna didn't recognize filled the limo with its soulful sound. "You know," said Sam, "I so love that she's not stick-skinny."

"Who?" Anna asked.

"Alicia Keys. On the CD."

"What are you talking about?"

"She's not a twig, but she still looks totally hot. I could never—"

Anna regarded Sam dubiously. "Has it ever occurred to you that you're obsessed with your weight?"

"Gee, you think?" Sam shot back.

For a moment, Anna couldn't figure out why Sam was being so nasty. Then she realized it had to be Cammie's tacky Vegas outfit contest. The idea of competing with Cammie in any kind of appearance-based contest had to be stirring up every last one of Sam's insecurities.

"We could always just show up at Lush in our regular clothes," Anna suggested. "Cammie would be the only one dressed to thrill. She'd win the contest for sure, but she'd look like an idiot."

Lush was a well-known club not far from the Strip. The guys had insisted that this was the place they had to meet, at nine o'clock, in their showgirl costumes; Anna had no idea why. They claimed they had an awesome first prize all cooked up.

"Cammie's my friend," Sam commented quickly. "And yeah, I know about all the bitchy stuff she's done to you. But she's been my friend since we were little kids, and old habits die hard."

Fine, Anna thought. Psychological overload. Let it go.

Feelings USA was located in a strip mall—the limo driver pulled into a parking lot that also served a cell phone store, a palm reader, a taco takeout place, and a nail salon called Sexxy Nails. Anna and Sam got out of the limo, told the driver to wait, and stepped inside.

The store itself was actually quite small, brightly lit with fluorescents. A Las Vegas rock radio station blared Green Day from its loudspeakers. Anna scanned the aisles; there were rack upon rack of shiny, cheap women's clothing that gave new meaning to the word *tacky*. Not a single natural fiber in sight.

Sam grinned as she took in the selection. "Well, well. We've hit the mother lode."

The place was deserted, save for a cute college-age brunette behind the cash register. She wore a Playboy bunny getup, complete with ears, and was intently reading a book.

Anna couldn't help herself. What could a sales-person in store like this possibly be reading? She cocked her head to take in the book's spine. *The Collected Poems of Sir Walter Scott.*

"Umm, excuse me?" Anna got the girl's attention.

The salesclerk looked up, startled. "Sorry. I didn't hear you come in."

"I love his poetry." Anna chucked her chin at the book. "Sir Walter Scott."

The girl put a blank sales slip into her book to mark her place and then closed it on the counter. "I'm a junior at UNLV and I've got a killer midterm tomor-row. They make us take one literature course. This is it. I should have just called in sick."

" 'O what a tangled web we weave when first we practice to deceive,' " Anna quoted.

After a momentary blank look, a light of under-standing washed over the salesgirl's face. "That's from

Hamlet, right? I *hated* my Shakespeare class. Why couldn't he just write like everyone else?"

"Actually, the line is from the guy you're reading," Sam corrected. "From a long poem called *Marmion*."

Anna glanced at Sam with admiration. Sam was smart. She read actual literature. She thought about things. If she got a little testy sometimes, so be it.

The salesgirl puffed some air out of her lips. "I wish you two could write my essay for me tomorrow. Anyway, sorry and all that. How can I help you?"

"The Hey, Baby clothing line?" Sam prompted.

"In the very back," the girl pointed. "Next to the feather boas."

Anna hesitated. "Do you mind if I ask you a question? I hope this doesn't seem rude. Does the store make you dress like that for work?"

"No." The girl blinked her big brown eyes, confused. "Why?"

"Just curious," Anna said with a bright smile. Anna had been to various far-flung corners of the Earth, and yet this was her first trip to Vegas. The place was just so . . . bizarre. "So . . . back there. Thanks."

She found Sam already pawing through a rack of black latex dresses. "These are for you," Sam intoned darkly. "If I tried one on, I'd look like an overripe black Bavarian sausage."

"One of us could wear what the salesgirl is wearing," Anna suggested.

"Way too early *Bridget Jones*," Sam decreed as she

made her way to another rack and extracted a very short, cherry-red dress. Imitation leather strings laced it up from nonexistent neckline to crotch. Sam twirled the hanger around. "Check it out. It even has a built-in underwire bra."

Anna looked tentative. "You meant for you, right?"

"No, I meant for Parker," Sam spat sarcastically. "*You*."

Anna flashed back to her first date with Ben, how she'd gotten up all her nerve and suggested they go into the giant Hustler sex store on Sunset Boulevard. She'd wanted to shock him, and she had. She'd loved the way Ben had looked at her—Anna, the proper girl, suggesting something so nasty. She'd actually purchased some vinyl pants with a zipper from front to back, bisecting her crotch, so tight she had barely been able to breathe. It had been so much fun to wear them for Ben, to see the look on his face, to feel his arms around her. . . .

"Uh, Anna Percy? Hel-lo?" Sam waved a perfectly manicured hand in front of Anna's face.

Anna blinked. "Sorry."

"Where'd you go?"

"Ben."

"Ah. You did call him from the plane, right?"

"Right."

Anna hoped Sam would let it go at that. She didn't.

"Did you actually talk to him?"

"No. Just voice mail."

"So call again." Sam pulled another dress from the

rack, possibly even shorter than the other one: a slinky yellow tube number with a cutout middle.

"Sam, if he cared even the tiniest bit, he'd get the voice mail and call me back."

"Okay, so he sucks. It's on to the next." Sam turned the dress around. The rear of the skirt was cut out too, evidently to expose butt cheeks and a thong.

"Not in this lifetime," Anna avowed. Something white with crystals at the neckline caught her eye, and she took it from the rack. A crystal collar attached to a silver O-ring connected the collar to the dress. There were crystals along the hem of the dress, which was a tiny bit longer than the other two horrors.

"Try it on," Sam admonished.

Anna realized that Sam hadn't yet selected anything for herself.

"When you do," she retorted.

Then she spotted something: purple chiffon harem pants and a matching purple bra top covered in ornately hideous gold scrollwork. Anna knew that Sam was especially self-conscious about her figure from her hips to her ankles. Well, the flowing pants would cover all that, while the bare midriff would be sexy enough to qualify her for the contest

"What do you think?" She took the outfit off the rack and thrust it at her friend.

Sam smiled a truly genuine smile. "Thanks."

"You're welcome."

They went into the tiny changing cubicles and tried

on their outfits. Everything fit perfectly. Anna thought she looked like someone trying way too hard to get into a party at, say, the Playboy mansion. Sam looked like she was going to a costume party and was going to lose the contest for best costume. But then, they weren't entering a best-dressed contest. "I guess we're set," Anna surmised as they surveyed themselves in a two-hundred-and-seventy-degree mirror.

"To work here, maybe," Sam cracked. "But actually, we aren't set."

"What else do we—"

"Think, Anna. Put that New York private school education to use. *Accessories.*"

They found a glinting purple faux stone that Sam decided should be attached to her navel. The salesgirl gave her some false-eyelash adhesive, and it stuck perfectly. Then Sam went to a small shoe rack and removed a pair of platform shoes, Anna trailing along. The shoes had six-inch hot pink heels, and hot pink lips hung suspended in clear liquid in the soles' two-inch Lucite platforms. Sam dangled them in front of Anna.

Anna shook her head. "You must be on drugs."

"Come on, you want to beat Cammie, don't you?"

"I couldn't even stand in those things!"

"What about all those years of ballet you told me about? Come on, you're graceful enough to walk on stilts." Sam turned one of the shoes over. "It's destiny. These are size eight. Your size."

Anna raised a dubious eyebrow. "What about you?"

"I'm a harem girl. Flat thongs."

Muttering under her breath, Anna tried on the dreadful shoes. She took a couple of steps. Okay, she could walk in them. Barely. Then she checked out her reflection again in the three-way mirror.

"I'm six-foot two in these things! I look like a freak."

"Uh-huh," Sam agreed smugly. "And we are so going to get our freak on tonight."

"I don't know, Sam. . . ."

"Consider them a gift. And by the by, we aren't changing, since we're going straight to Lush."

Anna sighed. There was no use protesting.

Sam marched back to the girl in the Playboy bunny outfit and paid for all her stuff, as well as for Anna's shoes. The salesgirl applauded their choices.

"I haven't committed to keeping this stuff on," Anna pointed out as she handed over her credit card. "I can always change."

"Oh, you'll wear it," Sam assured her. "Because as much as you don't want to look like a 'ho, you *really* don't want Cammie to win."

Baby Voice

Dee paid the taxi driver and walked through the massive mirrorlike doors that led into the Venetian Hotel on the Strip. Wow, this place was so incredible! It was much larger than the Palms and infinitely fancier. Everywhere she looked, there was ornate Italian art, gilded angels, and pasty-faced royalty. There were even frescoes on the soaring ceiling of fat ladies who had never heard of a suntan, lolling on jewel-toned cushions.

Renaissance art, she'd tell her friends. This time she was certain she'd be using the right word, because just inside the front doors of the Venetian had been an oversize video monitor that guided visitors through the hotel's extensive collection and the bigger collection of the Guggenheim Hermitage Museum housed in an annex to the hotel. The video boasted how the Venetian had invested hundreds of millions of dollars in its arty image.

She checked her D&G C'est Chic platinum watch with the tiny free rubies scattered over the face; there were still twenty minutes before the past-life-regression yoga class she wanted to attend. It was to be taught by a renowned Indian master in the Venetian's Canyon Ranch SpaClub.

Dee had read in *Casino Player* magazine that the second floor of the Venetian had been designed to look exactly like Venice, Italy. So she got directions from a helpful concierge, then cut through the crowded hotel casino—to get anywhere in most Vegas hotels, you had to go through the casino—and rode the escalator to the second floor.

A short tourist-dodging walk past a gallery of upscale boutiques—Prada, Chanel, Le Petit Enfant—took her around the corner to a sight that made her gasp: It was Venice's Grand Canal, right there inside the hotel! Two-story storefronts lined the canal on both sides, along with broad walkways for pedestrians. Above was a magically blue sky with fleecy clouds lit from behind to look as if the sun were peeking through the clouds. Dee felt almost dizzy, because it just seemed so real.

It reminded Dee of what Jim Carrey saw at the end of *The Truman Show*: how it all looked real but wasn't. Here, by this mock Grand Canal, it was daytime 24/7. The weather was always perfect, the sun always shining.

Dee sighed. She wished life could really be like that.

The fake Grand Canal was a big tourist attraction. All along the canal, Dee saw tourists leaning against the restraining fence. She went to the restraining fence that bordered the canal and found room for herself just as an authentic Italian gondola boat swished by. The gondolier was completely authentic—he wore a red-and-white shirt with black pants and a black Italian beret. In the stern of his wooden vessel were two couples in their late twenties—one girl wore a silver Britney Spears T-shirt, the other a cropped shirt from which her stomach pooched before disappearing into her too-tight jeans. The guys, who both sported goatees, were clicking their girlfriends' photos with disposable cameras.

Then the gondolier started to sing—an aria from *La Traviata,* he announced to his passengers and the people looking down on them. His voice was rich and romantic; it echoed off the fake second-story storefronts and the false sky.

Wow, this had to be even better than the real Venice. You didn't have to deal with weather problems. Like, if it was hot, you might sweat and mess up your makeup. Or if it rained, it could totally wreck your blowout. Best of all, no one spoke Italian.

A woman to Dee's left nudged her. Dee turned to see that the nudge had been unintentional—the woman was kissing her boyfriend. Dee stared indiscreetly for a few moments, deciding that the guy looked like a "before" participant on *Extreme Makeover*, with a vampirelike overbite and pockmarked skin. But clearly his girlfriend/wife loved him, anyway. Unless she was a hooker. This was Vegas, so he could be paying her to *pretend* to be into him. But no, Dee decided, they were really in love.

She scuffed her size-four baby blue Dolce sandal with the daisy between the toes against the restraining fence. The truth was, Dee was lonely. In this romantic setting, she wished she had someone there with her.

Even if the guy did look like the alien in that movie *Independence Day*, Dee knew she could love him if he loved her. Looks could be fixed; a guy could always go for plastic surgery from Ben's dad. No one had to be unattractive anymore. That was the best thing about living in the twenty-first century.

Of course, Dee knew she didn't have a boyfriend, even though with her cute looks, huge blue eyes, and baby-girl voice guys came on to her all the time. For some reason, it never worked out. Most of the guys she fell for turned out to be gay.

It wasn't like she had good role models for a relationship! Her parents were still in Europe, Dad doing business, Mom trying to mend their marriage. Her father was a serial cheater—Dee had known that forever. Her mother always got the best jewelry afterward. But lately her mother seemed unhappy with their arrangement. Dee didn't want them to break up. She was the only person she knew whose parents were still married to each other. She was well aware that it might not work out—that her dad might come home with a different wife, and her mom might not come home at all. It happened all the time.

That was why Dee thanked Hashem—the common Hebrew name for God, though Dee had learned at the Kabbalah Centre that the actual name of God had been lost for thousands of years, which was just so mystical and awesome—on a daily basis that He'd brought another family to her. A family by choice, one that would always be there for her.

It was amazing, really, how one day she'd run into Sam's new stepmother at the Kabbalah Centre and how they'd instantly bonded. When Poppy had asked Dee to move in and help prepare for the baby, Dee had felt more needed than she'd ever felt in her life. Now that Ruby Hummingbird was alive and thriving, the three of them were like one soul with three bodies. That was how close they were.

If only they could be with her now! A couple of the baby nurses would need to be there, too, since someone had to feed the baby and change the baby's diapers and all that yucky stuff. But still, it would be so fun.

Dee dug her new cell phone out of her Donna Karan sports bag and touched the digit 1 three times—speed dialing Poppy's private number. But after just three rings, Kenny Rogers singing "Ruby, Don't Take Your Love to Town" came on.

Dee smiled. Until the day before, it had been the Rolling Stones' classic "Ruby Tuesday." She'd been the one to suggest that song to Poppy, and Poppy had done it!

Then Poppy's voice: "Hi, it's Poppy and Ruby. We've taken our love to town, so leave a message after the beep!"

Dee left a message and then dropped her phone back into her bag. She'd been uncertain about going on this trip, what with Ruby and Poppy needing her so much. But Poppy had been amazing about it. Sure, they'd miss Dee. But Dee really did need a break with kids her own age. Dee had reminded Poppy that age was meaningless. Poppy was only a few years older than Dee, anyway. Plus, all three of them were very old souls. Whenever

Dee looked deeply into Ruby Hummingbird's eyes, she knew they'd been together in a former life.

She couldn't talk about stuff like this with Sam and Cammie. She knew that they just tuned her out, and she tried not to judge them too harshly. She and Poppy were simply more *evolved* than Sam and Cammie. So it was no wonder she'd grown closer to Poppy and the baby—two people who wanted and needed and understood her.

Sometimes she did wish life could go back to how it was before Anna Percy showed up in Beverly Hills. Not that it had been Anna's fault or anything. Dee wasn't into placing blame. But back then, it had been like being in the coolest, most exclusive club in the world—her and Cammie and Sam doing everything together. She remembered how they'd first started talking about the senior trip to Vegas when they were in ninth grade.

Only now that the trip was here, and it wasn't anything like she had imagined. She thought they'd run around Vegas being crazy, flirting with guys, and everything would be perfect. That was the picture she'd had in her mind. Dee gulped hard, tears threatening. Funny how a person could feel so lonely in the middle of a crowd.

No—she refused to be negative. She was simply vibrating on a higher plane now, and she had learned that it could be lonely at the top. People misunderstood, even your best friends. Dee was happy that she finally had some direction and focus, even if her friends didn't understand. Sam had always been the smart and talented one, Cammie the hot and bitchy one, and Dee had been . . . well, just Dee. The tagalong. The loyal friend. She liked being the evolved one better than being the loyal friend. If she and Sam and Cammie had grown apart, at least it was for a very good reason.

It wasn't Sam's fault that she wasn't as far along on her spiritual path. And Cammie . . . well, Dee was pretty sure that Cammie was a lost cause. But that didn't mean she wasn't fun to hang around with—when she wasn't picking on Dee.

The gondolier reached the end of the canal and held a high note that rang out, then finished his song with a flourish. Everyone applauded him.

"Gnocchi! Gnocchi!" Dee yelled down, clapping along with everyone else.

A pretty girl with dark curly shoulder-length hair turned to Dee, who had to look up at least six inches to see the girl's eyes. "Excuse me. Why did you shout 'gnocchi' just now?"

"I wanted to thank the gondolier for the song," Dee explained earnestly, happy that someone was engaging her in conversation. "Gnocchi is Italian for 'thank you.'"

Sometime last year Dee had been buying cashmere boy shorts by Australia's Nude Sleepwear when she'd run into an Italian guy named Giancarlo, who was shopping for a Leigh Bantivoglio bustier for his girl-friend. They'd flirted, gone out for coffee, then made out in front of Fly Boutique for a while. Then he'd invited Dee back to Le Parc Central Hotel in West Hollywood, since his girlfriend wasn't with him on this visit to Tinseltown.

When Dee turned him down, Giancarlo hadn't been

upset. He'd just kissed her hand and whispered, "Thank you for a lovely afternoon. Gnocchi."

" 'Thank you' is *grazie*," the curly haired girl corrected her. "Gnocchi are little potato dumplings."

Dee's eyebrows furrowed. "Are you sure?"

"Of course I'm sure! I'm Italian."

"Oh. Well, maybe he was telling me what he wanted for dinner."

The girl gave Dee a cockeyed look and stepped away from her.

Sheesh, Dee thought. No one would have gotten that upset over one little word in Los Angeles. People could be so mean. She'd have to make sure that Ruby Hummingbird wasn't tainted by any mean people.

"I hate mean people, Ruby," Dee uttered aloud. Then she shook her head. The baby wasn't with her, obviously. But sometimes she had the most powerful feeling that Ruby Hummingbird could *intuit* what she was thinking, because of their cosmic bond.

She slapped a dreamy smile on her face and took off for the spa so she wouldn't be late for the yoga class. Maybe this would be the night that she'd come to truly understand the cosmic nature of the soulful connection between her and the baby. The wonderful, perfect part of it all was that no matter how lonely or isolated or weird Dee ever felt, she always had Ruby's spirit with her. Always.

"Right, Ruby?" she whispered.

Dee could have sworn she heard a baby's voice whisper back, "Right, Dee."

In a Tacky, Vegas Kind of Way

Cammie lay with her cheek resting against Adam's chest, listening to the steady beating of his heart. That same organ had been pounding just a few minutes earlier—she knew just what to do to make Adam insane with lust. But Cammie wondered why it always felt like she was giving some kind of performance. Not that she didn't adore sex, because she did. With the right partner, it was better than drugs. But she was always aware of the need to prove how hot she was. She was never able to entirely lose herself in the moment, and it irked her.

Adam gently kissed her forehead. "You good?"

"I'm great," she assured him, even though it wasn't entirely true.

What the hell was the matter with her? She and the guy she loved were in the killer Rock Star Suite at the Palms (the Palms was much too happening to have anything as gauche as, say, a presidential suite).

The thousand-square-foot space, located on the second-to-top floor of the white tower, was bigger than many apartments. The bedroom had a huge king-size bed tented in white netting, with dozens of silk and velvet pillows in various shades of white, taupe, and black. An indoor garden flourished under special black lights, sprouting exotic blossoms in a riot of colors that scented the air; an automatic sprinkler system periodically sprayed the plants. The marble-tiled bathroom had a hot tub, a Jacuzzi, and a shower with eight jets. The floor was heated so that the temperature stayed at an even seventy degrees. There was a separate sitting room with a red velvet couch, large-screen TV, and Dolby sound system. The mirrored bar area was stocked with every type of alcohol, mixers, and munchies. There was also a music room with Bose amps, speakers, keyboards, and six-foot whiteboards with markers in case lyrical inspiration struck. The whiteboards were the only similarity to the Screenwriter's Suite on the same floor, which had an office walled in whiteboards, plus a top-of-the-line Dell computer, fax machine, high-speed color printer, and three phone lines. Cammie knew this because her father had once represented a successful but incredibly arrogant young director, another poker aficionado who liked to stay at the Palms, who had once trashed the suite during an argument with a player he'd suspected of cheating.

Okay, so the place they were staying rocked. Plus, she and Adam had just made love—and with Adam, that was truly what it was.

Except for that niggling voice in Cammie's head. The one that told her she had to keep proving that she was the hottest girl in the world. The one that told her Adam was simply too good to be bad, and bad was what she craved. Hell, maybe bad was even what she deserved. Was it the bad-girl part of her that had made sure she had a certain Vegas phone number in her purse before she left L.A., a phone number she definitely had not shared with Adam? Maybe.

"So, did you come up with something hot for the contest?" Adam asked. He lay on his back, her head resting on his chest as he stroked her hair.

Cammie mentally put aside the call she planned to make as soon as Adam was out of sight. "I just picked up something downstairs by Skin," she murmured. "I was in a hurry to get up here to you."

"And I was in a hurry for you to get here." He cocked an amused eyebrow. "But what's Skin?"

"The outdoor club by the pool—there's a small boutique," Cammie explained. She stretched luxuriously. "So tonight should be fun. First I win your little contest, then we gamble the night away."

Adam shifted so that he could look at her. "Is that your idea of a good time?"

She gave him a soft, sexy kiss. "Well, there *are* other things I like better. But a girl can't spend her entire life in bed."

"Oh yeah, she could." Adam returned her kiss. "But I don't know about the whole gambling thing, Cam. It's mostly poor people who get sucked in and ripped off at casinos. I feel weird supporting the casinos."

"No one makes them risk their money, Adam," Cammie pointed out, propping herself up on one elbow.

"Yeah, but the lure of it can be irresistible. It doesn't seem right, you know?"

No, she definitely did not know. First of all, if poor people were stupid enough to take whatever poor people earned per week and risk it on a spin of a roulette wheel, they deserved whatever they got. Second of all, she definitely wasn't poor. So it had zero to do with her.

Yet Adam looked so earnest. So caring. She just couldn't tell him how she really felt. She kissed him lightly, teasing him until it turned into more.

"Down girl," Adam laughed. "Got to jump in the shower and get this show on the road. I'm a judge in the contest you're about to win, and we have, like, a half hour to pull it together and get over to the club." He swung off the king-size bed. "You want to take a shower with me?"

"Well, I would," Cammie cooed, holding her hair off her neck, "but that might lead us to things that will make us late for the contest. And we wouldn't want the judge to walk in late with one of the contestants. How would that look?"

He leaned over to kiss her. "Pretty good to me. But I see your point."

He padded into the bathroom—the boy had a killer behind—and closed the door. Cammie waited until she heard the shower running; then she grabbed her petal pink Gucci baguette purse from the nightstand and fished out her new cell. She'd programmed in the number she wanted before they'd left Los Angeles. She dialed and waited as it rang. Once. Twice. Three—

"Hello?"

His voice was deep, inviting, and sexy as hell.

"Hi there."

"Camilla."

Ohhhh, that voice. Cammie smiled and licked her lips. Perfect. She could hear Adam singing in the shower. "Hi."

"You're here?"

"I came, I saw, I conquered," Cammie quipped, toying with a lock of her hair. "Or maybe I saw, I conquered, I came."

"My kind of girl. Now how soon can you get your ass over here?"

Overgrown foliage surrounded the cozy green-topped tables at Lush, whose bases had been made to look like chopped-off bonsai trees. Stuffed parrots dotted the foliage; monkeys swung from the trees. The waitresses wore minuscule bikinis that looked as if made of jungle flowers, with leafy garlands around their heads. There was a rain forest backdrop behind the stage. None of it was real, of course, which Anna decided made it perfect for Vegas.

By the time she and Sam pulled up in the limo, Cammie, Adam, and Parker had already snagged a banquette in the corner. The huge, illuminated sign in the front window had flashed in giant neon letters:

LUSH! EVERY TUESDAY NIGHT! AMATEUR
SHOWGIRL CONTEST! $500 PRIZE! 9 P.M.!

The Lush amateur showgirl contest was clearly a popular happening. The club was packed. Girls dressed to thrill sat at various tables, some with other girl-friends, some with guys. A lot of them, from the way they were stretching out their calf muscles, were

preparing to enter the contest. Anna saw girls in silver
lamé G-strings and glittery pasties and even a curvy
redhead who looked like a giant fruit pie: Huge cherries
covered her nipples, and a tiny skirt made to look like a
piecrust encircled her hips.

"Hey, where have you two been?" Adam asked, slid-
ing over to make room for more chairs at their table.

"We went to Dee's suite to try and coax her into
coming," Sam explained. "But there was a just a note—
she went to the Venetian for some yoga class and then
was going back to the hotel. Something about having
promised her kabbalah rabbi that she'd study the
Talmud before bed. Of course, I'm the one who's half
Jewish. Dee is as WASPy as they come—except for
Anna, of course."

"With Dee it's New Age one day, kabbalah the
next," Parker mused. "I guess she's looking for the
meaning of life."

"Honestly?" Sam queried. "I don't think Dee knows
what she's looking for."

Anna hadn't known that Sam was half Jewish; she
never talked about it. It had to be on her mother's side.
But come to think of it, Sam never really discussed her
mother. Anna had no idea who she was or where she
was. Funny how much about her life Sam hadn't shared.

"Anyway," Sam went on, "we wrote down for Dee
where we'd be, in case she changes her mind."

"She won't," Cammie predicted. "These days she's
either ready to shave her head, put on a wig, and move

to the Fairfax district, or Velcro herself to Poppy and the baby. I have no clue why she even came with us."

Could Cammie really be that dense?

"To be with you," Anna said pointedly.

Cammie assessed her coolly. "Come again?"

"She came because you and Sam are still her best friends. She wanted to be here with you."

"Please," Cammie scoffed, leaning into the leaf-printed faux leather banquette. "She's too busy breast-feeding Ruby Hummingbird, or whatever the hell she does over at Sam's house."

"Geez, Cam," Adam chided.

"I'm just kidding," Cammie assured him.

But it was obvious to Anna, and, Anna was sure, to everyone else at the table, that Cammie was definitely *not* kidding.

"So, Cammie, what's up?" Sam asked. "You didn't make much of an effort for the contest."

Anna had been wondering the same thing. Cammie had on low-slung Dolce & Gabbana black jeans with diamond studs on the fly, and a black DIRTY GIRL T-shirt. The effect was underwhelming, especially after Anna and Sam had expected Cammie to show up in the most outrageous outfit in North America. And, Anna recalled, the contest had been Cammie's idea in the first place.

Cammie just shrugged, craning around for a wait-ress. "It'll work. Anyway, who do you have to screw to get a drink around here?"

"Well, you and Sam look hot," Parker told Anna. He flashed his patented megawatt grin.

"In a tacky, Vegas kind of way," Adam added.

"Emphasis on the tacky," Cammie put in, with a smile that never reached her eyes. "So I guess one of you wins the little contest."

"Tell me the prize, and I'll tell you if I forfeit." Sam glanced at a girl walking by clad in a sixties mod miniskirt that was entirely see-through, showing off her black-and-white op art–print thong beneath. "Although I think I have a clue."

Adam and Parker shared a grin.

"Winner's in the showgirl contest," Parker said.

"Not loser?" Anna ventured. She figured that was why Cammie had come so underdressed.

"Then I forfeit to Anna!" Sam sang out. "Congratulations, Anna. May the farce be with you."

"Forget it!" Anna protested, though she laughed as she said it. But there was just no way was she getting up on that stage to parade around in her stupid little white dress.

Parker folded his arms. "You girls did not play by the rules."

Cammie smiled. "That's what makes us fun, Parker."

The lights in the club dimmed and the stage lights rose as the curtain parted, revealing a trio of musicians playing rock music Anna couldn't identify. Three buxom girls in very high heels and sequined bikinis made to look like flowers came out and began a slinky dance routine. A harried waitress scurried over to their table and took their drink orders. Maybe it was because the lights were low and she couldn't see how old they were, or maybe she was just so busy that she didn't care, but she didn't ask any of them for ID.

The dancers finished their warm-up routine to a smattering of applause. Then a voice came over the sound system. "Ladies and gentleman, please welcome your host, recently retired from the World Wrestling Federation and a new addition to the Vegas comedy circuit, Monty Markam!"

Monty Markam—an energetic guy with a shaved head and the burly looks of the former wrestler he was, trotted onstage to a drum roll and a cymbal crash from an onstage trio of guitar, piano and drums. Then he immediately launched into his comedy routine. Fans of the WWF might have found him funny. Otherwise, it was a lost cause. All his jokes were about other wrestlers.

"He's gonna need to broaden the range of his material," Sam observed. "In Los Angeles, people would throw beers at him."

Finally, Monty stopped his jokes. "Okay, let's get this party started!" he boomed as the musicians went into a funk groove. "We've got twenty-three contestants this week, and these girls are hot, hot, hot!"

"Make it twenty-four," Parker urged Anna. "Come on, it'll be a hoot."

"How about if I loan you my dress, and *you* make it twenty-four?" Anna asked sweetly.

Parker's laugh was drowned out by the emcee. "Let's

introduce this week's three celebrity judges," Monty went on. "Voted Best Showgirl on the Strip in 1995 and again in 1996, Miss Doily LaFlame!"

A spotlight hit a woman seated in the front; she stood and turned to nod at the crowd's applause. Her raven hair reached the bottom of her low-cut black dress.

"Number two judge, choreographer *extraordinaire*, who's done shows at MGM, Harrah's, and the Crazy Girls Fantasy Revue at the Riviera, Mr. Rock Hard!"

The crowd applauded as a slender man with a bad rug stood and gave the crowd a royal wave.

"And finally," Monty continued, "there should be silence before I introduce our third judge." He waited and waited, until the club was as quiet as a funeral parlor. "Our third judge is a very special guest. Frankly, it's an honor even to be in the same room with this man. We're talking legend here, folks. The one, the only . . . Mr. Wayne Newton!"

A chubby-cheeked man stood and waved as the room erupted into cheers and applause.

"Who's he?" Anna was baffled.

"A singer," Adam informed her. "My grandmother used to listen to him."

"Mr. Newton, I salute you," The emcee put two fingers to an eyebrow. The band went into a different groove, and Monty moved to the side of the stage. He read from index cards. "Our first contestant is a local fave. Give it up for Lucy Gianni!"

Lucy sashayed out onstage to Michael Jackson's "Billie Jean." She was a short girl with stubby, muscular legs that even her bright pink platform heels couldn't do much to improve. She wore a glittery gold one-piece swimsuit; a giant Cleopatra headdress made of pheasant feathers and crystal stones adorned her head.

The spotlight followed her as she paraded around the stage. Meanwhile, a lone table of friends behind Anna hooted and hollered for her.

"Why would a chick with those thighs enter a show-girl contest?" Sam asked.

"And why would she dance to 'Billie Jean?' " Cammie wondered aloud. "That's like guaranteeing you're gonna lose."

"She's never gonna win if she can't afford a decent freaking costume," a pear-shaped, spiky-haired redhead at the next table said loudly to a friend. The redhead was obviously going to compete later on—her red sequined dress and stiletto heels gave it away. "She should shop at Show-Off!"

Then the redhead caught Anna's curious gaze. "You a tourist?" Her voice was raspy—the voice of too many cigarettes.

Anna nodded.

"Well, there's a place called Show-Off! where everyone gets their showgirl outfits," the girl explained. "The headdress costs like three hundred something. But if you don't shop at Show-Off!, you don't win. I think the owner here has an interest in the place."

Sam, who'd been listening, nudged Anna's arm. "Damn. We should have gone to Show-Off!, huh? Who knew?"

When Cleopatra Headdress was done, the next girl paraded out. She wore a green hula skirt made of raffia with a floral bikini top and did a Hawaiian dance. More contestants followed in quick succession. A tall, thin girl in a bikini made entirely of sequins, with matching long sequin-encrusted gloves. A woman in a mermaid showgirl outfit with a fantail. Most of the would-be showgirls merely paraded around the stage and posed like they were in the Miss America Pageant. A few did original things—a dance or acrobatics. At the moment, a skinny girl in an ill-fitting red-white-and-blue two-piece bathing suit and Uncle Sam stovepipe hat was wobbling onstage in cheap high heels, looking more than a little uncomfortable.

"No tits, no ass, no problem!" Cammie chortled to the others at the table. "This is such a hoot!" She pushed back her chair. "Pee break." She took off for the ladies' room.

Leave it to Cammie to say something bitchy about the poor girl, Anna thought. Cammie made a career of putting down everything and everyone. Maybe it was genetic, Anna mused, the result of some strange virus in her father's pool. Or maybe Cammie had done it for so long that it was as automatic as breathing.

Anna glanced at Adam. It still amazed her that he was with Cammie. Two boys Anna had been with,

Adam and Ben—both of whom Anna knew to be sensitive and deep—had been with Cammie. It was disturbing to think that they'd settle for a girl with so little character, with such a lack of heart, just because she was the hottest thing in the zip code.

Onstage, the skinny girl stumbled and started to dance again, her face as red as the stripes on her bikini. She stumbled again and finally wobbled off stage with a tiny wave to the crowd. Most people in the club clapped politely, which made Anna think that maybe the rest of the country—the part that Sam always called flyover country—had better manners than the rich and famous.

"Hey, at least she's got guts," Adam told the table.

"I agree," Anna chimed in.

More guts than I have, she added in her head.

Next up was a tall, beautiful girl with long platinum blond hair and a showgirl's body and walk. She wore an angel outfit worthy of the grand finale of a Tony Kushner play; transparent wings spread from the sides of her gossamer bikini top when she spread her arms.

"Hey! Disqualify the bitch!" the redhead at the next table shouted, getting halfway out of her chair. "She worked at fucking Harveys in Lake Tahoe last year! I know—I was a blackjack dealer!"

What would it be like, Anna wondered, to be a blackjack dealer? Or a showgirl? Both jobs were solar systems away from anything she would ever actually do. Even for one night, even in this place. What was the famous saying? "What happens in Vegas stays in

Vegas?" It irked Anna that she wasn't willing to try it out, unlike so many of the girls and women she'd already seen compete. So many of them—like the painfully skinny girl she'd just seen—had no chance of winning; they were doing it because it was, in some way for them, fun.

So here she was, in a tacky Vegas outfit, looking in from the outside. That was as far she was willing to let herself go. Except for wondering what it would be like to be the kind of girl who could get up in front of a nightclub full of people and—

"And our final contestant, all the way from Beverly Hills, California—Miss Cammie Sheppard!" the emcee boomed.

What?

Anna's attention snapped to the stage, where the spotlight hit Cammie. She wore the same black T-shirt and black jeans she'd worn earlier, the same Constança Basto sling-back aqua heels.

"That bitch!" Sam cried, but she was laughing as she said it. "I thought she went to the john!"

Cammie strutted across the stage, followed by the spotlight. She'd chosen "Miles Apart" by Yellowcard, and there were a few protested shouts over the music that the blond bitch wasn't in a real costume. But then Cammie stopped, crossed her arms at her waist, and slowly inched her T-shirt over her head before flinging it into the cheering crowd. All she had on now above the waist was her pale pink satin Dior push-up bra, pushing up the best breasts that money could buy.

Next off were the heels—she kicked them into the vicinity of the three judges. Then she slowly undid the diamond studs on the fly of her jeans, one after the other, swiveling them down her hips until she could step out of them. Her pale pink satin G-string matched her bra, exposing the slender twenty-four-karat gold chain she wore around her belly. Then Cammie stood on her toes—Anna figured this was to compensate for her lack of high heels—and paraded around the stage, swinging her sexy curls over her shoulders.

Guys stood and whistled. Adam and Parker, Anna noted, among them. Some stomped their feet. The red-headed girl and her friends, though, stood on their chairs and booed through cupped hands. "Disqualify her!" they bellowed. "No costume! Disqualify her!"

Sam leaned into Anna's ear, shouting to be heard over the crowd and the music. "This is just such a Cammie Sheppard moment!"

Sam was right. Which meant that it was the exact opposite of an Anna Percy moment. Anna knew she could never pull that off, not in a million years. Sure, her best friend, Cyn, from back in New York, definitely could. Anna smiled at the thought of Cyn being there. Cyn would strip down to her Brazilian wax just for the pleasure of vanquishing Cammie. Scott Spencer would be right there, too, clapping and whistling for her the way Adam was clapping and whistling for Cammie.

Maybe that is what guys want, Anna mused. At least guys who are in high school. Maybe that's why as much as I was crushing on Scott, he never gave me a second glance and fell for Cyn instead. I don't have a wild bone in my body. I'm too proper, too well bred, too . . . too boring.

Damn.

The music ended and Cammie bowed to the audience, which was still going wild for her. Anna had to give Cammie credit: She had guts, and she'd—

"Anna! Anna Percy! Yo, Anna, where are you?"

Anna turned.

No. *It couldn't be.*

But it was. She stood up and waved her arms.

Her friend Cyn saw her, grinned wildly, and pushed through the crowd toward her table. Her chin-length, choppy black hair was mussed to perfection. She wore an ancient thrift-store black cashmere cardigan unbuttoned to her navel, revealing naked skin and the hammered-gold Bing Bang necklace Anna had given her for her fifteenth birthday. Below that were camouflage pants that barely cleared her bikini wax. And below the pants, red-and-white checkerboard Vans sneakers.

Anna just stood there, dumbfounded by the moment. Not only because it was as if she'd conjured Cyn up by thinking about her, but because of who was trailing behind Cyn.

Dee Young.

And Scott Spencer.

Sugar Daddy

As Anna hugged and shrieked over what was evidently the unexpected arrival of her two friends from New York, Parker gave them a quick assessment. The chick wasn't Hollywood gorgeous, but she was definitely hot in a sexed-up Ashlee Simpson kinda way. The guy with her was very Chad Michael Murray—a guy Parker loathed. He'd been up for the same small part on *Gilmore Girls* that had gone to Chad, and from that Chad had been cast as the lead on *One Tree Hill*. Parker knew he could have played the hell out of both of those roles. He'd try not to let that color his opinion of this guy from New York. For all Parker knew, he could be someone in the business who could help Parker's career. Or he might know someone in the business.

Anna took the opportunity to introduce her friends while the judges were deliberating and the band covered Green Day's "Boulevard of Broken Dreams."

"This is Cynthia Baltres," Anna told the group excitedly, with her arm around Cynthia's waist.

"Please, it's Cyn," the girl clarified, hugging Anna again.

"I still can't believe you're here!" Anna exclaimed. "Oh, and this is Scott Spencer," she added, nodding in the direction of the Chad look-alike.

"They wouldn't be here if I hadn't brought them," Dee pointed out with a pout. "They'd still be at the hotel waiting for you."

"Sorry, Dee," Anna exclaimed, her heart pounding just from being in the presence of Scott. "Thank you!"

"I missed you soooo much!" Cyn cried, throwing her arms around Anna again.

"Me too."

Parker saw Anna's eyes fill with tears of happiness as she quickly told the group how she and Cyn had been best friends for more than a decade. As Anna spoke, Scott just stood there, the epitome of cool.

"When we heard you were coming here, we just had to come too," Cyn declared.

"But how'd you find us?"

"Thank your friend Dee," Cyn reported. "We'd called your dad—he knew where you were staying. And then we were knocking on the door of your suite— okay, pounding—when Dee came out to see what all the noise was about."

"They looked harmless. I asked what they wanted; they said they were looking for you. I knew where you were," Dee brushed her long bangs out of her eyes. "It was no biggie to bring them here. A mitzvah, really."

Scott turned to Sam as soon as he figured out who she was. "Hey, your dad just got robbed on Oscar night, right?"

"Nah," Sam joked. "I get confused with that girl all the time." She gestured to her outfit. "My father is a sultan from Brunei. Hence the harem outfit."

Cyn put her hands on her hips and stood back to scrutinize what Anna was wearing. "So what's your excuse?"

"We were having a contest," Anna explained. "Tackiest Vegas outfit—"

"And she lost," Cammie added, sidling up to join them. "You are?"

Her eyes flitted over Cyn, who introduced herself. So did Scott.

Cyn leaned closer to Anna to speak confidentially, but Parker could still hear her. "Cammie's the one who you told me has been such a bitch to you, right?"

"Exactly."

"You just missed Cammie doing a serious strip thing onstage," Adam informed the New Yorkers, as he snaked an arm around his girlfriend's waist. "You rocked, girl!"

"Yeah," Parker agreed. "You so have this thing locked up."

Cyn appraised Cammie from top to bottom, then met her eyes again. "You're hot shit, huh?"

"We'll let the judges decide," Cammie replied confidently.

The sound system was pumping out the Rolling Stones classic "Honky Tonk Woman" while the judges deliberated. Before Parker knew what was happening, Anna's friend had jumped on their table. She began to do what had to be the hottest dancing Parker had ever seen. Heads in the room swiveled, guys started whistling and cat-calling, and Cyn's boyfriend seemed totally down with it. She inched her low-rise camouflage pants south, exposing a tattoo of an angel with a quiver, his arrow pointing south. Just as a waiter was rushing over to pull Cyn from the table, she spanked her own butt once, then jumped down herself. She stood in front of Cammie and blew her a "fuck you" kiss. That this was Anna's best friend opened a whole new side of Anna that Parker had never even imagined. As for Cammie, she looked ready to spit ice picks because Cyn had waltzed in and stolen her thunder.

"There's a thin line between hot and tacky," Cammie addressed Cyn. "You might want to brush up on that." She waggled her fingers at Adam. " 'Scuse me, sweetie. I have to go retrieve my shoes before some fetishist gets hold of them."

As she headed back toward the front of the club, Parker noticed that not only did Adam's eyes follow her, but so did Scott's. Parker understood, though. Cammie had the same effect on guys that Parker knew he had on girls. He hadn't asked for it, hadn't really worked for it. He just had it. He felt Cyn's eyes on him, checking him out at that very moment. He gave her his patented perfect slow grin. Meanwhile, the wheels turned rapidly in his head. The Ashlee Simpson chick and Chad Michael Murray dude were clearly a couple. But how tight were they? They'd be getting a room together, for sure. But maybe if he made a play for her, it would lead to a breakup with Scott, and then Cyn would have to change suites, and maybe she'd want to come to his suite to make Scott even more insane. Parker could forget his credit card, and she'd use hers to pay his half of the hotel bill, and no one would find out that he had exactly three dollars in his pocket.

Parker had pulled the same scheme in the past. Once on a group ski trip to South Lake Tahoe, where he'd hooked up with a woman from Georgia who'd come to the resort by herself. And another time, when he'd decided he'd better practice lest his skills atrophy, he'd taken a solo trip to Disneyland, figuring that he might as well set up a true test for himself. Even that excursion had been successful, as he'd managed to insinuate himself into the bed of a college girl from Pomona. She'd come down with a friend but had lost her for the night to one of the cartoon characters—out of costume, of course.

Parker knew full well he had to make something like that work here in Vegas. He'd already pegged which waitress at the buffet he would hit up for free food and booze.

"An amateur showgirl contest—*so* hilarious," Cyn declared. "I gotta record this shit, because no one at home will believe it." She pulled out her Nokia cell and started snapping pictures of the garishly dressed girls all waiting to hear who'd won. Parker knew it wasn't much of a competition; Cyn's impromptu table dance wasn't actually in the running. It was either the chick with the angel wings or Cammie.

"Oh man, there was the funniest article on showgirls in *The Onion* last month," Scott recounted for the group. He was on his knees on his chair so he could get a better look at the stage.

"'Showgirls and Nuns, Career Options,'" Adam quoted. "A riot. *The Onion* rocks, dude."

"Right with you, my man," Scott agreed. They shared a fist bump.

Parker grinned and nodded as if he shared their love of the satirical newspaper. He'd heard about it, of course, even knew it had a high hip factor. But he'd never actually read it. Well, he was gonna start the minute he got back to L.A. It was just so hard to keep up with everything. You had to watch *The Daily Show*, because everyone thought Jon Stewart was god. And you had to watch Dave Chappelle, of course, or you were totally out of it. Then there were *Daily Variety* and the *Hollywood Reporter* to read, so that you could talk about what was going on in the business. And aintitcool.com and drudgereport.com, so you could know the scuttlebutt. Then there were auditions, more auditions, going to the right parties, and chatting up the right people. At the very bottom of the list came school. Whenever a guidance counselor told him to buckle down and work harder, Parker would point to the diploma on the counselor's wall and ask, "Dude, do you have any idea where Jackson Sharpe went to college?" Of course, the counselor never had a clue. Which, Parker always said, was the whole point. No one gave a damn. Jackson hadn't become America's favorite movie star by pulling a 3.5 average in sociology. He'd done it the old-fashioned way—by getting a small part in a police drama twenty years ago and stealing the show. That had led to a bigger role, and then to a bigger role, and it hadn't been long before Jackson was on top on the world.

That was just what Parker planned to do. He had the looks, he had the charm, and he was willing to do *anything*. He knew that wasn't all it took; you had to be smart and good as well as willing. There was no way he was going to fail, not in the long run.

The drummer gave a brief flourish, and Monty returned to the stage. Parker watched Cammie scurry back to their table, having reclaimed her shoes. She plopped down directly in Adam's lap.

"Drum roll, please," Monty told the drummer. "Lush is proud to announce its showgirl of the week. And the showgirl of this week is . . . Daphne Whitestone!"

The hot girl with the long platinum blond hair and the angel showgirl outfit climbed onto the stage to claim her crown and the check for five hundred dollars.

The redhead at the next table shot Cammie a nasty look. "No costume, disqualified, and the other chick at your table dances better than you do, anyway."

Cammie's face clouded. Cammie's face never clouded. She gave the redhead the finger.

The girl stood and got in Cammie's face. "You want a piece o' this, bitch? Bring it on."

"Girl-on-girl action, I love this shit!" a drunk frat-looking guy at the next table crowed to his friend.

"Let's get out of here." Adam rolled his eyes, pulling some money out of his wallet and tossing it on the table. "This'll cover everyone."

"Nah, I took care of it."

Parker turned—a middle-aged man with a ruddy complexion, and clad in Texas-style clothes tipped his cowboy hat to Cammie. "Hey, you are one sweet peach, little lady. I'd like to eat you with some whipped cream."

"Well, you aren't going to get the chance to—" Adam began to protest, but Cammie slipped a hand over his mouth.

"Aren't you sweet," Cammie purred to the oversized Texan. "You could be Jessica Simpson's sugar daddy with that accent."

"I'd rather be your sugar daddy, sweet thang," he drawled, winking at her. "I already picked up the tab for your table, little lady. And I'll be seeing you in my dreams. I'm staying at the Bellagio. You can find me in the poker room there. Texas Hold 'Em is my game." He tipped his cowboy hat one more time and moseyed out of the club.

Parker could see that Adam was pissed, but Cammie was reveling in the good ol' boy's attention. Not that Parker cared much how either of them felt. He was just grateful that the cowboy had picked up the check.

Anna leaned against the side of the hot tub and closed her eyes, the steamy water loosening her muscles and relaxing her until she felt as liquid as the water itself. Was there any bliss quite like the first five minutes in a hot tub?

Well, yes, actually. Ben. Sex with Ben had been that kind of bliss. It amazed her how much she'd loved sex, right from the very start. She'd heard horror stories from friends about their first time having sex: pain or embar-rassment or a "that was *it*?" moment of disappointment.

For Anna, none of the above had occurred. It had pretty much fulfilled every fantasy she'd ever had of what sex would be like. And then some. Evidently Ben didn't share her opinion, though, or her phone would have rung by now. Anna reminded herself: Ben had done the horizontal with Cammie (also probably the vertical, the hanging from chandeliers, etc.). Cammie was very experienced and had no inhibitions. No way Anna could compete with *that*.

Now she wondered: Would sex with Scott offer that kind of bliss? According to Cyn, definitely. Cyn hadn't paid any attention to the part of the *This Is How We Do Things* Big Book that underscored how discretion was the better part of living. Not that such a book literally existed. But Anna and every other old-money rich girl from Manhattan's Upper East Side had been raised on the same metaphorical tome. Cyn loved to share. In detail. Her steamy confessions of how amazing Scott was in bed could be . . . well, overwhelming.

Not that Cyn had a clue about Anna's feelings for Scott. Of course, Scott didn't know anything about them, either. Anna had vowed that neither one would ever know. She could never, ever do that to her best friend—what Sturm und Drang that could unleash. Boys might come and go, but best friends were forever, so—

"Fucking Scott," Cyn was saying.

Anna opened her eyes and popped out of her stream of consciousness. She, Sam, Dee, and Cyn were all in the hot tub at the Palms' spa. It was just the four of them, Cammie having taken off for parts unknown. They'd come back to the hotel to chill out and dress before going out for the night. Their destination would be Rain, the hottest nightclub in Las Vegas, located right downstairs in its own wing of the hotel. Even as they'd come to the spa, they could see the long line for the nightclub. But they knew that since they were hotel guests, they wouldn't have to wait to get in.

Anna wore a white Dior one-piece with a halter neck and high-cut legs that she'd had forever. Cyn had on a yellow-and-lime-green polka-dot bikini with lime green fringe that looked like something from the fifties, and it was just so Cyn. She had a great, lean body, with perfect C-cup breasts. Anna knew for a fact that they were real, because she'd watched Cyn grow them. Sam's Donna Karan black two piece with a boy-short bottom flattered her bottom-heavy figure, and Dee's baby pink frilly bikini with tiny white hearts all over it looked like it had come from the children's department.

"Pardon?" Anna asked Cyn. "Something about Scott?"

"She was talking about her boyfriend," Dee filled in, waving a hand languidly through the hot water, "and how he's starting to get on her nerves. Maybe he's gay."

"You're the one who hooks up with gay guys, Dee," Sam reminded her.

"Scott is *definitely* not gay," Cyn stated.

"Oh, I'm sorry," Dee apologized softly. "I'm sorry. I thought I heard you tell me that telepathically." She let a hand trail through the water.

Cyn fiddled with one of the many small gold hoops in her right ear. Then she leaned back, and Anna could see her breasts pressing against her fringed bathing suit top. There was an obvious new addition—a ring through one of her nipples. Anna winced just thinking about it.

"Dee, are you, like, shining me on?" Cyn asked.

Dee shook her head and pushed her shaggy bangs out of her eyes. "Why would I do that?"

"Cyn, don't worry. Dee's on her own planet," Sam explained. "Ignore her."

Anna switched positions so that one of the pulsing water jets pressed into the small of her back. Scott was starting to get on Cyn's nerves? This was news. How could a guy that cool be irritating?

"What were you saying about Scott?" she asked, as nonchalantly as she could.

"I don't know about this couple thing," Cyn muttered. "Maybe I'm just not cut out for it."

Anna was shocked. Scott was the first guy about whom Cyn had really, truly cared. She'd shed a lot of her usual wild-child ways as soon as they'd hooked up. No more stealing guys with wedding rings away from the wives just because she could (it was a game she played that never went beyond furious make-out sessions; Cyn said it helped her keep a realistic and jaded view of the male half of the human race). No more getting wasted at parties and dirty dancing with handsome waiters who neither spoke English nor had a green card. Nor more taking E and sneaking into the Little Red Lighthouse under the George Washington

Bridge and reading *The Little Red Lighthouse* to the wheeling terns.

"You mean you're bored?" Anna asked.

"Kinda." Cyn shrugged. "We don't *do* anything anymore. Like, instead of going to clubs, now he wants to stay in, throw some popcorn in the micro, and rent movies."

"Is the popcorn popped in palm or coconut oil?" Dee queried. "That could be the problem, because they're both totally poison. Even if you flush your system clean with a high colonic you—"

"Dee, leave the enemas out of the discussion," Sam snapped, and then cocked her head at Cyn. "The clubbing thing can get tired, though. I mean, it's so been-there-done-that. Even King King on Hollywood Boulevard is full of wannabes from the valley these days. And House of Blues? Unless you're there on a private party night, it's toast."

"The valley, meaning G.U.?" Cyn laughed.

Sam nodded. "Geographically undesirable."

"Area code 201 where we come from. I get your drift." Cyn reached for the bottle of Evian that rested on the ledge of the tub and took a long swallow. "Scott's desirable. I mean, just look at him. But dammit, I'm not even eighteen years old. I can sit at home with some guy farting Orville Redenbacher when I'm, like, forty."

"He farts popcorn?" Dee was incredulous.

Cyn drank some more water. "Not literally, but you know what I mean. He wants us to actually watch the damn movie and then discuss it afterward. Sometimes he'll even take notes for a future screenplay of his own. I can't believe it, because we used to jump each other, like, three times a night. When we went out to the movies, we'd sit by a wall and do it during the boring parts."

Anna tried not to look as shocked as she felt. "You mean . . . you had sex . . . in a movie theater?"

Cyn laughed. "Put your jaw back on your face, Anna. We're not the only ones. It's not that hard to pull off. You just—"

Anna raised a hand to stop her friend. "Oversharing."

This was too personal, and the whole conversation was upsetting in the strictest sense of the word. When she'd seen Cyn and Scott come into Lush together, she'd been sure everything was status quo. But obviously, based on what Cyn was telling her, everything wasn't hunky-dory. Meanwhile, Anna knew full well, despite how much she was missing Ben, a part of her still had feelings for Scott, if for no other reason than that she'd been feeling them for years. That moment when he'd come into Lush, she'd wanted him. In her heart of hearts, she wanted him still. Maybe more than she'd wanted any guy, ever. Maybe even more than she'd wanted Ben.

"How about behind a statue at the new MoMA?" Cyn asked innocently.

"Aren't you the nasty girl," Sam chuckled. "Trying to get into the *Guinness Book of World Records* for being first in that museum?"

"Well, semisex," Cyn qualified. "And no, not me giving him a blow job, either. That is so over."

Sam grinned. "Without something in return, of course."

"No kidding. I don't know where that blow-jobs-aren't-sex shit started. Probably with some writer for *Rolling Stone* who wasn't getting any and decided to try and start a trend by writing about it."

Anna nodded. Even with her somewhat limited experience, she agreed.

"I've got it," Sam declared. "Your relationship is all about the physical. That always gets old when the sex isn't new anymore. Do yourself a favor and save yourself six months of heartache. Blow him off."

Cyn shook her head. "No. I really care about him. But I don't know." She cupped her hands in the hot water, scooped some up, and let it drip down her face. "We don't screw, we don't talk. . . . I don't know what we do anymore. Shit. Relationships suck."

"Not Sam's," Dee put in loyally. The conversation with the voices in her head had ended satisfactorily for all concerned. "She's in love."

"Maybe," Sam replied cautiously. "But Eduardo's in Paris. It's not like we get to hang out on a regular basis. We never have, really."

"You will," Anna encouraged.

"I wouldn't rush it. Distance can be a good thing. You'll never get bored of each other." Cyn rubbed her temples thoughtfully. "Maybe that's the best kind of relationship of all."

"I don't know, man," Scott declared. "Cyn's cool. But it's like the fire's gone. You know what I'm saying?"

Adam nodded, even though he was only half listening. They were sitting on high leather stools at the Roller Lounge, off the main casino area of the Palms. It was a small private bar with a few tabletops and a few more leather banquettes, along with a bar, waitress, and barkeeper. The place was tougher to get into than the Derby on a busy Saturday night. It admitted only the most exclusive clientele—the high-roller gamblers for whom it was named. Once admitted, guests were exquisitely well cared for. They drank only top-shelf alcohol. A top-of-the-line humidor housed Cuban cigars that had been smuggled illegally into the country—Padrón cigars, from the manufacturer's 1964 anniversary series.

Without being known and approved by the pit bosses and casino personnel, mere mortals wouldn't have had a chance of being admitted to a lounge where Vince Vaughn and Will Smith were both puffing cigars. But a few words between Scott and the boss of the Roller Lounge had secured them the best table in the place.

Knowing how much longer the girls would take to get ready for the rest of the evening, Adam and the other guys had some time to kill. It was why they'd decided to stop for a drink. Cammie had bowed out; stopping in their suite only long enough to change outfits, claiming she had some things to do downtown. When Adam had asked her, she'd just smiled enigmatically. What was *that* about?

"Maybe it's time to move on, man." Parker lifted a

Baltika beer, imported from St. Petersburg, Russia, to his lips. "Good," he pronounced. "Really good. How'd you get us in here, anyway?"

Scott smiled, took a swallow of his Glenlivet and water, and then hoisted the glass to Adam. "A toast. First, to my family name. My uncle is Roger Spencer. He helped to develop half the hotels on the Strip. That means something in this town. Second, to your lady, Cammie. Nicely done."

"Oh yeah," Adam agreed. He could hear the edge in his own voice.

"You good, Adam?" Parker asked him.

"Sure. Why wouldn't I be?" Adam sipped his Coke. He wasn't big on alcohol.

"I didn't get which chick you were with," Scott told Parker.

Parker shrugged. "I'm freelancing these days."

"I hear you, man," Scott agreed. He took another sip of his drink. "I used to kinda wonder about Anna Percy, back in New York."

"Wonder what?" Adam asked. Funny how he still felt protective of Anna, even after she'd treated him so badly. There was just something essentially good about her, though she did seem to act—in her own refined rich New Yorker way—like getting guys to like her was a right, not a privilege. Then he stopped himself. Why worry about Anna Percy? It was over with her. Long over.

"There are like a million variations on Anna at Trinity—where I go to school," Scott explained. "You know what I mean: rich, blond, WASP, smart."

"You've got that right," Adam stated definitively.

"It's interesting, because Cyn is her good friend and she's a wild girl," Scott observed. "So it's kind of intriguing, you know?" He stared contemplatively into his drink. "I guess I should say Cyn *used* to be wild. Or I used to think she was wild. Can't quite figure out how we got where we are, you know?"

"Well, as far as I know, Anna is flying solo these days," Parker put in. "If your thing with Cyn isn't working, maybe you should check Anna out."

God, what a moronic thing to say, Adam thought. But he let it slide. He actually liked Parker—at least most of the time. Adam suspected that Parker had a depth that most of his peers had no interest in plumbing. Though he couldn't quite put his finger on it, something about Parker put him just a little out of step with the Beverly Hills High School A-list. He could relate. He still felt like an outsider. Or at least he had before he'd hooked up with Cammie.

Adam watched Scott rub his jawline thoughtfully. He realized that he didn't know the history of Scott and Anna from when they lived back in New York. Anna was a big girl; she'd have to deal with that one herself.

He had other things on his mind. He glanced at his watch. Where the hell was Cammie?

Between Lust and Love

Dee sat on the edge of her suite's massive oak-with-white-canopy-netting bed and tried Poppy's private line. Voice mail again. It worried her. A lot. Where could Poppy possibly be with Ruby Hummingbird? It was eleven o'clock at night! Ruby should be home sleeping in her pink-and-white Lacoste crib, tucked in next to her limited-edition Steiff stuffed zebra that had been a gift from Ashton and Demi.

"Hi, Poppy, it's me. I know this is like my fifth message, but I'm really worried about you guys. You know how I have this cosmic connection to Ruby, and it's telling me that something isn't right. If I were closer I'd just come over, but I'm in Las Vegas, so that's kind of impossible. So please, you have to call me back right away. Thanks."

Dee hung up but still jiggled one foot nervously against the other. Maybe she really should go back, just go to the airport and catch the next shuttle to Los Angeles. It wouldn't be hard—she could be at the Sharpe compound in two hours, tops. Her mind raced with horrific possibilities of why Poppy had not

returned her call. What if some crazed lunatic had broken into the Sharpe compound and then kidnapped
Ruby? Maybe it was a whole gang of them—they'd
bound and gagged Poppy and all of the baby nurses so
that the infant girl could be held for ransom.

"Don't worry, Ruby Hummingbird—I'll save you," Dee
muttered, confident that on some cosmic, inexplicable-
by-ordinary-man level, the baby could understand her.

What was that?

Dee whirled around. Had she just heard a baby's
cry? "Ruby?" she whispered.

She listened carefully, closing her eyes to concentrate.

But Ruby didn't answer.

There was only one thing to do. She had to tell Sam
to call the Beverly Hills police.

Still in the red-and-black satin La Perla nightgown
and robe she'd put on when she'd come back from
delivering Anna's friend to that sleazy nightclub, Dee
padded down the hall to Sam's suite. Usher was wailing
from the sound system inside, so she knocked hard on
the door. Nothing. Maybe the music was too loud. She
should go back to her suite and call their suite and—

"Mama!"

It was a baby's cry. Dee whirled, eyes wide.

"Ruby?" she called out. "Ruby?"

Nothing. Certain that Sam's baby stepsister was desperate to contact her, Dee pounded harder on Sam's door.

It opened.

"I miss you, too," Sam was cooing into her cell as

she opened the door, acknowledging Dee's presence with a brief wave, then motioning with another for her to come in.

"Sam, I have to talk to—"

Sam held up a wait-a-minute finger and laughed—Dee was almost positive that she was on the phone with Eduardo in Europe. But this was far more important. This was life and death!

"No, señor, I'm not telling you what I'm wearing," Sam told Eduardo in a deep, teasing voice, turning her back.

Dee marched over to her and tapped her shoulder. "Sam, seriously, you have to listen to me. It's about Ruby!"

"Just a sec." Sam put her hand over the mike of her cell. "Not now, Dee. Can't you see I'm kinda busy?"

"But Ruby's in trouble—"

"No, she's not. My dad and Poppy would call me right away if the baby was sick. So whatever is so urgent is going to have to wait. Okay?"

Dee slunk away, wondering what to—

Cammie. Cammie would listen. Cammie *had* to listen.

She bolted out of Sam and Anna's suite and ran in the opposite direction toward where Cammie and Adam were staying. Raised voices came from inside.

"Dammit, Adam, would you just chill out?"

"What, you think it's crazy that I want to know where my girlfriend disappeared to for an hour and a half?"

"I'm not on a leash, okay?"

"Geez, Cammie, I'm not trying to keep you on a leash! I was just asking you where you were!"

Dee backed away. Cammie and Adam were obviously having a fight, and this was no time to interrupt. Cammie would be furious if she did, and she didn't want to endure her friend's wrath. Hold on, she thought. She'd left her cell back in her suite. Poppy could be calling her that very minute and Dee might be missing the call! She charged back the way she'd come, opened her door, and checked for messages.

Nothing.

And then, as if by magic, her custom-designed cell phone ring tone—the haunting melody from the Avinu Malkeinu prayer from Rosh Hashanah, the Jewish New Year—sounded.

"Hello?" Dee answered by the end of the sixth note.

"Dee, this is Tarshea, one of the baby nurses for Mr. and Mrs. Sharpe," the woman announced on the other end of the phone.

Thank Hashem.

"Right, right, I know exactly who you are," Dee assured her. "I'm so glad you called! Is Ruby okay?"

"The baby is just fine," Tarshea assured her. "Mrs. Sharpe is out with Mr. Sharpe and she forgot her cell. She called in for messages and asked me to call you, sweetheart."

Dee sagged onto her couch with relief. "So everything is okay?"

"Everything is just fine. Mrs. Sharpe asked me to tell

you that you don't need to be calling here while you're on your school trip, sweetheart."

"Oh, I don't mind. I think it's my responsibility to stay in touch."

Silence.

"Don't take this wrong, sweetheart," Tarshea finally told her. "But Mrs. Sharpe is askin' you *not* to call. She said she'll call you when she gets a chance."

"Oh."

"Just you go have fun with your friends. See you soon." Tarshea hung up.

Dee just sat there. What could that possibly mean, don't call? Maybe Tarshea had misinterpreted Poppy's message? Yes. That had to be it. She dialed Poppy's cell again and got the machine.

Well. It didn't matter what the nursemaid told her. No way was she going out with the others, not with all this going on at home. She'd wait until she heard from Poppy. She could read the Zohar, a book of Jewish mysticism she'd brought with her. Then she'd go to sleep. In the morning, she'd go to Chabad for the morning minyan, just like she'd promised Rabbi Yaakov at the Kabbalah Centre.

But meanwhile, she'd be still and listen very carefully. Maybe Ruby Hummingbird would send her another psychic message.

Anna sat on the black wool love seat in her suite and tried to read *Vanity Fair*. But it wasn't working. The suite's walls weren't so thick, and she kept hearing Sam on the phone with Eduardo.

They'd already dressed for their evening downstairs at Rain, the Palm's hipper-than-thou club. Anna wore a black Helmut Lang shrunken cashmere sweater with the shoulders cut out, purchased last year on a shopping spree at Saks with Cyn. Anna recalled her mother's frown when she'd first seen Anna in the sweater, and her comments: Didn't Anna find it rather tacky to cut the shoulders out of black six-ply cashmere? Did Anna intend for it to be so cropped that it looked like it one of the maids had mistakenly thrown it into the washing machine? Anna recalled how she'd changed out of the sweater after that, the joy of wearing it gone.

Well, she didn't carry her mother's disapproving voice in her head anymore. At least she tried not to, so she was damn well going to wear the sweater tonight. She'd paired it with white silk pants from the Vanessa Bruno Athe' collection. Stila lip gloss. Shiseido brown mascara. Hair straight and loose to just past her shoulders. And her grandmother's Akoya pearl necklace. She was good to go, just as soon as Sam finished the call. Of course, that could be in the next century, from the sound of it.

Anna was happy that Sam had found such a great guy. She really was. But with Scott's arrival and Cyn's complaining about him, Anna was feeling as out of sorts about guys as she had in months. Really and truly, what did she want? One thing she knew for sure, she'd spent the hour since they'd gotten out of the hot tub thinking way too much about Scott Spencer. It was a proven fact: Her body went to mush every time she looked at him. She told herself it was just some bio-chemical thing, utterly meaningless. The problem was, her self didn't seem to be listening. Even now, she didn't seem to know the difference between lust and love. It wasn't like she really knew Scott. It was just some . . . some hormonal reaction.

With Ben it had been that and so much more. Anna felt dizzy.

Ben. Last year at this time—possibly even in this exact suite—Ben and Cammie had been insane with lust for each other.

"Hypocrite," she muttered softly, though no one was in the room to hear her. She was lusting after two boys at the same time, but she would feel horrible if Ben lusted after some other girl while he was with her.

For all she knew, Ben had a new girlfriend at Princeton. Just because his father had said that Ben was pining away for her didn't make it reality. She eyed her PalmOne Treo 600 Smartphone (a new purchase that had helped her organize her life, since it also served as a digital camera and a PalmPilot and allowed her to access her e-mail) on the nightstand where she'd left it. Sam had programmed Ben's number into it.

It would be insane to call and invite Ben to Vegas. So not her.

Exactly.

She forced herself to put down *Vanity Fair* and picked up her phone. After four rings, she got voice mail again. "Hey, yeah, it's me. Leave a message."

Anna's heart jumped a staccato beat at the sound of his prerecorded voice.

"Uh, hi, it's me again. Anna," she added quickly, which made her sound like an idiot, since she'd already left a message for him earlier. "So . . . I'm calling you from Vegas. We're at the Palms. And I just. I just . . ."

Damn. She could do this.

"I was thinking how much fun it would be if you were here." She took a deep breath. "The thing is, I still think about you. A lot. Wherever I go, you're still there inside my head. That sounds crazy, I suppose, considering how we parted. And I'm rambling, and . . . well, I just wanted you to know. . . ."

As she was thinking of what else to say, Sam knocked on her door and opened it. Anna took the moment to hang up.

"Eduardo just told me the funniest story about one time when he was here and—" Sam stopped dead in her tracks. "Did someone die?"

Anna shook her head.

"Then why are you standing in the middle of the room, clutching your phone, with your face the color of overcooked pasta?"

"I called Ben again."

"Oh." Sam reslung her purple Balenciaga leather motorcycle clutch over her shoulder—it was two shades darker than either her Zac Posen velvet-and-paisley shirt or her slimming Joe's jeans, both of which she'd purchased at one of the boutiques on the main floor of their hotel. "Well, geez, it took you long enough. Did you tell him to get his ass to Vegas?"

"Not exactly."

"Well, whatever you want with him, I hope you get it."

Anna smiled gratefully. Since Sam and Eduardo had fallen for each other, Sam was even a nicer human being. Amazing what being in love did to a person.

"Thanks."

"Yeah. Hey, we're rich, we're young, and we're hot—in my case I'm using the term loosely." Sam laughed. "So let's not cry into our Cristal."

"You're absolutely right. Enough navel-gazing."

"Speaking of, Dee was here a little while ago having a woo-woo moment. I really can't deal with her tonight."

"She knows we're going to Rain," Anna pointed out. "If she wants to come, she'll come."

"I might have to duck out early. Have you ever had phone sex? I thought maybe it could be a warm-up with Eduardo until we're together again for the real thing."

Anna smiled at her. "This is the happiest I've ever seen you."

"Yeah," Sam agreed softly as they walked out of the suite. "I know."

Flexing Her Sexiness

Eminem blasted from the supercharged sound system, and Cammie took a look around Rain. She nodded at her surroundings with cool approval. She remembered when George Maloof had bought the hotel—her father had sent a congratulatory bouquet of roses and a hard hat. She also recalled her father's comment that Georgie had to have ice in his veins— that the hotel business was treacherous and capricious, that today's hot spot was tomorrow's toast.

At least in Rain, Cammie thought, George had done everything right. The place was as deep and wide as two football fields; it spread out on multiple levels, and the main ceiling was at least seven floors high. There was a central raised dance floor. Above it, giant spigots spewed low-heat fire that pulsed to the beat. Behind the main service bar was a wall of Plexiglas, and behind the glass rain fell continuously. As Cammie watched, the rain became an indoor waterfall. The effect was breathtaking. She'd been to all the great clubs in Vegas. Rain was the best, by a wide margin.

"Dance?" Adam yelled over the music.

Cammie nodded. Their fight was over. The truth was, she hadn't gone much of anywhere when she'd left their suite. She'd merely gone across the street to the Rio Hotel, parked herself at the sushi bar, and consumed three California rolls and two small bottles of sake. She'd needed time to think. Alone.

Or no, maybe that was a lie. Maybe she'd done it so that guys could flirt with her. Without being superglued to Adam, she was free to flirt back. She'd come back to the Palms' casino where some guy in baggy blue Fubus, a huge black T-shirt, and what Cammie assumed were his initials—DR—in giant diamond letters around his neck, had asked her to roll his craps dice for him. She'd been amused to see that his bet was for twenty thousand dollars. She'd rolled craps and lost all his money. He hadn't seemed to care. He had a limo waiting. Where did she want to go? The answer: nowhere with him.

Then she'd strolled the perimeter of the casino—guy after guy had hit on her. Old, young, short, tall, bald, ponytailed—they'd been on her like white on rice. None of it had given her the thrill that she'd expected, the old zing of flexing her sexiness and seeing the kind of power she had over men. She couldn't decide if it was because being with Adam was taking that excitement away from her, or if she had just gotten incredibly jaded.

Then she'd seen something that had stopped her in her tracks. A pretty, modestly dressed brunette in her thirties had walked by, her arm linked through that of an ordinary-looking man with thinning brown hair and a largish nose. She was only about five foot three, and her husband wasn't much taller. Cammie noticed their matching wedding rings. The woman gazed up at him like the sun, eyes only on him.

What had taken Cammie's breath away was how much the woman looked like her mother. Same soft brown eyes, same lustrous brown hair, same easy step as she walked.

The stab of the moment came on so quickly that Cammie's hands flew involuntarily to her own heart. Cammie had been eight when her mother had died, the victim of a freak boating accident just a few miles off the Pacific coast. There one minute, gone the next.

Cammie suspected that her father, lovingly known to those in the movie business as that sonofabitch agent Clark Sheppard, had actually loved her mother. He'd never been the same since she'd died, even though he'd remarried. And neither had she. After her mom died, Clark used to admonish Cammie to toughen up.

"You're my flesh and blood, for God's sake. I can do it; so can you."

Her father's harsh words had hurt back then. Thinking about them now, they hurt still.

Eminem's tune segued into a slow song by Beyoncé, and Cammie slipped into Adam's arms.

"We good now?" Adam whispered in her ear.

She wanted them to be good. So much. So she nodded and held him tighter as they swayed to the music.

Sam came up next to them. "Hey, we're going to the upstairs VIP room." She motioned to the second level of the club. "You guys coming?"

"After this dance," Adam nodded.

"You're not gonna freaking believe who's up there in the Rain suite next to ours," Sam intoned. "A whole bunch of Academy Award losers. And not just from this year, either. Best Supporting Actor loser. Best Actor loser. Best Picture loser. They all wanted to know if my dad was here."

Adam chuckled "That's hilarious. It's like a losers' convention."

"I'm cursed, I swear," Sam decided as she glanced around the dance floor. "God, half the people in here are from, like, Boise or something." She shuddered, her gaze landing on a nearby couple. The girl was chunky, in a loud floral skirt stretched so tight across childbearing hips that it revealed a visible panty line. It was not a thong, either. "Do you realize that chick actually went into a store, tried that skirt on, checked herself out in the mirror, and said, 'Wow, I'm so buying this'?"

"Taste is a gene," Cammie declared. "She's missing it."

"That's gotta suck." Sam laughed cheerfully. "So I'll see you guys up there." She edged her way back through the crowd.

Cammie smiled at Adam as Beyoncé wailed sexily. She felt antsy—not really in the mood for night clubbing. "Want to go play the slots, just for fun?"

"I told you, Cammie, I'm not big on gambling."

Cammie felt irritation creep up her neck. "It's not like you're taking food out of the mouths of poor people, Adam."

"It's the principle of the thing. Let's just hang here. With our friends."

Fine. Great. Swell. Cammie knew she was needling him on purpose, but she couldn't seem to stop herself.

"Has anyone ever flung the term 'bleeding-heart liberal' in your direction? Rich Beverly Hills boy, all sanctimonious—"

"First of all, I'm not rich—"

"Your parents probably make—"

"And second of all, who the hell cares?" He backed away far enough to frown at her. "What is up with you, Cammie, for real?"

She hated the frown: like he didn't know her, or if he did know her, he didn't like the her he saw.

"Why do you want to be with me?" she asked plaintively. "When I'm such a jerk?"

"You're hot," he joked.

"No, I'm serious."

"So am I, but it's a lot more than that. I don't know, Cam. You're . . . I guess I see a part of you that you don't let most people see."

Cammie felt a warm sensation in her chest. Oh my. A guy who thought he could peer into her soul. How could you give a boy like that up, just because you wanted to be able to flirt with other guys? God, what would she do if she lost him? How could she possibly want him and not want him at the same time? Maybe she was losing her mind.

She took his arm. "Hey, let's go upstairs, order something lethal to drink, and get utterly wasted."

He led her off the dance floor. But instead of taking her up the winding stairs to the balcony level, he led her into the long corridor entrance to the club, lit only with recessed black lights. Two couples were leaning up against the wall, hot and heavy in the purple glow. Another girl was crying to her girlfriend.

Adam stopped, folded his arms, and turned to Cammie. "Now tell me what's going on."

"I told you—"

"No, you didn't," Adam insisted. "You're acting strange, and I want to know why."

"Maybe because I *am* strange," Cammie shot back.

Adam rubbed the star-shaped tattoo behind his ear, something Cammie knew he only did when he was stressed. "I just—why won't you talk to me?"

He sounded sad and hurt. The horrible truth of it was, Cammie didn't know why she was treating him so badly. She edged back against the wall to let some boisterous partygoers pass on their way to the club.

"Did you ever just feel something that you couldn't even name? Like . . . like this feeling of wanting to crawl out of your skin or be someone else?"

"No," Adam replied softly, his voice soothing. He moved closer to her. "But I'm listening. Is that how you feel?"

"I don't *know*."

She didn't know how to make him understand— how as much as she loved him, she felt both suffocated by that love, and, like with her mother, certain in her knowledge that it could disappear overnight. That as much as she wanted her freedom, she'd say anything and do anything so she wouldn't lose him.

"I love you, Adam," she murmured, and snaked an arm around his neck.

"I love you, too." He put his arms around her and kissed her softly. She rested her head against his chest. Then she slowly began kissing down his collarbone, taking advantage of the darkness to take his hands and slip them under her own shirt. She wore no bra, just a simple camisole.

"What are you doing?"

"What does it look like I'm doing?" She put her own hands atop his, but he quickly withdrew them.

"I'm serious, Cammie. Not here. It's not cool."

"Oh, come on," she coaxed breathily. "What happens in Vegas stays in Vegas. Loosen up."

"I don't want to loosen up."

"Please? For me?" She rubbed up against him.

Adam stiffened. "Dammit, Cammie. Cut it out."

"Fine," she snapped, heat rushing to her face. "Just forget it, then. Forget everything."

She whirled and headed out of the club, striding past the reception area, where she could feel dozens of male eyes turn to watch her go. But she ignored them and pushed out the glass doors toward the valet stand. Part of her hoped that Adam would follow her; part of her was glad when he didn't. She told the black-clad bellboy she needed a taxi and pressed a bill into his hand when he opened the taxi door for her—she didn't know what denomination it was and she didn't care.

"Where to?" the middle-aged driver asked, eyeing Cammie in his rearview mirror.

She pulled the scrap of paper from her Balenciaga bag and read the address to him. Twenty minutes later, they were climbing a private winding road toward the top of a mesa. The taxi driver told her that that if she was into flying saucers, she could probably see Area 51 from her seat. She told him to keep his eyes on the road. Finally, they reached the top of the mesa. At the very top, overlooking the bright lights of Vegas, was an enormous, modern-looking white house that had a commanding view of the city. In the circular front driveway, Cammie paid the driver. He tipped his blue baseball cap and headed back down the hill toward the city. She ran to the front door—tall, huge, and plain white, with a heavy brass knocker. Cammie ignored it and hit the illuminated doorbell. Seconds later, the door opened.

"Camilla. It's been too long."

She went into his arms.

So Damn Sexy

Anna peeked outside—the sun that shone brightly over the Strip was practically overhead—and then padded quietly toward the suite's small kitchen in search of coffee. Her head was pounding; had she really had that much to drink the night before? Maybe the headache was just from spending so long at Rain.

It had been a strange evening. Fun, but strange. Shortly after they'd been brought to their five-thousand-dollar-a-night VIP suite on the second floor of Rain, overlooking the bedlam down below, Sam had departed. Orlando Bloom was next door with Jude Law, and Sam knew him from a dinner party her father had hosted to raise money for the Kerry campaign. Sam had gone to ask him to dance. Then Cyn and Scott had disappeared, too. Anna was left with Parker, who grinned and flashed a small hip flask that he said was full of Stoli. Whatever they were drinking, they could fortify if they wanted.

The suite was great—big enough for twenty, open to the club, comfortable couches and pillows on the floor, great video monitors, and a waitress who only served their section of Rain. Parker morphed into his usual charming self; and he and Anna spent a long time in the midst of the throng on the dance floor. By the time they came back, Cyn was giving Scott a lap dance on one of the couches. It made Anna wonder: Why was she gyrating like that on him if she had so many doubts?

Anna found the coffee, got a pot started, and checked her watch—it was just after twelve. Well, they'd been out until nearly four, so that wasn't surprising. While the coffee was brewing, she brushed the fuzz from her teeth, then downed some cranberry juice from the living room minibar. What she needed to clear her head, she decided, was a swim. So she donned the vintage canary yellow bikini she'd found at Darling down on Horatio Street—the label had faded and she really couldn't remember who had designed it—then pulled on her ancient Levis and a plain white Calvin Klein tank tee over it. Taking a cup of coffee for the road, she took her white key card and headed out the door.

The see-and-be-seen scene at Skin, the outdoor pool area at the Palms, was just beginning for the day. A few couples were having a late breakfast at the tables just behind a small filigreed iron gate. Around the Olympic-size rectangular pool, girls in string bikinis posed and preened. Other gorgeous girls leaned over the balconies above, taking in the view. The day was already hot—it had to be in the low nineties, and Anna remembered that they were out in the desert. Even a day in April here was bound to be a lot warmer than in L.A.

As soon as she found an empty rose-colored chaise, a pool girl in a tight Palms shirt and low-slung denim short shorts scurried over. Did Anna want a cocktail, a towel, anything at all? She accepted the proffered towel, turned down the drink, pulled off her clothes, and executed a perfect dive into the deep end of the crystalline pool. Funny, she was the only person actually swimming.

After a few laps in the cool water—fortunately, the Palms wasn't one of those places that heated its pool to body-basting temperatures—Anna's head felt clearer. She stopped to catch her breath and shook her hair off her face.

"My dog does that."

Anna squinted up into the bright sun and then used her hand as a visor so that she could actually see. Scott Spencer stood by the edge of the pool, wearing nothing but blue-and-white surfer jams and a killer smile. God, he looked great.

"Your dog?"

He crouched down. "Yep. A chocolate Lab. Her name's Marge. Don't think you two are acquainted. She shakes her head just like that."

Anna laughed. "You just compared me to your dog."

"Hey, she's a beauty, take it as a compliment. So, looks like everyone else is still asleep."

"Evidently."

" 'Evidently,' " Scott echoed. "Why is it you Vassar types don't ever say 'yeah' or 'for sure'? No, you say 'evidently.' "

Anna frowned. "I never thought about it, I guess. I mean—"

He splashed some water at her; she neatly put her hands up to block it, treading water as she did. "Hey, I'm teasing you."

"Where are you going to school next year?" Anna asked.

"Colby. In Maine. Want to see my cannonball?"

"No. And neither do the overly made-up girls sitting way too close to the edge of the pool."

"Yeah, I saw the DON'T SPLASH ME, I MELT signs." He scooched over to the lip of the pool and slid in, going all the way under before popping up again. "Oh man, this feels great."

"I know." Anna cocked her head at him. "Just what is a Vassar type, by the way?"

"Like you don't know. Half the moms at Trinity. On the committees of all the best charities. They all went to Vassar. Unless they went to Bryn Mawr or Goucher. Where'd your mother go?"

Anna thought for a moment. Had Scott ever met her mother? She didn't think so. He'd moved to New York from Boston fairly recently, and they didn't exactly travel in the same social circle. Yet he'd pegged Jane Percy perfectly.

"Goucher."

Damn.

"Okay, point taken," she allowed, "but that doesn't mean you know me. I'm going to Yale. And how would you like it if I called you a Colby type—just as financially stable as anyone else but who still likes to ski in the winter and rock climb in the fall? And hates fraternities on principle? And whose mother drives a Saab instead of a Mercedes?"

He laughed. "Okay, I deserved that. So, we gonna swim or we gonna take turns insulting each other?"

"Race you to the far side," Anna challenged.

"You're on," Scott agreed. "Loser buys lunch. On your mark, get set—"

They both took off, Anna doing a smooth freestyle honed during summers in Southampton. Yet Scott beat her easily.

"Swim team," he breathed hard, when she reached the other side four strokes after him. "I joined this year."

"You could have fooled me," Anna puffed. She latched onto the pool wall to catch her breath.

He grinned at her. "I'd rather have you buy me lunch."

They were treading water so close that their feet actually got entangled. She let her toes linger momentarily before pulling them back. It was involuntary. She told herself so, even as she imagined doing things that she definitely should not be imagining doing with her best friend's significant other.

"So . . . where's Cyn?" Anna asked brightly.

"Still sleeping."

"Maybe we should wait until she wakes up."

"Maybe we shouldn't."

God, Scott was just so damn sexy. And she felt so . . .

clearly her body didn't have the same scruples as her mind. It was everything she could do not to let her toes drift toward his legs. Instead, she swam a few strokes away from him.

"Okay, let's go."

She got out of the deep end and dried off; his chaise was on the other side of the pool. He looked just as good far away as he did up close. Scott got his stuff and joined her, then nodded toward the tables behind the filigreed gate. "How about we eat right over there?"

"Sure," Anna agreed, slipping her tank top over her bathing suit and picking up her jeans. They headed for the tables. It's just a friendly lunch, she reminded herself. People go to lunch with people all the time and it doesn't mean anything.

"So, how are things back in New York?" Anna finally asked, after they'd ordered.

"Droll," Scott replied coolly.

"I heard about your piece in the *Times*."

"Yeah, Cyn told you on Webcam; I was there, remember?"

Of course she remembered. She'd been in a terrible mood and had e-mailed Cyn, who had insisted they turn on the Webcams they'd both just bought. One of the first things that Cyn had told her was that the *New York Times* had just published a humorous op-ed piece by Scott, about what would happen if the Bush twins joined the Peace Corps.

"You were celebrating your publication."

With your tongue down my best friend's throat, she added mentally.

"My mother who drives a Saab has connections."

Anna bit her lip. "I really didn't mean to insult your mother."

"Why not? I insulted yours."

Anna ran a finger over the condensation on her water glass. "It's just that I don't buy into those stereotypes, so it's hypocritical of me to be propagating them."

"Hey, my mom's a cliché and I admit it." He reached for the Foster Grants with the circular lenses he'd laid on the table and slipped them on.

"Which makes you a son of a cliché."

He raised his beer glass and clinked it against hers. "Touché."

The waitress—another scantily clad blond Palms Girl type in a variation on the T-shirt-and-hot-pants ensemble—brought Anna her Cobb salad and Scott his gorgonzola cheeseburger. Anna smoothed her napkin onto her lap. "So you want to be a writer?"

"The next Hunter S. Thompson."

"My father knew him," Anna confessed. "One of his clients helped to finance that movie of *Fear and Loathing in Las Vegas*."

"Doesn't surprise me." Scott took a swallow of his beer, then put it down again before he continued. "I guess what I want to be is a *great* writer. Problem is, I'm a lazy perfectionist. I mean, if I were a real writer, I'd have a notebook with me at all times, to write down the pearls of genius as they appeared." He spread his palms up. "No notebook. Not even a minidisc recorder."

Anna smiled. His self-deprecation was charming. It was a quality she appreciated and that she found in short supply in Los Angeles.

"Maybe you're taking notes in your head. Are you working on anything these days?"

Scott shrugged. "*Working* might be too strong a term."

"What is it?"

"A novel, actually. A sort of future history of Manhattan over the next twenty years or so. Everyone with children leaves because they can't afford to live there, so the whole place gets gentrified. Then Bill Gates—obviously he's old by then—buys it and gives it back to the Indians."

"Sounds . . . interesting."

"It would be," Scott allowed, "if I could get past the outline."

"Cyn says you're a really good writer."

There. Anna had brought up Cyn. That proved she had no designs on Cyn's boyfriend.

"Maybe great sex dumbed down her opinion," he suggested. "Ever happen to you?"

Anna bit into a forkful of her salad. "What?"

"Have you ever had such great sex with a guy that you thought he was someone he wasn't?"

Since Anna had had sex with only one guy, she really

didn't have a basis for comparison. But she wasn't about to tell Scott that.

"Why would that be any of your business?"

He shrugged easily. "It isn't."

"Are you asking me personal questions because you don't want to talk about your writing?" Anna pressed. "Do you think you only got published in the *Times* because your mother called in a favor?"

"Ouch." He washed down another bite of his burger.

Anna instantly felt terrible that she'd attacked him. It was probably only because she was so damned attracted to him. She knew she shouldn't be. She knew the smart thing to do would be to bring this lunch to a rapid conclusion, go up to her suite, and read *Vanity Fair.*

She stayed put.

"I'm sorry I said that," she finally murmured.

"It's funny," Scott began. "Back in New York you always seemed so . . . tense."

Only around you. Because I wanted to throw myself at you every time I saw you.

"It's not like you knew me," she pointed out.

"True. Maybe I should have gotten to know you." Scott's direct gaze met hers. He had a single freckle right next to the left corner of his lips—

"Am I interrupting?"

Anna almost dropped her fork. Cyn was standing at their table clad in a very Cyn outfit: vintage burnt orange bellbottoms and a forest green long-sleeved pullover under a ratty pink shrug. She wore her giant black Chanel sunglasses, so Anna couldn't see her eyes. But her nose ring was in. And the accusing tone—that Anna couldn't miss.

"No, of course not!" Anna exclaimed. "We saw each other here when we were swimming. Then we got hungry. That's all."

"Whatever." Cyn slid another chair up to their table. "Is Vegas a pit or what?"

"Morning, babe." Scott leaned over. She raised her lips for him to kiss her. He did.

"I missed you when I woke up," she told him. She put her hand on her stomach. "God, I'm concave I'm so hungry. Where's the waitress?"

"You know what? I'm done, actually," Anna declared, pushing her seat back. "So I'll see you two later."

"Much," Cyn winked at her. "We may have to go back to bed for a while."

"All righty!" Anna agreed a bit too gaily. "Have fun."

She trotted toward the simple glass doors that led into the lobby. As she stepped inside, the casino assault hit her: the noise, the pounding music, the shouts of winners and losers at the craps tables and the slot machines. Anna headed straight for the bank of elevators that would take her back up to her suite. She wanted to shower and change clothes. She wanted to start the day over.

God, she had acted like such an idiot when Cyn showed up. As if she and Scott were guilty of some secret flirtation.

But they weren't. Anna was sure they weren't.

Well, pretty sure, anyway.

Lime Green Heels

TONIGHT! LIVE IN THE JUNGLE ROOM: DRAKE MESMER IN HIP-NO-SIS. VOTED BEST HYPNOTIST IN VEGAS BY LAS VEGAS INSIDER!

Parker sat at the small wooden bar just outside the Congo Room at the venerable Sahara Hotel chatting up a redhead from Dallas. The redhead claimed her name was Kendall, though Parker suspected that she'd borrowed the moniker from Erica Kane's daughter on the soap opera *All My Children*—a soap on which Parker had once done an under-five.

This particular Kendall appeared to be the kind of insecure rich girl who had to advertise her money: gumball-size diamond ring, gold necklace dripping with jeweled charms that disappeared into her eye-popping cleavage, shocking-pink-mink-trimmed Dr. Romanelli leather bomber jacket. The jacket was a limited edition. Parker knew for a fact it went for six grand, because he'd been moseying through Kaviar and

Kind in Hollywood over the holidays and had seen
Naomi Watts purchase the exact same jacket, only the
fur trim on hers was baby blue.

The million-dollar question was, why was this Kendall
in this hotel? She obviously had plenty of money. But the
Sahara these days was so far down anyone's notion of
where to stay in Vegas as to be off the list. Its heyday had
been forty years ago: The corridor leading past the ubiquitous all-you-can-eat buffet had been lined with photo-
graphs of literati and glitterati from the 1960s—everyone
from President Kennedy to the Beatles to Truman
Capote. But now the Sahara was toast.

It was exactly why Parker had decided to come
trolling here. The others were eating dinner at the sushi
bar in the Bellagio. Parker had claimed he wasn't
hungry so he could go off on his own and meet . . .
well, someone like Kendall.

He was a man with a plan. Which was why he
changed the subject from which casino on the strip put
the most alcohol in its free drinks to something a bit
more personal.

"You know, Kendall, you have the best hair." Parker
fingered one of her curly locks.

"You think?" she drawled, noisily sipping the last of
her Singapore Sling through her straw. It was her third
drink—Parker was counting. "I always hated being a
redhead when I was kid. So, tell me more about your
acting."

"I just booked a U-five on *Everwood*," Parker lied,

"and I'm about to shoot this indie film. Sean Penn is directing. Fox Searchlight is going to release it."

Kendall's radiant blue eyes, lined with way too much kohl eyeliner, grew huge. They were glassy from the alcohol. "For real?"

"Well, it's not the lead or anything," Parker excused himself modestly, making it up as he went along. He was interested in this girl. Very interested. Kendall screamed money. Kendall might be a perfect short-term solution; that was all he was looking for, anyway. She was cute. She was a sophomore at some junior college in Dallas—Parker hadn't caught the name—and had come to Vegas with her best friend for a midweek get-away. The best friend didn't have a lot of money, so they were staying at the Sahara, because Kendall didn't want her best bud to feel bad. When she'd heard that Parker was staying at the Palms, Kendall's inebriated eyes had lit up. That was where she'd wanted to stay.

Well, maybe that could be arranged.

"So, what's up for you tonight?" she asked, looking at him flirtatiously through her MAC-clumped lashes.

"My friends and I are going to see the hypnotist's show." Parker nodded in the direction of the Jungle Room. "It starts in like ten minutes."

"Oh, my friend saw that; she said it's great."

"Hey, you should come with us!" Parker exclaimed, as if he'd just thought up the idea.

Kendall feigned reluctance. "I wouldn't want to horn in or anything."

"No, really, my friends are cool. Like we came out here in Jackson Sharpe's private jet—"

"Shut *up*!" Excited Kendall almost slid off her bar stool.

"Yeah, his daughter, Sam, is one of my best friends. Come on. Let's go in and get a tabletop. I'll introduce you to her."

"That'll be fifteen dollars even," the bartender told Parker, removing his glass and wiping the condensation from the bar.

"Got it." He flashed his winning grin. Reached into his pocket. Felt around. "Oh man, I can't believe this, I must have left my wallet at the Palms!"

"I do stuff like that all the time," Kendall assured him. " 'S no problem. I got the night covered." She pulled a crisp twenty out of her purse and laid it neatly on the bar.

When her first step in her Constança Basto lime green heels went wobbly, Parker reached out to steady her. "Careful." He made serious eye contact. His hands remained on the small of her waist.

"Thanks," she cooed.

"You are so welcome."

"So, Sam Sharpe?" she breathed.

"Yeah, she'll tell you all about her dad. I hang out over there all the time."

"What's he like?"

"Cool."

"And what's she like?" They reached the admissions

desk for the hypnosis show. Kendall took out more money. Parker took Kendall's hand the instant she'd paid and steered her into the theater.

"Sam?" Parker asked rhetorically. "Well, for one thing, she's not half as cute as you are."

"You may think you can't be hypnotized," Drake Mesmer told the packed theater as he prowled the long, narrow stage. He was a large bald man in a well-cut, expensive-looking suit. "But you may be wrong." He waved his hand and the enormous diamond on his pinkie ring sparkled. According to the program, when Drake Mesmer wasn't doing his show he was a "hypnotist to the stars," jetting all over Hollywood and curing the rich and famous of various phobias and addictions. And based on the size of the giant rock on his finger, he must have made pretty good money doing it. "*You* five hundred esteemed guests are the show, ladies and gentlemen. None of you know me, correct? Mom, put your hand down."

The crowd tittered.

"What a hoot," Sam muttered to Anna. She took a long pull on the Bud Light she'd ordered. There was nothing else available at the Sahara that appealed to her.

"Hey!" The cheesy, overblown redhead whose outfit screamed, "Get me a makeover!" that Parker had brought to the show flailed at the air with her hands. "I can be hypnotized! Pick me!"

So polluted, Sam realized. Had a few too many before she even ordered the drink that's in front of her.

Drake asked everyone in the audience to lift one arm in the air. Sam checked out the crowd. Pretty much everyone did it. What the hell. She raised her arm, too. She was certain she couldn't be hypnotized; she was way too self-conscious to ever give up control in public.

Coming to this show had actually been her idea. Jackson had mentioned that he'd seen Drake's show last year when he was on a special episode of *Celebrity Poker* for charity. He said it had been worth coming all the way to the Sahara. Nor had Drake made a big deal out of having Jackson Sharpe in the audience, either. Jackson had been impressed by that, too.

"You will listen to me now." Drake's voice was strangely commanding. "You will listen only to my voice. You cannot lower your arm. No matter what you do, you can't lower it."

Sam lowered her arm. So much for that. She looked around. Many others in the audience had lowered their arms, too, including all her friends. But the drunk moron with Parker was reaching for the ceiling with both hands, like a ref signaling a winning Super Bowl touchdown. Then Drake instructed everyone in the room to stare at their two extended index fingers.

"You will find them moving closer to each other. Keep staring, keep staring—they are moving closer and closer and closer. . . ."

Sam didn't even bother to do it, until she saw Anna's friend Cyn with her eyes locked on her fingertips; ditto for the guy from New York, Scott. In the other direction, Cammie and Adam were doing the same thing.

Oh, fuck. Why not?

Sam put her index fingers a foot from her face and stared at them like they were the Academy Award statue her father had been robbed of winning.

"You are becoming sooo relaxed, sooo happy, sooo tired," Drake assured the audience. "You can't even keep your eyes open. Just let them close. That's it. Let your eyes close." Drake crooned on and on in a hypnotic tone. Sam closed her eyes. She knew she wasn't hypnotized, though, because she'd made a *choice* to close her eyes. She was just going along with it for fun.

"Your eyelids are getting heavier and heavier, but you're completely and totally relaxed," Drake intoned. "When I count to three, you will try to open your eyes, but you will be unable to. No matter how hard you try, you will not be able to open your eyes. "One, two, three."

Sam opened her eyes. What total bullshit. She surveyed her friends. They all had their eyes closed. Next to her she could see Anna's eyelids fluttering, as if she were trying to open them but couldn't. Okay, that was freaky. Anna was not the type to fake it. For a moment, she wished that Dee had decided to come with them to the show instead of staying in the room with her kabbalah text, waiting for a crucial phone call from Poppy that she said she was expecting.

This was right up Dee's alley. On the other hand, it might have influenced Dee—so many things did. Dee Young deciding to become a hypnotist was a scary proposition.

"You feel no panic, no concern," Drake went on as he strolled the stage from end to end. "Everything is fine. You are totally relaxed, but you cannot open your eyes. Listen to the sound of my voice. You know you are safe when you hear my voice. On the count of three, you will be able to open your eyes. You will feel relaxed. One, two, three."

Anna's eyes opened. "That was amazing," she hissed to Sam. "It felt like they were locked shut."

Drake swept a hand over his the audience. "Remember how I said you are the stars of this show, ladies and gentlemen? All of you who could not open your eyes when I said you couldn't but could open them again when I said you could . . . come on up!"

Canned rock music began to play as Drake waded into the audience, urging people to go up on his stage. Parker's drunk friend was the first one to lurch up the steps. She was followed by at least three dozen others— Sam was shocked to see that all her friends were partici- pating. Even Anna. Could they *really* have been hypnotized by this guy? It was hard to believe.

With the stage filled to his satisfaction, Drake moved bodies around. Sam could see he wanted the arrangement to be boy-girl-boy-girl. Everyone went along with this willingly. Sam couldn't imagine that some of these people weren't just goofing on the hyp- notist, playing him for laughs. Or that some of them weren't plants. But if they were indeed plants—inserted into the show by the hypnotist—they were wonderful plants. They looked just like tourists from Anywhere, USA.

"Another beer?" a cosmetics-queen waitress clad in a leopard-print mini uniform with lace-up feathered stilettos whispered to Sam. She nodded, studying Drake. He'd be a wonderful character in a screenplay, too.

Drake walked up and down his two lines of subjects, moving in and out. "When I touch your forehead, you will fall asleep." He used the same commanding voice as before. "You will have no worries, no cares; you will just fall instantly asleep. Trust me. Let yourself sleep."

He went up to people at random, put his palm of his right hand in the center of their forehead, counted to three and told them to sleep, and they fell over like a stack of bricks. It reminded Sam of those bizarre tele-vangelist shows she'd seen on TV, where Benny Hinn wandered through the audience taking the devil out of people by touching their heads. Being a big guy, Drake managed to ease everyone's fall and direct them onto a chair or the floor of the stage itself.

Sam watched, astonished, as Scott went out like a light at Drake's command. Then the hypnotist had Cyn go to sleep half atop him. The guy next to her landed on her right butt cheek. Cammie fell straight out in the center of the stage. Adam landed on her right Manolo but didn't seem to feel anything. Anna ended up entwined with a skinny guy sporting serious bling.

Un-freaking-believable. Maybe it *was* for real. There was no other way Anna Percy would be sprawled onstage draped over some guy she didn't know.

The audience applauded. Drake encouraged the applause, telling the crowd that the people onstage would not be affected by the noise. "They're mine until I wake them up." He kept talking to those onstage in that soothing voice. As he did, he walked around, stepping over sprawled bodies. He stopped by the redhead who'd come with Parker. He took her right hand, lifted it up, and watched it drop.

"I love you, I can't use you, good-bye," Drake said into the microphone.

Her eyes snapped open. Sam couldn't imagine how Drake could have determined that she was faking, but he most definitely had.

"But I'm *hypnotized!*" she screeched.

Sorry, sweetheart, can't use you." She rose and huffily made her way down the stairs with the help of two guys from the audience.

"See, if you've had a little too much to drink, it interferes with the hypnotic suggestion. And I have a feeling that girl's had a whole *lotta* 'a little too much too drink.' "

Drake told his subjects to get up and take seats at the rear of the stage. They all complied, then sat patiently, waiting for what would come next.

A drum roll. He began putting couples together at random, placing them around the stage. Anna was opposite a hot guy who looked a lot like Mark Anthony but taller. Cammie ended up with Adam. Cyn was with a muscular tattooed guy with a blue Mohawk—nice looking if you went for that sort of thing. Scott was put with a short girl whom either nature or surgery had blessed with gargantuan breasts. She wore a red skin-tight T-shirt—obviously on purpose. Trying way too hard, Sam decided. This she'd known since her first trip to Fred Segal with whatever nanny had been employed at the time. The key to style was to work your ass off and spend whatever was necessary to look as close to perfect as possible, without looking like you'd done anything at all.

"When I give you the signal, you will do everything you can to seduce the person across from you," Drake instructed. "You think they are the sexiest, hottest person in the world, and you want to prove to them that you are the only person for them."

As Drake gave the signal, Barry White's deep bass voice crooned sexily from the sound system. Instantly, the couples were all over each other. The short girl with Scott literally jumped on him, her stubby legs encircling his waist. Cammie and Adam were making out furiously. And Anna—Anna, of all people!—was practically rubbing herself up and down on the gorgeous Marc Anthony guy as if she were a Siamese cat in heat.

Leave it to Anna to get paired with a sizzler.

After a few minutes in which the audience could barely control itself, Drake called a halt to the proceedings. He sent all his subjects back to the row of chairs at the rear of the stage and commanded them to sleep. They slept momentarily and then, just as the waitress brought Sam another beer, Drake asked Adam to step forward and open his eyes.

"He's still under," Drake advised the audience. "Don't worry. What's your name, young man?"

"Adam."

"How's it going tonight?"

"Fine," Adam droned.

"Enjoying the show?" Drake asked, with a wink at the audience. "Feeling comfortable?"

"Yes."

"Can you do something for me, Adam? I'd like you to walk over to any person on this stage right now and say one honest thing to him or her. Right now. Do you understand, Adam? One honest thing. Do not worry; the person will not react to you. In fact, that person will say thank you. Do you understand?"

"Yes."

Sam sat forward in her chair. This was unbelievable! What would Adam do? There was complete silence in the theater as Adam stepped directly to Cammie. "Her."

"What's her name?" Drake prompted. "Do you know her?"

Adam nodded. "Cammie."

"Cammie? Can you take a step forward, please?"

Cammie stepped forward.

Drake went to Adam and draped an easy arm around Adam's shoulder. "Okay, Adam, what do you want to say to her that she doesn't know?"

Adam turned to Cammie. "You're my girlfriend, but sometimes I'm really attracted to other girls."

Holy shit. Sam was so startled that when she nearly

knocked over her beer. This was amazing. If Cammie wasn't hypnotized, she'd *kill* Adam for saying that. No, she'd break up with him first and kill him second.

"Thank you," Cammie droned.

Oh no, this was *not* happening!

"Cammie, do you have something you want to say back to Adam?" Drake queried. "Something honest? Don't worry, he'll thank you."

"Adam, I'm really into you, but you're too nice. Guys who are nice bore me."

"Thank you," Adam responded.

Sam shook her head, her jaw hanging open. If she hadn't been seeing this, she would never have believed it.

"Thank you, Cammie. Thank you, Adam." Drake nodded to them, then turned to the audience, a broad grin on his face. "How many of you want to take hypnotism classes from me starting right after the show? How many of you would pay me whatever I asked?"

The audience applauded and whooped, but Sam shook her head. She was baffled and worried. Would Adam and Cammie have any recollection of what had happened here onstage?

Next, Drake brought up the guy with the Mohawk, who told the guy he was with that he wanted to worship him and that he'd like to see him in red high heels.

All righty, then.

Next, Drake brought up Parker.

"He's mine!" the redhead Parker had hooked up with screamed drunkenly from the audience. Sam was beyond thankful that she'd chosen another table.

"Oh yeah?" Drake asked.

"Yeah!"

"What's his name?"

"Parker!"

"Okay, Parker." He draped an arm around Parker's broad shoulder. Is there one honest thing she doesn't know that you'd like to tell her, man?"

Parker stepped to the edge of the stage and peered into the darkened audience. "I think you're cute—"

"See? See?" The girl interrupted triumphantly, stabbing the air with her finger.

"But that's not the only reason I hooked up with you," Parker went on.

"Tell her the other reason," Drake urged him.

"The other reason is . . . you seem like a beautiful person on the inside, too," Parker said. "And I really care about stuff like that."

"I fucking love you!" she yelled, jumping up from her seat and waving her arms in the air. Someone nearby pulled her down, thank God.

Drake cupped his hand to his ear. "Do I hear wedding bells? Maybe they'll come back to Vegas and get married by an Elvis impersonator—you never know!"

The audience cracked up.

Sam looked from the drunk redhead up to Parker, then back at the redhead. Okay, this made zero sense. The girl was not that cute, plus her *uni* was worthy of the headline "Would You Be Caught Dead in This Outfit"? Plus, Parker had just met her—how would he know if her insides were beautiful? *Très* strange.

Parker took his seat onstage; Drake called Anna up.

"So, Anna? Tell someone in this room one honest thing they don't know."

Anna spun around and looked directly at Cyn's boyfriend, Scott. "Scott?"

Drake urged Scott forward—he stepped up opposite her.

"Yeah, Anna?"

"What I want to tell you is . . ." Anna hesitated.

For a moment, Sam wondered if Anna would be the one who could resist Drake's hypnotic suggestion. If anyone could do it, it would be her. She would open her eyes, look at Drake with that direct gaze of hers, tell him thank you but no thank you, and return to her seat.

It didn't happen. She was completely under. What Anna said instead made Sam choke on her beer.

"Scott, I've wanted to have sex with you ever since the first moment I saw you."

Cammie's Mystery Destination

" **O**n the count of three you will be fully awake
and aware, no longer hypnotized. You will have
a wonderful, refreshed feeling. One, two, three."

Sam watched the people onstage slowly open their
eyes. Drake had them all standing in a row—each of
them was looking around, maybe a little bit dazed, but
no one upset, perturbed, or concerned about their
experience.

The audience, of course, had loved it. Drake thanked
his participants for being such good sports and thanked
the audience for being such a pleasure to entertain.

"And just in case you want a souvenir of the best
show in Las Vegas, we've got instant DVDs of your
experience at Hip-No-Sis on sale in the lobby for
thirty-five dollars. I'll be happy to sign the case for you.
Thanks for coming; it's been a great night!"

Once more, there was hearty applause from an
audience that had been both amazed and entertained.

"Man, I love this guy's show," Sam overheard
a husky guy behind her tell his companion—a biker-

chick girl in a black tank top and black jeans. "I've seen him three times and he kills every time."

Sam touched the burly man's arm to get his attention. "Excuse me," she interjected. "I happened to overhear you say that you've seen Drake's show before."

"Yeah?"

"Do you know if people remember what happened? The people who were hypnotized, I mean?"

"Hell no!" The guy guffawed heartily. "First time I went up there, I didn't remember jack afterward. Drake had me twirl around the stage like a figure skater. A chick figure skater. It was hilarious. You gotta buy the DVD."

The house lights went up and people started to file out of the club. Appearing no worse for the experience, Anna stepped in next to Sam.

"Tell me the truth. Was that bullshit?" Sam demanded. "How do you feel? Do you remember what happened?"

"I feel very relaxed and peaceful for some reason, to tell you the truth."

"So you were under?"

Anna nodded. "I guess so."

"Remember what happened?"

"No. I really don't. That's kind of . . . odd."

Sam caught a glimpse of Parker furiously making out with the wasted redhead; evidently there was no accounting for bad taste.

The line to leave the club slowed by the DVD sales

booth, where an older gentleman with a terrible toupee was loudly hawking souvenirs. "Get your DVD of tonight's show, ladies and gentlemen; you'll be amazed!"

Adam and Cammie were waiting for Sam there. "You guys ready to book?" Adam asked.

"Tell me if you two remember what happened when you were onstage," Sam demanded again.

They looked at each other and shrugged.

"Nope," Adam declared.

"You're shitting me," Sam exclaimed.

"Why?" Cammie asked easily. "What happened?"

"You're telling me that you don't find it bizarre that you were just hypnotized in public and you *don't know what the hell you said or did*?"

"What did he do? Make us cluck like chickens or moo like cows?" Anna asked. She edged toward the souvenir stand. "Should we buy a DVD?"

Whoa. This was deeply, deeply weird. Sam understood in that moment that she was the only one out of all of them who knew what had been said and done. And if no one bought a copy of that stupid DVD, what happened in Vegas would definitely stay in Vegas. Actually, it would stay in the Jungle Room.

But if someone *did* buy the DVD . . .

Shit.

Parker joined them, one arm draped around his new girlfriend, who had her hand on his ass. "Hey, you guys met Kendall, right?"

"Oh my God, you're Sam Sharpe!" Kendall gushed. "I saw you in *Teen Vogue*! Oh, and in that *Vanity Fair* article, too. Wow, you're so much cuter in person."

"Thanks," Sam said mechanically. Evidently Parker had picked up a suck-up, and not a very smart one.

"My father invested a few million in a movie last year," she went on. "It's about the ten plagues, but, you know, modern. Everyone in my family is *so* into Hollywood!"

"Uh-huh," Sam uttered.

The hawker raised his voice to catch the last people leaving the theater. "Hip-No-Sis! Get your DVD of tonight's fun! Relive the excitement! Just thirty-five bucks!"

"Shall we?" Adam asked the group, motioning toward the short line.

It was a serious moral dilemma. Sam knew that the DVD would change everything for everyone. Maybe she should secretly order a copy so she'd have it for the future, kind of like an insurance policy for when Cammie—

"Guys!" Cyn hustled over with Scott. "I bought one! I bet it's a hoot."

No more moral dilemma. Fate—well, Cyn—had intervened.

"You want to go back to the hotel and watch it?" Cyn suggested.

"Please," Cammie scoffed. "What do you do, watch your parents' home movies for fun?" She swung her curls off her face, eyeing Parker and his "date." "You are . . . ?"

"Kendall Cunningham. You have great hair. Who does it?"

Cammie merely blinked at the girl, as if she weren't even worthy of a reply, then turned back to the group. "I've got a better idea. Remember I told you guys that I knew a place where we could gamble?"

"Cammie—" Adam began.

Cammie waved him off. "Adam doesn't approve of gambling," she told the group.

"You came to Vegas and you don't approve of gambling?" Scott shook his head in mock disbelief. "You're a better man than I am, my friend."

"It's no biggie," Adam offered easily. "I came to hang with my friends and my girlfriend."

"Which is so sweet, really." Cammie stood on tiptoe to kiss her boyfriend. "And you can relax, baby. Because the place I want to take you is totally private. And you can gamble for fun, not for profit. No animals will be harmed in the process." She kissed him lightly.

"Can we check out this DVD there?" Cyn pressed.

"Whatever. Let's go—I'm sick of this place," Cammie declared. "We can figure it out later."

What happens in Vegas stays in Vegas was definitely *not* about to stay in Vegas. Sam panicked as they made their way through the cavernous hotel to their waiting limo. As soon as her friends saw that DVD, the shit was going to hit the Vera Wang. And who knew how far it would fly?

Anna peered through the glass of the black stretch limo as the mesa-top mansion came into view. It was about time, she thought. The freeway run out of Vegas to the north and then the winding drive up the mesa to Cammie's mystery destination had made her feel a little queasy. So had the two bottles of Cristal they'd cracked open and emptied.

"This doesn't look like a private club." She leaned forward to look at Cammie as the limo rolled past the front door. "It looks like someone's place."

Cammie smiled enigmatically. "Doesn't it, though?"

"An enormous place," Cyn opined, taking in the three-story-tall mansion that was as long as a football field. "Do you mind telling me where the hell we are?"

"O ye of little faith," Cammie pronounced, opening the limo's windows so her friends could take in the panoramic view of Las Vegas. "Let's just say this is one of Sin City's best-kept secrets."

"Or you could be setting us all up for the Mafia hit that will put you out of your misery," Scott joked half-nervously.

"Trust me." Instead of stopping by the front door—more like the entrance to a grand hotel than a front door, with its white colonnaded facade with laser lights shooting into the sky in all directions—the driver followed Cammie's instructions and brought them to a side entrance, where three sets of double glass doors led to a lower level. The driver asked Sam if it would be okay if he went down to the valley again to wash the limo. Sam said that was fine. She'd call him if he wasn't back when they were ready to leave.

As the limo pulled away, the group regarded the

glass doors. They were tinted and it was impossible to see inside.

"Quick, who knows the secret knock?" Scott whispered.

Cyn laughed and kissed him, which made Anna squirm. Yes, she'd flirted with Scott at the pool. Well, kind of. Well, badly. But it had been harmless. And she'd never, ever, ever actually move in on her best friend's guy, even if she had the remotest notion of how to do such a thing. Which she didn't.

Cammie stepped forward and pressed a tiny doorbell—Anna realized that if you didn't know it was there, you'd never find it. Moments later, a man in his early twenties with a hipster goatee and a platinum blond buzz cut, clad in black Armani, slid open one of the doors.

"Yes?"

"Cammie."

"Of course." He ushered them in.

Once inside, Anna could see that the room was approximately three times the size of the family room in her father's Beverly Hills home. But where Jonathan Percy's taste ran to the classic, this room was done entirely in futuristic chic. In one corner was a replica of a female Japanese anime character with spiky black hair and outsize breasts that stood twenty feet high. On the far wall was a two-story fireplace; above it was a box of inlaid glass bubbles of turquoise and taupe. Recessed into the bubbles was a flat-screen TV. Bubble chairs made of Plexiglas hung randomly throughout the room, suspended from the ceiling by clear chains. There were postmodern paintings of soap bubbles on the walls. In each corner was a bubble-shaped white leather love seat lit by an Arco stainless-steel-and-marble lamp. Anna could see a full bar off to one side.

What was *really* special about the room, though, was the center: It was devoted to gaming, with all the trappings of a mini casino. There were a blackjack table, a craps table, a roulette wheel, and a row of video poker slot machines.

"Welcome to the House," announced the goateed gentleman who'd let them inside. "Can I get anyone anything?"

"Your name would be nice," suggested Cyn.

"Craig."

"Craig," Cyn repeated. "Where are we?"

"Do you mean in the existential scheme of things?" he asked coolly.

"I'll explain," Cammie put in. "For now, just have a good time and do all the gambling that you're not allowed to do down in the valley. How about apple martinis all around. Munchies?"

"Is there, like, a menu or something?" Scott asked. He looked around the room, taking it all in.

"Quaint notion." Cammie smiled. "Craig, how about some foie gras, beluga caviar with French bread, gherkins, an assortment of charcuterie, two fresh fruit platters, and two pitchers of apple martinis, stirred not shaken."

"Very good. You'll excuse me." Craig took his leave,

heading through the entryway into the barroom.

Very strange. Anna couldn't imagine what the connection was between it and Cammie. "Seriously, Cammie. Where are we?"

"An old friend's house," Cammie replied. "His father keeps this cute little casino for guests, friends, private parties, bar mitzvahs, you know. It's kind of like a hobby."

"What friend?" Adam queried, an edge to his voice.

Craig had just swung back through the door. "You kids want to play for fun or for money? I can convert the machines with a flick of a switch. And we've got the loosest slots in town."

"Nah," Adam answered quickly. "We'll play for fun."

"Fair enough," Craig agreed. "I'll be back shortly with the refreshments. Sound system is by the side of the fireplace, and then we can open whichever gaming table you like. Cammie can show you the gym and the virtual reality room. Please feel free to explore. Really."

"Cammie can show you?" Adam repeated. "How does Cammie know?"

"Enough with the intrigue shit," Sam demanded. "Whose place is this?"

"My place." A voice came from behind them. "Brock Striker."

Anna turned—a ruggedly handsome guy with broad shoulders, spiky hair, and blond stubble on his dimpled chin stood with his arms crossed. He wore hip, baggy jeans and a long-sleeved black T-shirt.

Sam was staring at him in disbelief. *"Brock?"*

He smiled. "Sam Sharpe. You remember me?"

"How many Brocks are there?" Her face broke into a huge grin. "I can't believe it. You used to be such a little shit! I wondered what happened to you."

As the others watched, Sam threw her arms around the guy, who hugged her back, warmly. "God, remember that time in, like, fifth grade when your parents took us out on their yacht?"

"And we played spin-the-bottle with Chassagne-Montrachet '77 from your father's wine cellar," Cammie recalled, laughing. "He found us and said, 'You *drink* this, you *play* with each other.' Then he made us all drink some."

" 'Take in the bouquet,' " Brock intoned somberly, evidently imitating his father. "Didn't Dee Young get sick?" He looked around the casino room. "Where is she, anyway?"

"Seeking enlightenment in the mysteries of the Zohar, up in her suite at the Palms," Sam scoffed. "She didn't want to come."

"When did Dee convert to Judaism?" Brock sounded incredulous.

"Oh, there are many souls living in Dee's teeny-tiny body," Sam joked. "So you never know."

Brock motioned to the far side of the room, where there were white couches and an entertainment center. "Why don't we go over there and wait for the food? It'll be a lot more comfortable."

"Um, at the risk of being rude, how do you know

this guy?" Cyn asked Cammie and Sam as they made their way across the mini casino.

"From the Brentwood Country Club," Cammie explained.

"His family moved away maybe five years ago," Sam chimed in. "He really was a little shit. Smallest kid in our class."

"I've grown." Brock grinned. He settled into one of the plush couches. "It was six years ago, but who's counting? When Camilla called and told me you were all coming to Vegas, we reconnected."

Camilla? Anna thought as she found a seat on a love seat. Parker plopped down next to her. He calls her Camilla?

Cammie introduced everyone to Brock, saving Adam for last. Brock gave Adam a strong handshake. "So, you're her guy. I heard a lot about you."

Adam's face looked tight. "I didn't even know you existed."

"No reason you would," Cammie said easily.

"So, what's your poison?" Brock asked the group. "Blackjack? Craps? Craig'll be back in a minute. If you don't know how to play, he'll help you."

"Blackjack," Adam declared loudly.

"My man!" Scott laughed, sharing the latest variation of a fist-shoulder bump.

"Let's play for money," Cyn decreed. "Otherwise what's the point?"

"Let's play for services rendered," Adam suggested.

"Ooh, you naughty boy," Cammie said, patting Adam's butt.

Anna smiled. It was nice to see that Adam could hold his own with Cammie. "Excellent," Brock told him with a chuckle. "You'll have the best dealer in the world. Me. And let's make things interesting. A new 3Com Palm IX for the winner?"

Parker spoke up. "Brock? There isn't anything past a Palm VIII right now."

"O ye of little faith." Brock smiled. "Adam, I suggest you play hard this evening. I have a feeling. Tonight, you're going to get lucky."

Anna motioned to Brock with her right hand. "Hit me."

"You sure?" he asked. "You've got seventeen."

She took a sip of her Grey Goose apple martini— really good. Anna was still nursing her first while everyone else had moved on to seconds, or even thirds. Anna contemplated the big stack of chips in front of her, knowing she shouldn't take another card. It was statistically foolhardy; there were so many chances to go over twenty-one and lose.

"Don't do it," Sam cautioned from her stool to Anna's right. "It's a sucker play."

"Let the girl do what she wants," Cyn opined. "If she wants to throw her chips away, she should have that privilege."

"How supportive," Anna quipped. "I know what I'm doing. I think."

It was almost an hour later, and the blackjack game had been going hot and heavy. Anna knew the game but had never really played it with any kind of stakes—not even with chips for fun, like she was doing right now. And she had to admit, it was fun to watch her stack of chips grow and grow, while Cammie's and Cyn's were shrinking and shrinking. Sam, meanwhile, appeared to be just about breaking even.

The guys had disappeared. Probably to check out the virtual reality gaming room on the top floor.

"Okay, this is my last hand," Anna declared. "So hit me, Brock."

Brock pushed a card in her direction. Anna flipped it over. Four of diamonds. She punched the air with her fist. "Twenty-one."

Sam flipped her cards. Eighteen. Cammie hers. Seventeen. Cyn took one more card on a hand of twelve. Jack of hearts. Busted. Finally, Brock flipped his cards over. Twenty.

"Nice job, Anna," their host complimented her. "You should think about doing this for a living."

"And skip the whole Yale-education thing. Highly overrated." Cyn pushed back from the table. "Tell you what. Let's get the guys and watch the DVD from the hypnosis thingie."

"Bad idea," Sam responded quickly. "I was there. It wasn't that great. Let's play some more."

Anna ran a finger over the top chip on her pile. "I'm kind of curious, actually."

Cyn pulled the DVD case from her oversized Dior

by John Galliano white goatskin satchel—Anna recalled
how Cyn had filched it from her mother when they
were in junior high and had been invited to their classmate Babette Biscomb's grandparents' oceanfront
manse on Hilton Head Island for the weekend. Cyn
had stopped being friends with Babette years ago, after
Babette had caught Cyn making out with her boyfriend
at some drunken party in SoHo. Cyn had lost the
friend but kept the bag.

"DVD?" Brock asked with a sly grin. "That can be
arranged."

"What can be arranged?" Adam asked.

Cammie smiled as the three guys returned to the
casino room. "Perfect timing. We're going to watch the
hypnosis show. Should be cool."

Brock brought them back to the area with the
couches and pillows and opened a cabinet recessed in
the wall by the fireplace. Inside were the controls for
the TV and DVD player. As the group gathered
around the fireplace to sit on a lush white Berber rug,
Anna saw that Sam was a bit pale.

"Are you okay?"

"Shit," Sam muttered.

"Okay, let's roll 'em." Brock pointed the remote at
the DVD player and pressed the play button.

Anna leaned closer to Sam. "What?"

"You're about to find out."

The replay began playing on the flat-screen plasma
television on the wall above the fireplace. There was loud

music, a card listing the date and time of the show, and
then the actual show. Anna was amused to see herself
climbing onto the stage with all the others except Sam.

"You look hot on camera, girl," Scott told Cyn,
wrapping an arm around her shoulders. She leaned into
him as Drake put everyone into a trance.

"This is like watching a train wreck," Sam declared
in a low voice.

Sam's trepidation was really starting to bother Anna.
"*What*?"

"The kind where you don't want to look but there's
this sick fascination."

"What are you talking about?" Anna wanted to
know what was on that tape.

"Just watch," Sam hissed. "You'll see."

On the video, people starting "fluffing" the nearest
member of the opposite sex, thinking the person was a
pillow. Everyone cracked up. Anna laughed, too; it
really was funny. Weird, too, to think that she didn't
remember any of it. But this harmless stuff couldn't
be what Sam was so upset about. So what had happened? Anna blushed when she saw herself rubbing
against some very cute guy; everyone else in the room
hooted and applauded. Scott cut his eyes at her as if he
was reconsidering his opinion of her all over again.
How could she not remember? That had to be what
Sam had been warning about—her publicly seducing
a stranger. Well, Anna could handle it. It wasn't really
so terrible.

"No problem, Sam," Anna told her. "It's odd, but it was just a silly show."

"Uh, this might be the point where you want to leave," Sam suggested.

Anna's stomach began to clench, because Sam could only mean there was worse ahead. She watched intently as Drake the hypnotist had Adam step forward. She sneaked a quick look at the couple snuggled together on the floor and then one at Sam. The couple looked fine. But Sam was blanching.

The next thirty seconds of the video made it clear why.

"Cammie, you're my girlfriend, but sometimes I'm really attracted to other girls."

"Adam, I'm really into you, but you're too nice. Guys who are nice bore me."

Oh. My. God.

Anna saw Cammie jerk out of Adam's arms and twist around so she could see him, eyes wide with shock and hurt.

"Cammie, I don't even remember . . ." Adam began to apologize.

"Fuck you!" She stomped over to the glass doors leading outside, pulled one open, and slammed out into the night.

"Cammie, wait!" Adam jumped up and went after her.

Next Parker was on the recording, confessing his true feelings for Kendall. Anna was surprised. Kendall hadn't struck her as much except drunk. Not that she was judging. Strong feelings could develop quickly; look at her and Ben Birnbaum. Sometimes the right person entered your life not with a whimper but with a bang.

A moment later, she saw herself beckoned forward by Drake.

"Turn the damn thing off," Sam declared as he grabbed for the remote. Brock tossed it to her. Meanwhile, Anna's heart thudded in her chest. What had she said or done that had Sam so upset?

"Leave it," she insisted as she watched herself step forward on the screen. "I have to know what happened."

She watched herself summon Scott. "Scott, I've wanted to have sex with you ever since the first moment I saw you."

Brock snapped off the TV, and Anna wanted to die. In fact, she wanted the Berber rug to part, then the gray slate beneath it, and then the foundation of the house. That way, she could just plummet into the middle of the earth and never have to face Cyn.

She immediately forced herself to look at her friend. "Cyn, I—"

"Don't, Anna," Cyn cut her off. "Just fucking spare me, okay?"

Cyn stood up, too. But instead of following Cammie outside, she went into the corridor that led to the virtual reality games room. Anna felt like she'd stepped into a virtual reality of her own. A *horrible* one, where the truth had not set her or her friends free but where it had inflicted awful pain. The worst part of it was, she wasn't an observer. She was a full participant and in a big way, she was responsible.

Secret Knock

Brock suggested that maybe some food would be a good idea. But no one got up to follow him to the buffet table. Having heard Parker's "confession" about her—how truly into her he was—Kendall called a taxi and went someplace with Parker where there was a bed and room service. Scott asked where the bathroom was. Adam and Cammie had not yet returned from outside. Only Anna and Sam were left.

Anna put another birch log on the fire and then sat down again on the carpet. Her heart was *pounding*. In fact, she couldn't remember a more mortifying episode from her life. But having been raised on the metaphoric *This Is How We Do Things* Big Book (East Coast WASP edition), she knew that sangfroid was everything. What was that quote from Kipling? If you could meet the twin imposters of triumph and disaster with the same face, you would always keep your head while others were losing theirs?

Right. Far more easily said than done.

"You know, Sam, I could have happily lived out my life without ever having seen that tape." She swallowed hard.

"I tried to warn you."

Sparks flew up from the log as it ignited. Anna felt like she wanted to go up the chimney with them. "So, what to do now?"

"Go back to that town in Mexico and do about fifty shots of that souped-up mescal?" Sam joked. "That kinda took us out of reality for a while."

"I'm serious."

"Well, I *know* you're not asking me. When it comes to relationships, I'm not exactly the oracle."

"How could I have done that?" Anna rubbed her temples hard, as if the motion could wipe away the last fifteen minutes of her life. "God, I'm a terrible person!"

"Yeah, you suck," Sam cheered sarcastically

"I'm serious, Sam. I have no idea what I'm supposed to do. Do I find Cyn and apologize, or do I go talk to Scott or . . . God, how could I have *done* that?"

Sam twirled a lock of her hair. "The truth is supposed to set you free. Right?"

"Oh, very helpful," Anna groaned.

"Look, everyone lies, Anna. Especially in Hollywood. It's like, you tell the truth if it suits you and you don't if it suits you better. Kiss-kiss, hug-hug, honey, baby, sweetheart, stab 'em in the back if you don't need 'em anymore." Sam took off one black pump and rubbed her instep. "Dee and Cammie have been my best friends since, like, forever. I don't tell them jack. They don't even know that Adam and I made out at the New Year's Eve party."

Anna's perfectly arched brows rose. "You did?"

"That's not the point," Sam folded her arms.

"There *is* no point!" Anna groaned. "Cyn is going to hate me."

"There *is* a point. It's a friendship, Anna, not a confessional." Sam stood, got the fireplace poker, and pushed a couple of logs around. "Besides, Cyn is supposed to be a wild woman, right? She'll understand."

"Hey. Anna?"

Anna turned—Scott stood behind her, looking perfectly comfortable, as if this whole thing wasn't bothering him at all. The most mortifying moment of her life, and his voice was as even as if he were reading the telephone directory. Her heart started to pound again. Dammit. What to say, what to say?

She settled for hi, but wouldn't make eye contact with him, much as her good breeding told her how impolite that was.

"I think maybe we oughta talk," he suggested.

"Sure."

"Pick your poison," he said easily. "Here? Outside? Video poker?"

"Video poker works for me," Anna decided, rising from the couch. Stiff upper lip—she was not about to give away how totally humiliated she felt.

"I'll just sit here and contemplate how I can use this material in a future award-winning film," Sam cracked, waggling her index finger at Anna.

Great. Terrific. Now she was fodder for the future of

American cinema. She had a horrible flash of the Academy Awards sometime around 2020, with Sam accepting the award for Best Original Screenplay. *Hypnosis* was the title of the picture. And Sam was giving her acceptance speech, saying how the movie had been inspired by something that had happened to her when she was in high school, when her friends had all come to Las Vegas and—

Stop it, Anna commanded her own mind. *Just stop it.* She tried to remain cool as she followed Scott to the video poker area.

He slid onto a leather stool and patted the one next to him. Anna idly scanned the poker machine in front of her, just for something to do. At the Palms, they took coins or bills to begin operating them. Here at Brock's house, all it took was the press of a button. Scott began playing on his machine, so Anna did the same. The machine pretty much told her which cards to hold, so the exercise wasn't exactly absorbing. She pretended it was, though, because she was dreading whatever it was Scott was about to say to her. Cyn was somewhere in this strange mansion alone, and Anna was sitting here with Cyn's boyfriend—the boyfriend whose bones she'd wanted to jump since forever. Now they both knew it. Everyone who had been at that damn hypnosis show knew it.

"Royal flush!" Scott crowed as his machine came up all hearts: ten, jack, queen, king, ace. "Sweet. How come it never happens when I'm playing for money?"

Anna didn't give a rat's ass about his royal flush. She hadn't joined Scott to make inane conversation about gambling. If he wasn't going to get to the point, she was. She gulped hard and forced herself to swivel her stool in his direction. "About what happened . . ."

"Uh-huh?"

Uh-huh? Evidently he wasn't going to make this any easier.

"Look, Scott, I can't deny I said what I said. But I would never . . . I'm not . . . " She was at a loss for words.

"I have to admit, hearing you say what you said—it was hot," Scott confided. An easy grin spread across his face.

Anna had no idea how to respond. Hot was not what she'd been going for. She gulped. The truth was, she had no idea what she'd been going for. She'd been hypnotized. Out of control. A condition to which she was thoroughly unaccustomed.

"Truth is . . ." Scott continued, and his grin grew even wider. He stretched his arms overhead so thoroughly that Anna could see the muscles ripple in his forearms. "There's something I think you need to know."

Here it comes, Anna thought. He's going to tell me that he and Cyn are having problems. That he's attracted to me, too, and—

"Truth is, I'm just not all that attracted to you."

Anna felt the color rush to her face. "You—what?"

Scott hit the video poker game again and two pairs came up—aces and jacks. "I admit, I flirted with you a little at the pool. No big thing, right?"

"Uh . . ." Coherent words were simply not coming out of Anna's mouth.

"I hope you know it didn't mean anything," Scott continued, hitting the button to get a new card. It came up an ace. "Full house. There's no justice, huh?" He turned back to Anna, gesturing toward the video machine. "That was just a game, like this is a game, you know what I'm saying? But you knew that, right?"

"Right," Anna nodded, lying through her teeth. She hadn't known it; she'd felt pretty confident it had been about more than a little flirting, and when her friend Cyn had shown up, she hoped that her blush hadn't been too obvious.

"I'm never opposed to harmless flirting," Scott added with a rueful shrug. "As long as both people know what's going on. And I'm a writer. Or at least I want to be. Writers need to have experiences. So sometimes I'll do things not because I want to but because I need the experience or want the experience. You know what I mean? I hope you didn't take it the wrong way, now that I heard what you said."

"Of course," Anna replied smoothly, though she didn't feel smooth at all. "I can . . . understand that. It didn't mean anything to me, either."

She thought back on those moments by the side of the pool. Had that been harmless flirting? If so, she was pretty sure Scott had been taking it to a level beyond harmless. Now here he was, backpedaling furiously, making it look like she was the one who'd misunderstood. A maneuver worthy of a Hollywood mogul. What was it that Sam had said about lying being par for the course? And what was all this about writers needing experiences? Had Tolstoy and Emily Dickinson used the same reasoning that Scott was? Anna had recently read biographies of both writers. If they had, it was news to her.

"Actually, I'm not sure you're telling me the truth," Scott opined. "I mean, you might not admit it right now, but you were hoping at the pool that I'd give you my room key. Right?"

"Wrong," Anna responded pointedly, crossing her legs as she spoke. "Besides, that was then. Not now."

He smiled and glanced at his watch. "Then was about eleven hours ago. Anyway, just so I'm clear: I don't feel that way about you. Never did."

"Yes," Anna managed. "I got your point."

"Okay, cool." Scott nodded. "I mean, I admit I was kind of curious about you. Or I've gotten curious about you. You seem so much more laid back here than you seemed back in New York."

Oh, really? Anna sat up a little straighter, like the ballet dancer she'd been before she'd given her life up to play inane West Coast mind games. She slumped a little. Who was she kidding? Before the inane West Coast mind games, it had been inane East Coast mind games. Whatever kind of mind games they were, she wasn't interested in playing them with this guy. She might be more laid back than she'd been when she left New York, but she thought she was also at least a bit smarter.

"Scott, face facts. You didn't know me then. You don't know me now."

He nodded affably. "Point well taken. Of course, you didn't really know me, either. If you had, you'd have known that you're not really my type. Or maybe you didn't pay that much attention."

Anna began to feel angry, and she liked that feeling much better than the embarrassment and humiliation that had previously flooded her. "Shouldn't you also point out that you supposedly have a girlfriend? A girlfriend who's my best friend?"

"Well, yeah, that too," Scott agreed. "But even if I wasn't with Cyn, I don't think we'd be hooking up."

Anna stood. "You know what? You just taught me something."

Scott stood too. "Yeah? What's that?"

"It's possible to be attracted to a guy who doesn't care about anyone else's feelings but his own. And who you thought was a lot cooler than he is."

Scott put a hand to his heart. "A little harmless flirting and she says I don't care about her feelings. I bet you're used to guys being all over you, right? If you're interested, they're interested?"

Right.

"Wrong," she lied. "That isn't the issue. Not that it matters anymore. Are we done?"

Without waiting for an answer, Anna walked away. Her hands felt clammy and her breathing was shallow. Most of all, she was angry at herself—angry for letting herself be taken in by her own illusion of a guy instead of by the guy himself. But right now, that didn't matter.

She knew exactly what she had to do next. She was going to do it, too, no matter how much it hurt.

Cammie found a redwood swing at the edge of the expansive backyard that overlooked the shimmering city below. The night was warm—she sat there, knees to her chin, arms wrapped around her legs, gazing first down at Las Vegas, with its many boulevards of broken dreams, and then up at the impossibly starry night. Cammie felt suspended between two places and two versions of herself—the self that Adam loved, and the bitch who kept spewing to the surface, again and again. It was the bitch's fault that Adam was still attracted to "other girls." It had to be. It just hurt so much.

She knew she was a total hypocrite, because she was attracted to other guys, too. Half the time she pulled Adam closer and half the time she pushed him away. God, she was just so fucked up. Every once in a while, she wondered where that had come from. It wasn't from her mother. Everyone she'd ever talked to about her mom had told her that she was one of the truly good spirits on the planet. It wasn't from her father, either. He was different from her. Certainly a philanderer but always clear about where he stood. If Clark Sheppard was with you—whether you were his client or his lover—he was with you. If he wasn't, watch out. He didn't have that ambivalent thing that Cammie knew was as much a part of her makeup as MAC lip gloss. One day maybe she'd drop fifteen or twenty thou in therapy and see if she could get to the roots. On the other hand, Sam had Dr. Fred on retainer, and look what good *that* had done her.

Someone was approaching. Adam. She felt his weight settle next to her on the swing. He reached over and wiped the tear that was tracking down her cheek. Wordlessly, she buried her face in his shoulder. His arms went around her, and she sobbed her heart out.

"I hate crying." Cammie edged away from him and wiped her face with the palm of her hand. "I'm a mess."

He handed her some Kleenex—evidently he'd come prepared. "You're fine."

No, she wasn't. She wiped her eyes and blew her nose. "When you said that you're still attracted to other girls—"

"I didn't mean I'd ever act on it, Cammie."

"Oh, well. Doesn't *that* just make it all better," she sniffled. "Do you have any idea how many guys want me?"

"Yeah, I do. Can you honestly tell me that you're never attracted to any of them?"

Of course she was. Plus, Cammie knew that he'd heard her say that nice guys bored her. She did not intend to let Adam get the upper hand here, and she knew how difficult this would be, since she was used to appearing as if she had it all together. Perfect on the outside made her strong. Perfect on the outside struck fear in the hearts of others. But tonight she was water-logged, red-nosed, makeup-streaked. Her facade had slipped badly. No one was afraid of her.

"We're talking about *you*," Cammie insisted. "Or should I say, you and Anna."

Adam looked confused. "What are you talking about?"

"Other girls. You meant Anna Percy."

"No, I didn't."

Cammie pushed her hair off her face. "Let's get Drake the Snake out here to hypnotize you again, then we'll see what you say."

Adam rested his hands on the thighs of his jeans. He was quiet for a long time. "Okay," he murmured. "Let's say you're right—"

"I *knew* it."

"But I'm attracted to lots of girls, Cammie. Just like you're attracted to lots of guys. That doesn't mean we don't love each other. Does it?"

Cammie didn't answer. She wanted him to suffer a little.

"So tell me the truth for a change. Why did you really come to see this guy Brock? And why did you keep it some big-ass secret?"

She folded her arms defiantly.

"Here's what I think," Adam began; she heard a certainty in his voice that she'd rarely heard before. A fearlessness. "I think that every time you and I get really close, it flips you out. So you pull some kind of stunt to push us apart. That's why you said that nice guys bore you. Because they—I—scare the shit out of you. You can't be in control and in love at the same time."

The truth of this hit Cammie somewhere at her very center. It was a truth almost as scary as loving Adam.

"What, you're just supposed to let the other person control you?"

"Not at all," Adam insisted. "But love—it makes you vulnerable, Cam. That's just the way it is."

Cammie looked down at the shimmering city for a long time before she spoke.

"Brock knew my mother. His parents were on the yacht the night my mom drowned."

"Wow."

She felt Adam's strong hand begin to rub her back, very gently. It felt good.

"I always wanted to ask him if he knew anything about what really happened that night."

"Did he?"

Cammie nodded. "He did."

Adam raised his eyebrows. "You want to talk about it?"

"It isn't pretty," she warned.

"I think I can handle it."

"He said that at the time my mom died, his father was screwing her. Not at the exact time, but that they were having an affair," Cammie said bluntly.

"You think it's true?"

"Nope, I think it's horseshit. I remember my mother. She wouldn't screw around. Maybe my father would do that—hell, definitely my father would do that." Cammie frowned. "He doesn't know anything. But why would he? We were just kids."

Cammie felt Adam's arm tight around her shoulder. "This must be very frustrating for you," he murmured.

"No shit."

"Can I be honest with you?"

Cammie pursed her lips. "Seems like this is the night for it. Fire away."

"I was sure you were sleeping with him," Adam declared bluntly. "Brock."

A few crickets chirped while Cammie considered her answer. She didn't want to lie. "I thought about it. That's true. But we didn't. That's also the truth."

She saw Adam sag with relief. "I can tell you're being honest."

"Not completely," Cammie confessed. "I thought about it a lot. What would you have done if I had?"

"How the fuck should I know?" Adam responded with a grin.

A moment later, the two of them were exploding in laughter so loud it echoed off the canyons.

"I guess that's honest," Cammie managed to choke out.

Adam caught his breath. "I wish you'd told me before about your mom."

"I did."

"But I didn't know it meant so much—I mean, that, that it bothered you that much. I mean, it would bother anyone, but—"

Cammie put one finger on Adam's lips, then kissed him sweetly. "You don't have to say it. I know what you mean."

"I don't know if you do," Adam took her hands in his. "I want to help you."

"With what?"

"With finding out what happened. To your mom. So you'll know. There's a lot that I can do. That we can do. Especially if we work together."

Cammie shook her head. "It was almost ten years ago. What are we going to find out?"

Adam got to his feet. "I don't know." He started to pace. "But I'll tell you this—I am very bad at taking no for an answer. Very bad. So, what do you say?"

Good question.

"I don't know," she admitted. She loved the idea of Adam being her partner. But it was scary was hell. Both because of what she might learn and because it might bring them even closer. "Love sucks, Adam."

"Yeah?"

Cammie nodded. "I hate feeling all . . . like the other person can just decimate you. But . . . I do love you,"

"I love you too, Cam." He sat, put an arm around her again, and kissed her hair. "But I need to know. . . ."

Cammie guessed where he was heading. "Do I think you're so nice you're boring?"

"Yeah."

Cammie honestly didn't know. Had she lied so much that she couldn't even tell the truth from a lie anymore? Could she possibly be that fucked up? The only thing she felt certain about was that she really did love him, in a way she'd never loved anyone before.

"If I thought you were boring, would I do this?" She leaned over and kissed him tenderly.

He rested his forehead against hers. "We'll just play it as it lays, Cam. And really. What I said before, I mean. About finding out what happened."

"I'll think about that. I really will."

They rocked, neither speaking, the only sound the creaking of the swing's chains. There were a lot of things about which she didn't know the whole truth. Yet there were others about which she did. She still had Adam.

Adam was different from any guy she'd ever met, even Ben Birnbaum. He didn't just want her. He was willing to help her.

Anna had to look through the whole mansion before she found Cyn. Living room, family room, game room. A room devoted to Brock's father's hobby of hunting, complete with the stuffed heads of various American and African game animals, and a gun collection that made Anna gasp. Several bedrooms, each more ornate than the next—the master one had mirrored walls and a mirrored ceiling, along with a round bed. Two kitchens, a library, and a home gym that would have been the pride of most five-star hotels. It was in that gym—actually, the locker room attached to the gym—that Anna found her friend Cyn. That was only because of the pile of clothes outside the sauna door. When she peered through the small glass window, she saw Cyn perched on one of the wooden pallets inside, wrapped in a black-and-white-striped bath sheet.

Anna shivered involuntarily. The last time she'd been in a sauna, it had been at a spa in Palm Springs, on a weekend getaway with Sam. Cammie had been in that sauna, and Ben, too. Some very hurtful things had been said.

Anna hoped that she wasn't about to repeat the experience as she opened the wooden door. She was hit by a wave of heat. "Can I talk to you?"

If Cyn was surprised to see her, she didn't betray it. Instead, she motioned Anna inside. "Sure. You might want to get naked first, though."

Anna disrobed in a small changing area and found a fuzzy towel of her own. She wrapped it around herself, tucking the end in, then stepped into the sauna. It had to be new—it still smelled like redwood. The hot rocks glowed neon red.

"God, this is heaven," Cyn whispered. She was spread out on the upper deck. "I'm going to stay in here until I melt away like the Wicked Witch of the West."

"Except *I'm* the wicked witch," Anna challenged. She backed up against the far wall and drew her knees to her chest. "I want to apologize."

"I can't fucking believe you, Anna."

She winced. "I'm so sorry, Cyn—"

"*Please*," Cyn snorted. She twisted her head from side to side, like she was trying to loosen a giant knot.

Anna felt the sudden ache of unbidden tears in the back of her throat. "You're my best friend in the world. I would never go after your guy."

Cyn rolled over and peered down at Anna. "You think that's why I'm pissed?"

"Isn't it?"

"No, you idiot!" Cyn bolted upright. "I'm pissed because you're *my* best friend in the world, and you never told me how you felt about Scott."

"Wait. You're not mad that I wanted to—"

"Screw him senseless from the first moment you saw him?" Cyn filled in. "Why the hell would that make me mad? The boy is hot. I saw one of my mother's bitchy friends try to slip him her phone number at the school play last January. And we did *Oedipus Rex*."

"So what—"

"Here's what." Cyn hopped down and sat next to Anna. "All those times that I went on and on about me and Scott, our first kiss and our first this and our first that, and all that time you pretended to be happy for me. But the inside, you were going nuts. Am I right?"

"Yes," Anna admitted, her voice low.

"So if I'm your best friend, blah, blah, blah—why couldn't you trust me enough to tell me?"

Why, indeed? Anna reached for the wooden pitcher of water and poured a little on the rocks. Steam rose to the ceiling; she inhaled deeply, her muscles relaxing. It was hard to stay tense in a redwood sauna. "What was I supposed to say, Cyn? I want *your* guy?"

"Sure. Why the hell not?"

"Because . . . because . . . I just couldn't! You're too important to me."

"Not important enough for you to tell me the truth."

Anna sat down next to Cyn again. It was hard to accept that all these months, since Cyn and Scott had hooked up in the autumn, she'd done the wrong thing by keeping her mouth shut. She'd been raised to appreciate the value of discretion; that discretion had proved useful so many times when she'd seen other girls blabbing and oversharing, almost always to their detriment. She tried to put herself in Cyn's shoes. If Cyn had been hot for, say, Ben, from the very first moment she saw him, would Anna have wanted to know?

"I don't know how I should have handled it," Anna finally admitted. "I mean, I know you're in love with him—"

"Nah," Cyn declared, shaking her head.

Anna couldn't believe it. "But . . . you're not?"

"I thought I was for a while there. Probably I was. Seduced the man of letters and all that. Plus he's smart and very cool. Not to mention incredibly fine. It was really intense there for a while, especially right when you left for California. But I have to say, it hasn't lasted. I think Scott and I are played out. In fact, I know we are. I need to tell him that. Flat out tell him, hold the mayo and the onions."

Anna was cautious. "Maybe you're just in a slump and you'll work it out."

"No, seriously. If you want him, go for it."

"This reeks of irony, Cyn."

"Meaning?"

"Well . . . Scott told me he's not attracted to me."

It took Cyn a beat before she burst out laughing. Then Anna started laughing, too—in great peals, the way they used to laugh when they'd roll in the autumn leaves near Gracie Mansion in Manhattan.

"You know what?" Anna asked, when she could finally catch her breath. "I don't care! I mean, my ego is a little bruised, I suppose. I remember how I used to see him in front of school, reading *The Onion*. It was like he was a young Jack Kerouac. I used to dream about him. But lusting after him and wanting all of him— they're two different things."

"Totally," Cyn agreed. She leaned back against a slanted wooden headrest, then sighed contentedly. "So I guess we're just wild women on the prowl again, huh?"

Anna leaned her head back, too. "Not necessarily."

"You're joining a nunnery? Taking a vow of chastity? What?"

"Ben Birnbaum," Anna admitted. She felt a little embarrassed to say so but loved how honest she was being with her friend. It felt liberating.

"You're back with Princeton Boy, and you didn't tell me that, either?"

"We're not together at all. I'm here, he went back to New Jersey in January, we've hardly talked. But I can't stop thinking about him."

"So hop a plane to Princeton, invite him out to dinner, and then jump him. That's what I'd do."

"Yes, but I think it's a well-established fact that I am not you. You've always been audacious. And I've always been . . . not."

"That Jane Cabot Percy part of you needs to be squished like a nest of cockroaches in the butler's pantry."

"My mother would die hearing that analogy."

"That's my point. Anna, you're not Jane."

"I'm getting better, really." Anna sighed. "I called Ben and invited him to Vegas."

"And?"

"I got his voice mail and left a message. He hasn't even returned my call."

"Okay, so it isn't meant to be." Cyn got up and stretched, then looked directly at Anna "The world is full of hotties. Speaking of hot, I've about had enough in here. Ready to go?"

"Sure." Anna stood, still thinking about Ben. He was definitely a hottie. But she also felt some special connection between the two of them. It wasn't that she was going to do what she used to do in elementary school when it came to boys—write her name in her spelling notebook as Mrs. Anna Cabot Percy Birnbaum. Sometimes, though, she thought she might come close. "He's more than a hot guy. Ben, I mean."

"As it turns out, Scott isn't," Cyn said. "I'm not looking for more than hot and temporary anymore: not for a while, anyway. On to the next."

"On to the next," Anna agreed, even though her heart was saying, "Back to Ben." But Cyn was right; it probably just wasn't meant to be.

"Pinkie swear?" Cyn asked, holding up her right pinkie.

"Like when we had the friendship rings from Tiffany that our mothers got us?" Anna grinned. "Definitely. And we'll swear to honesty."

"To honesty. Look how upset you got tonight. Over all the wrong things."

They touched pinkies and laughed, then headed for the showers.

As the hot water needled down on her, Anna thought how glad she was that the night hadn't hurt their friendship in any significant way, and how right Cyn was about honesty. Without honesty, you couldn't have love and you couldn't have friendship. Friendship meant everything to her—maybe even more than love. Ben might have been different, but it seemed like guys came and guys went, but true friends—especially true girlfriends—endured. If that was the lesson she was supposed to learn from this amazing adventure in Las Vegas, she was very glad she'd come.

His Famous Megawatt Smile

S am swung her taupe embossed leather Rena Lange open-toe pumps from her index and middle fingers as she and her friends stepped through the glass doors into the Palms. It was nearly dawn. Once again, her feet were killing her. Though the hour was late, the casino was still packed; the bells and whistles and music and alcohol-fueled excitement felt overwhelming after such a long night. Though she'd been here many times, it always struck her as extraordinary that this was a place where time lost all meaning—where morning and after-noon and night all melded into one thing called Sin City.

Scott and Cyn claimed exhaustion and went right up to their suite. Cammie and Adam did, too. Sam was impressed that the two couples had been able to recover from the evening's revelations. "Well, that was quite an evening," she commented to Anna as they passed the reception area—per usual, the video monitors were flashing the Palms Girls.

"It was . . . interesting," Anna replied carefully.

"Vegas isn't interesting," Sam quipped. "To quote Dee, it's sound and *furry*, signifying nothing."

"We should check on her before we go to sleep," Anna decided as Sam stopped at the cash machine to get some more money.

She stuffed the money into her back pocket carelessly, then caught a glimpse of someone familiar at the bar beside the video poker machines. "Parker's over there."

"Alone," Anna noted. "I wonder what happened to Kendall?"

"Me too." Sam's eyes were still on Parker. He was rubbing his forehead, and his foot was tapping nervously against the bottom of the bar. Something in her gut told her that all was not well. "Hey, I need to go talk to him a sec. You wanna wait here or you want me to meet you upstairs?"

"I'll wait." Anna sagged against the wall and yawned.

"Go play some slot machines," Sam instructed. "Better yet, hang around the craps tables. Some rich asshole who's winning big will give you thousand-dollar chips just for looking good."

Sam sidled up to Parker, who was staring into a tall glass of what looked like gin and tonic. "Hey." She slid onto a bar stool, and a beefy bartender with a bald head and a soul patch asked her what she wanted to drink. She considered a dry Tanqueray martini on the rocks with a twist of lemon but opted for a Campari instead. "And get my friend here a refill." Sam cocked her head toward Parker. "He looks like he needs it."

"Another *ice water*?" the bartender asked, his tone withering.

"I'm good," Parker mumbled.

So. Parker was sitting by himself drinking ice water with a lime in it. That made zero sense to Sam. "Where's your new squeeze?"

He shrugged, staring into his glass.

"Don't you care? I thought you were so into her and everything."

He shrugged again. "I'm not really in the mood to talk, if you don't mind."

Okay. She could just say good-bye and leave him be. But maybe if she probed enough. . . . "You're really into this Kendall chick, huh?"

Parker finally looked at Sam. "What part of 'Go away' don't you understand?"

"The part where you declared your devotion to the new love of your life and ended up sitting here alone at the bar looking like you're ready to slit your wrists."

"She left right after we got here. Her father called, screaming at her. She's on a plane back to Texas even as we speak."

"That sucks," Sam said soothingly. "You can go visit her and—"

"Geez, Sam, I don't even like the chick!" Parker exploded.

Her brain tried to process this information. Parker didn't like Kendall. But when he'd been hypnotized, he'd said how he was into her "inner beauty," or some such bullshit. Either he'd been really into her for a really short period of time, or—

Holy shit.

"*Sonofabitch.* You fucking scammed the hypnotist."

Parker looked at her balefully.

"Goddamn. You were *acting*!"

She was impressed. Not with herself because she'd figured it out, but with Parker, because she'd never thought that he actually had any talent. "Jesus Christ. Parker, you're good!"

"Tell that to *Everwood*'s casting director," he snapped.

"You shined all of us on, even the hypnotist." She waved a finger at him. "I knew your taste in girls couldn't have slipped that much," Sam mused. " 'My father invested in this Hollywood movie. We all love Hollywood.' " Sam laughed, mimicking Parker's date. "You couldn't have pretended you were hypnotized to get into Kendall's pants because, I mean, who would want to? You wanted to prove that you have talent! This is so hilarious!"

"Yeah, Sam. It's a laugh riot." His eyes slid to a bony blonde at the other end of the bar whose diamond necklace looked as if it weighed more than she did. He lifted his ice water and gave her that special smile.

"You're *still* acting." Sam laughed.

The blonde pouted at Parker, then looked to Sam, then looked at Parker again, a question in her eyes. "I'm about to go pick up that chick, so if you wouldn't mind . . ."

"Her? Why would you—"

"She's got money," Parker hissed. "She's in real estate; I overheard her say she took home seven figures last year. You happy now?"

Sam might have been raised by nannies, but those nannies had not raised a stupid girl. The last piece of her mental puzzle fit neatly into place. Kendall was rich. Parker knew the chick down the bar had some money. The only reason that Parker, with his A-list looks, would hit on C-list girls who had money was that he didn't.

He gestured to his glass of ice water. "You pay for your drinks unless you're gambling."

"You're . . ." Sam could hardly bring herself to say it. "Low on cash?"

"I'm broke," Parker replied through clenched teeth. "As in poor, as in pretending to have money like all the rest of you. As in low-rent." He ran a hand through his hair. "I hit on Kendall so that she'd pick up my hotel tab, but she split. If you don't get your ass out of here, I'm gonna lose out on the chick at the other end of the bar, too."

For once in her life, Sam was speechless. She had *no* idea how to deal with this. It wasn't like she was Miss Sensitivity. The truth was, she spent most of her time thinking about herself and her problems, not other people's difficulties. "I can pay your hotel bill," she offered awkwardly.

"I really don't want to have this conversation, if it's all the same to you."

"Well, it's not. I want you to know—"

"I don't care what you want me to know."

"Hey, I didn't steal your family's fortune, bucko."

"What fortune? My mother is a cocktail waitress."

At that moment a weary cocktail waitress with a trayful of drinks passed them, on her way into the casino. Sam studied her. She was thin and pretty, but there were already lines around her mouth and a hard set to her dark, almond-shaped eyes. She probably wasn't more than thirty, but in five years she'd be considered old. No hip hotel would want her serving drinks to the high rollers. Then what?

Sam shook her head despondently. The waitress's life wasn't her problem. She wasn't accustomed to thinking about the crappy lives of the teeming masses, and she wasn't about to start now.

"Happy, Sam?"

"I don't care that you don't have money, Parker. That's not why we're friends."

"Who's acting now?"

"Okay, you're right," she admitted. "All my friends are rich. Well, except you, evidently."

"Bingo." He took a long drink of his ice water and held up a one-moment finger to the skinny blonde, who looked antsy.

"Okay, so I'll . . . leave you to whatever," Sam muttered. "I won't tell anyone." She got off the bar stool.

Parker's facade slipped. He looked about twelve years old. But he quickly covered, a cool veneer closing down any hint of need. Then he leaned over and kissed Sam's cheek. "Thanks."

"You're welcome."

He kissed her again, this time lightly and sweetly, on the lips.

"Uh-uh-uh," Sam demurred. "I have a boyfriend."

"For now."

Parker's grin spread into his famous megawatt smile, and he moved down the bar toward the blonde.

Wow, who'da thunk it? Parker Pinelli had guts. Evidently he also lived off of rich girlfriends. But his guts, at least, Sam had to admire.

She went to the reception area and told them to put all Parker's charges on her credit card. Just in case things didn't work out with the blonde.

"How did it go?" Anna asked as Sam pressed the elevator button that would take them back to the top floor.

"You tell me first. Pick up any princes who showered you with chips?"

"None. So what happened with Parker?"

The shiny chrome elevator doors opened and they stepped out onto their floor.

"He hit on me," Sam said.

Anna looked incredulous. "Out of nowhere?"

"Who knows?" Sam mused breezily. She intended to keep her promise to Parker. Bizarre. She had just done something nice for a guy in whom she was not even interested. "You know, I *am* capable of being a really nice person."

"I already knew that."

"Yeah?" Sam's eyebrows rose and she opened her pocketbook to dig for their key card as they approached the wooden door to their suite. "Well, I didn't."

"Wait." Anna put her hand on Sam's arm. "We were going to check on Dee, remember?"

"Please. I'm so tired I'm about to pass out. I'm sure she's asleep. Why wake her?"

"Let's just knock softly and see what happens."

"I'm tired of being Oprah. Especially at five in the morning."

Still, Sam dutifully trudged after Anna down the hallway to Dee's suite and waited patiently as Anna knocked on the large white door. No answer. Anna knocked louder.

"Dee slept through the Northridge earthquake," Sam reminded her. "She'll never hear you. Let me call her cell."

But before she could, her own cell rang.

"Yeah?" Sam answered.

"Samantha Sharpe?" asked an unfamiliar voice.

"You're speaking to her."

"This is Nurse Maria Hernandez, Clark County Hospital. Your friend Dee Young gave permission for us to telephone you. We've got her here in our psych unit."

Thorazine

"**H**ow could they just bring Dee here against her will?" Cammie ranted as she, Adam, Sam, and Anna followed the signs to the hospital psychiatric unit. Clark County Hospital was a big and antiseptic place, bright fluorescent lights casting a deathly white glow against the white walls of its hallways. The place was alarmingly quiet: the graveyard shift. Cammie shuddered. She hated hospitals.

"We'll find everything out when we talk to the doctor," Adam assured her, giving her shoulder a little squeeze.

"If they don't release her, I'm suing their asses," Cammie thundered.

She sounded a lot like her father at that moment. And she was glad. It was better than freaking out. That had been her initial reaction when Sam had pounded on the door of their suite at dawn, just as she and Adam were drifting off to dreamland. They'd pulled on some clothes, and Cammie hadn't even stopped for a slick of Stila lip gloss, which meant she was damned serious.

Finally, they were in the psych unit, identified by a simple sign on a pair of double swinging doors.

"Over there." Sam pointed to the nurse's station—a low wooden counter with high Plexiglas sections separating the nurses from the general public. A middle-aged woman with her dark hair in a long braid over one shoulder glanced indifferently through the Plexiglas as they approached.

"Can I help you?" Her voice was slightly muffled by the barrier.

"I'm Cammie Sheppard. We're friends of Dee Young. You called my friend."

"Me," Sam chimed in. "Samantha Sharpe. My father is Jackson Sharpe. The actor." To prove her point, she held up a photograph of her father with his arm around her.

"Oh, really?" The woman peered at the photograph.

"How is she?" Anna asked, unconsciously picking at her cuticles.

Nurse Hernandez opened a file. "Here's what she authorized us to tell you: She was hearing a baby's voice in her head."

"Ruby," Sam told the nurse matter-of-factly.

"Right," she confirmed. "That's it. Anyway, we found your friend in the baccarat lounge at the Luxor. Evidently she was harassing the gamblers, telling them to repent and blessing them in Hebrew. In her underwear."

"Shit," Cammie muttered. This was way out there, even for Dee.

"The resident on call admitted her for observation. One of our staff psychiatrists will evaluate her today. That's all I can say. You kids might as well go for now. We'll call you again after the doctor has met with Ms. Young."

Cammie glared at the nurse. "Are you kidding? Dee is like our family. Would you leave your family at the nut house?"

"I assure you this is not—" Nurse Hernandez began.

"Whatever," Cammie interrupted. "Dee has a perfectly good and perfectly empty suite at the Palms. She'd sleep much better there. We'll watch her like a hawk, we promise."

Nurse Hernandez shook her head. "I'm sorry. It's against regulations."

"But she—she can't stay here. Sure, she's a little loony. You're only going to maker her crazier. Dee needs the comforts of home, like twenty-four-hour room service. What do you people serve for breakfast here? Gruel?"

"Cam, calm down," Adam murmured.

"No, I can't calm down!" Cammie insisted. "We have to get Dee out of here."

"Tomorrow. At the earliest," Nurse Hernandez declared. "That's standard procedure here.

Cammie felt like she was going to be sick. This could not be happening to Dee. She couldn't let it happen. She and Sam and Dee were the Three Musketeers in couture. They had power, looks, money.

Sure, they'd drifted apart lately, especially because of that twit Anna Percy—what was she doing here, anyway? She wasn't friends with Dee and would never be. But did anyone ever think that the Three Musketeers never argued? No matter what, they ruled Beverly Hills High School. And the girls who ruled Beverly Hills High ruled the world. *Everyone* knew that.

"Dee asked us to try to reach her parents also, as a courtesy," the nurse explained. "We've left several voice-mail messages."

"They're in *Europe*. I *told* you," Sam reminded her.

"Yes, I heard you, Ms. Sharpe. But until our resident evaluates your friend—"

"There's no reason to wait for the resident. Dee's birthday was last month. She's eighteen. She can sign herself the hell out of here."

"Not until she's evaluated, she can't," the nurse retorted. "Now, if you don't mind, I have to get back to this paperwork."

Cammie was not about to be dismissed so easily. "Excuse me," she said sweetly. "We're not leaving until we see her."

The nurse looked from Cammie to Adam to Anna to Sam. She sighed.

"Two of you, that's all. And only because I'm the biggest Jackson Sharpe fan in the world. If she's a little out of it, it's because we gave her a shot of Thorazine a couple of hours ago. Down that hall, last door on the right, room 13-B. Ten minutes."

"Thank you," Sam told her, then, wasting not a moment, she yanked Cammie down the hall. There was no conversation about which two of them would go; that was obvious.

The door was open, and Dee was sitting upright in bed inside a small, generic hospital room. White-tiled floor, white walls, a minimum of medical equipment—Dee wasn't even hooked up to an IV. Actually, she looked completely normal. Normal makeup, mussy blond hair, her blue eyes round and alert. The only thing out of the ordinary was her blue hospital gown, which eerily matched her eyes. She was watching TV on a set that was somehow suspended from the ceiling near the far wall—an old rerun of *Blind Date* with no sound.

When Cammie and Sam walked in, Dee barely acknowledged them. Her eyes flitted immediately back to the television, as if encountering her friends in the psych ward of a hospital far from home was the most normal thing on earth.

"I'm waiting to hear from her," Dee explained, eyes still on the television. "I have to keep watching. But I'm so sleepy, it's hard."

"From Ruby?" Cammie asked. She and Sam stood uncomfortably by the door.

"Exactly," Dee confirmed, eyes still on the TV, where a guy with a goatee was blowing cigarette smoke out of his ears to impress his date. "Right before they gave me a shot, Ruby told me that she'd communicate with me by television."

Cammie shuddered again but forced herself to stay as conversational as she could. "Dee, the sound isn't on."

"It doesn't matter. We do it telepathically." Her eyes went to half-mast, then she yawned. "I'm tired."

As Dee stretched out and pulled the blanket up to her chin, Cammie and Sam both carried chairs to her bedside. Sam took one hand; Cammie went around the hospital bed to take the other. "Dee? Can you tell us what happened?" Sam asked.

"I was reading the Zohar, and Ruby appeared to me on the page. She told me that the world was coming to an end," Dee confided, her voice low. "She said I have to save all the sinners. I tried, I really did."

"At the Luxor?" Sam queried. "In your *underwear*?"

"It wasn't my decision—that's where she told me to go."

Cammie and Sam shared a look. This was unbelievable, like something out of a movie. So many times, they'd joked to Dee about her needing to get help. Now it wasn't a joke anymore.

"You know, now that I think about it, maybe I'm just another big, fat, ugly sinner. That's why no one wants to be with me. Not Poppy. Not my parents. Not you two, either."

"That's so not true, Dee," Cammie insisted quickly. Except that it really was true. Even when Dee's craziness had been milder, Cammie had gone out of her way to avoid her.

Dee closed her eyes. "Remember how happy the three of us used to be?"

"You'll be happy again," Sam promised. "I swear it. It'll be just the way it used to be. The Three Musketeers, remember?"

"Maybe," Dee allowed. "They gave me this pill to try to get me to tell them where Ruby is. It made my head fuzzy. Did they give you one?"

Cammie saw Sam surreptitiously wipe a tear away; she hoped Dee was too out of it to notice. She reached over the bed's rail and squeezed her friend's hand, wondering all the while whether there was anything she could have done that would have headed off this moment here in Clark County Hospital. "I suck. I'm so sorry."

"It's okay," Dee said softly. "This isn't your fault."

"No, it isn't," Sam insisted, her voice cracking. "You needed help. Big time. And you needed me to tell you that. But I was too involved in my own stupid problems to see it."

"Actually, Sam, she needed me to tell her too."

"Cammie, the fact is, she's living with me. And my family."

"Oh, like you were going to make it all better?" Cammie's voice suddenly went cold. "You've been seeing Dr. Fred for how long and you're still a mess."

"Well, if you ever went to see a shrink, maybe you'd figure out why you keep trying to sabotage the only healthy relationship you've ever had with a guy!" Sam shot back in a low voice, as angrily as she dared. They were way over the ten minutes that the nurse had allotted them; she didn't want them to be kicked out of the room.

Cammie was ready to fire back but managed to focus. "So what's the game plan here? Dee, do you want to go home with us?"

Dee brightened. "Home. That's a good idea." She started to get out of bed, swinging her legs toward Cammie's side. Her blue hospital gown flapped open, exposing her tiny naked butt, which was four shades lighter than the faux tan on her legs. Cammie grimaced at the sight—it made Dee seem so young. Then she blocked her friend's way.

"But I want to go home," Dee said, bewildered. "Can't we just walk home?"

"Dee, we're in Las Vegas, remember? Home is Los Angeles. Two hundred and fifty miles away. "You have to stay here now. But not for long," Sam assured her.

"I can't come with you." Dee swallowed hard. "That's what you guys always say. That's fucked up."

Cammie leaned over to hug her friend, then held her tight. "No. *We* fucked up."

Her eyes met Sam's over Dee's frail, birdlike shoulder, and she waited for Sam to say something. But for once, her oldest friend was rendered speechless.

I Wanna Be Sedated

It was early morning when they had returned to the Palms and decided to sleep for a few hours before facing the rest of the day and figuring out what to do with Dee. Anna had set the alarm on the Bose Wave radio on her suite's mahogany nightstand to the single classical music station she could find. It was the second-movement funeral march from Beethoven's Third Symphony, the Eroica, that awakened her. She knew it well and laid in bed until the movement was over, thinking about the crazy happenings of the night before.

Still in the old Trinity sweats she'd worn to bed, Anna padded over to the giant window and drew open the shade. Gray skies and pounding rain greeted her— she could barely see across the road to the Rio Hotel and Casino. As for the Strip, it was out there someplace in the mist. Without the lights, the flash, and the glitz of the Strip in the distance, this little section of Las Vegas felt ordinary indeed.

"Coffee?"

Anna turned: Cyn stood in the doorway, a steaming cup of coffee in her hand.

"Gladly. How'd you get in?" she queried, as she went to her friend and inhaled the heady aroma. "Hey! There's brandy in this."

Cyn shrugged. "It's Vegas. What happens here, stays here."

"I wish." But Anna took a sip, anyway. It was sweet and hot; the brandy took away any bitterness. Really good. "I'm going to take a quick shower."

"Go for it."

"Where's Sam?"

"Health club," Cyn reported. "For a massage and facial."

Anna smiled as she headed for the shower. "After last night, I can't blame her."

"After last night, I think I may stay in your suite for the rest of the day," Cyn confided. "It's a big upgrade on a regular room."

Anna motioned toward the suite's living room. "Make yourself comfortable; have some more coffee. I'll be out in a bit."

"Okay if I hit the minibar?"

"Be my guest."

Twenty minutes later, Anna had dressed and rejoined her friend. She wore no-name jeans, her ratty cashmere sweater, and had stuck her hair up in a ponytail. No makeup. Cyn was braless under a boy's T-shirt, with a

man's flowered ascot tossed around her neck. A
Chinese brocade miniskirt cascaded over distressed
jeans; black velvet Chanel pumps peeked out from
underneath. She was the only girl Anna knew who
could make that outfit work. In fact, if they were staying for another day, Anna was confident that half of Las
Vegas would be buying up Chinese miniskirts and
ascots to copy the look.

"What now?' Anna went to the window and looked
out. Still pouring rain. If anything, more heavily than
before. Cyn got up from the couch to join her. She was
nursing a drink that looked like Scotch on the rocks.

"Big news. Sam called while you were in the shower.
They're letting your friend out of the hospital. I think
you're taking her home."

"What?" Anna exclaimed. "Since when?"

"Since she signed herself out. They deemed she's not
a threat to herself or others so they couldn't keep her.
She promised she'd go straight to the psych ward at
Cedars-Sinai. You guys are supposed to drop her there.
You're meeting downstairs in an hour. Sam wanted to
finish her massage first."

That was just so Sam.

"Crappy day," Cyn commented, drawing a little circle in the condensation on the window.

"What are you going to do? You and Scott don't
have to leave just because we are."

"Nah, the thrill is gone."

"I'm sorry if I wrecked this trip for you, Cyn."

"No, Miss Manners, you didn't. Come on, how could you know your friend was going to short-circuit? It's not that. It's Scott." She turned away and went to the maroon paisley sofa, where she flopped down and swung her legs up over the back, the same way Anna had seen her do since they were in fifth grade. "I guess I thought coming here would change something between him and me, but it didn't."

"So are you over?" Anna settled down on the couch next to Cyn and threw a comforting arm around her friend.

"We've been over for a while. It's just that it takes a while to get there and say it. Anyway, the whole relationship thing is highly overrated. Seriously. I mean, what's the point?"

"Love?" Anna ventured.

"I love you more than I'm ever gonna love any guy. And like we used to say in sixth grade—"

"Not in a gay way," Anna and Cyn mutually recited.

"Exactly," Cyn nodded. "But the whole you-have-to-be-true-to-me-blah-blah-blah—it never works out. I guess if you're, like, thirty and you want to breed, it makes sense—which, by the way, is a disgusting thought."

"Being thirty or breeding?"

"Both."

Anna looped some hair behind her ear. "It seems like the relationship thing for me isn't quite working out, either."

"The difference is, you want one," Cyn clarified. She turned to check her reflection in the long mirrored wall that separated the living room from the kitchen of the suite and raked a hand through her messy black hair. Then she pulled her MAC makeup case out of her vintage Chanel purse for a quick repair job.

Do I want a relationship? Anna had certainly failed at her attempts at the friends-with-benefits thing multiple times. Maybe in another lifetime, on another planet, where there had never been a Cyn-and-Scott, she could have had that with Scott. But of course, in this alternate universe, Scott would actually have been attracted to her. One thing he'd said had stayed with her—she'd gotten very used, very quickly, to the idea that any guy she was interested in would be interested in her too. How presumptuous. But his I'm-just-not-that-into-you brush-off still smarted. She couldn't even give herself credit for having taken a risk in telling in the truth; she'd only done it because she'd been hypnotized. Her thoughts went from Scott to Ben, the only boy with whom she'd ever had a real relationship that amounted to anything. How honest had she been with him, really? Did that have anything to do with why he was so clearly rejecting her, not returning her phone calls? It hurt a lot more than what Scott had said, really.

Cyn shoved her makeup back into her purse. "You're thinking about Scott."

Anna took a moment to answer. *Honesty.* "Ben, actually."

"What's up with that?"

"Nothing." She was surprised at how the sadness of that confession hit her.

"You can't always get what you wa-ant." Cyn teasingly sang the old Rolling Stones tune. Then she switched tunes. "And if you can't be with the one you love, love the one you're with."

"You don't believe that.

Cyn popped up from the couch, then reached a hand down toward Anna. "No. But it's a lot easier than saying that I feel like shit. And now I have to fly home on the same plane as him."

"Change your flight."

"You're a genius. And I'll get a massage and a facial, too."

They hugged each other with the affection that only comes with a friendship where best friends have grown up together and know every little thing about each other. Many things made a good friend—someone you could talk to with a totally open heart. Shared interests. A person you loved to hang out with. Yet there was one more thing that should go on that list: history. It was irreplaceable.

"One more adventure for the Cyn-and-Anna chronicles," Anna noted, giving her friend another squeeze. "I hate saying good-bye to you."

"Puh-leeze," Cyn scoffed, stepping back from her friend. "It's never good-bye for us. And it never will be. Right?"

"Absolutely," Anna assured her. At a moment that was all about honesty, that was nothing but the truth.

"So, Vegas was quite the experience," Sam stated as the limo started to pull away from the hotel. The rain had slackened to a drizzle, but the Palms still looked defeated in the gloom, like a showgirl who'd slept until noon after spending the night with a stranger. "Who wants champagne?"

Anna wasn't sure that going to pick up Dee at the hospital was a champagneworthy moment, but she didn't say anything. Everyone was coping in their own way. After they got Dee, they'd hit the freeway back to Los Angeles, where they'd take her to Cedars-Sinai and get her checked in.

"We *so* need a soundtrack right now." Cammie rooted through the box of CDs that Sam had brought along as the limo waited to pull onto Flamingo Road.

"How about the Ramones' 'I Wanna Be Sedated'?" Adam suggested.

"Sick." Cammie laughed. "I love that about you. How about this?"

She slipped a CD into the player and pushed play. She craned her neck toward Adam. "The Donnas. Great band."

He pulled her close and kissed her; then they gazed into each other's eyes. Anna had no idea who the Donnas were, or why Cammie's playing their music suddenly made Adam so happy. She was just amazed that after their true confessions, they were still a couple obviously in love.

Love. What was it, really? How did you know when you were in it? She wanted to tap Adam on the shoulder and ask him, since he seemed in such bliss. She'd read somewhere that being in love produced endorphins that caused a natural high. Did anyone ever stay in that kind of love? Certainly her parents hadn't. She searched her mind for a long-term couple who still seemed to be really, truly in love. Definitely not Ben's parents. According to Ben, his mother was having a nervous breakdown over his father's gambling. So now that he was in Gamblers Anonymous, could she fall back in love with him again? Or maybe when love was badly damaged, a couple could never really recover.

If only there were a love version of the money-back guarantee. Then if you fell hard, as she had with Ben, and it didn't work out, your mind would simply erase the experience from your memory and you'd be brand-new again, without that wound on your heart or the scar tissue that formed around it.

Anna sighed and sank back into the petal-soft leather upholstery. Parker and Sam were sharing a single flute of champagne; which seemed odd, since there were certainly enough flutes to go around. Hadn't Sam said that Parker had hit on her? If he was doing it again, why was she letting him? Meanwhile, Cammie had climbed onto Adam's lap and they were furiously making out. In the past Adam had not been a fan of

PDA—public displays of affection. Yet here he was, definitely PDAing.

Anna turned to take one last look back at the Palms. She could certainly file this under New Experiences, and, after all, that had been what she'd wanted. Of course, she hadn't planned on Dee's break with reality. Who knew who the real Dee was?

She saw a taxi pull up to the hotel entrance.

Anna's heart flipped, leaped, somersaulted, then somersaulted again as the limo began turning right onto Flamingo Road.

"Stop!" she bellowed. "Stop the limo!"

The driver slammed on the brakes; everyone jerked forward.

"What the hell, Anna?" Cammie demanded.

But Anna was already out the door, running back to the entrance of the Palms. Ben turned and saw her.

Stratosphere

"Hi," Anna uttered softly. Finally, after all this time, they were standing face-to-face. Her heart was pounding and her knees felt weak, her breathing shallow and clammy. Her luggage was at her feet and the limo gone, having made a U-turn to bring it to her before departing again. There was absolutely no turning back.

"I came for you. Is that good?"

She tried to form a complete sentence. But words—the ally of her life—would not come to her. All she could manage was, "Very."

People were going to and fro all around, in and out of the hotel and casino, taxis pulling up and departing, a tour bus emptying out. Anna and Ben just stood there, their eyes locked. It wasn't until a valet told them that they had to move that they went inside. Anna stood by as Ben checked himself in and got a key card for his standard room on the seventh floor. Anna was grateful for the distraction. She was so nervous and so overwhelmed to be in his presence again that she still could hardly put two words together.

They rode the elevator in silence, got out on floor seven, and went together to room 714. It was well appointed but nothing special, with striped wallpaper and a king-size bed. Ben slung his small gray knapsack onto the floor and then sat on the edge of the bed. That was when Anna got a sudden flash: He was wearing jeans and a Princeton T-shirt—exactly what he'd had on when Anna had seen him for the first time, diagonally across the aisle from her in the first-class cabin of the flight from La Guardia Airport to LAX. He'd stood and pulled off his sweatshirt to reveal a V-cut hard body. Short brown hair, electric blue eyes, tall and rangy—Anna had immediately paid attention. Half an hour later, they'd been thisclose to joining the Mile-High Club in the first-class lavatory. It had been such an un–Anna Percy thing to do. It was also a cherished memory.

"You're wearing what you wore that first day." She sat on a chair across from him, not trusting herself to be next to him on the bed.

"On purpose."

She smiled, feeling slightly less like she'd need a defibrillator at any moment. "Why didn't you tell me you were coming?"

Ben scratched his chin. "I thought I'd surprise you. And . . . I don't know. I hate talking on the phone about anything serious. Why did everyone leave? Your message said you guys were all staying until tomorrow."

"That was the plan." Anna briefly told him about Dee.

"Wow," Ben muttered. "Someone in that triumvirate was bound to crack eventually. Sam, Cammie, Dee—we're not talking stable. But then, who the hell is?"

Indeed. Anna studied Ben's face—same startling blue eyes, same heart-shaped mouth, same soft lips. It took her breath away, just as it had the very first moment she'd set eyes on him, on the plane to Los Angeles. She remembered that Jane Austen had first titled *Pride and Prejudice* something else—*First Impressions*. Ben had made a wondrous first impression. Second impression, too.

"Were you glad I called?" Anna asked.

"Of course. God, Anna, you must know that."

Silence. Her eyes flitted from him to the tapestry bedspread, to the window, and back to him. If they sat here any longer, she was going to spring across the room and in about two seconds they'd be in that bed, naked. She was that powerfully attracted to him. But she had to be honest with herself: That wasn't what she wanted. Yet.

"You know what? There's this place called the Stratosphere that's supposed to have the best view of Vegas," Anna suggested, thinking it would be a good place to talk—better than any of the noisy restaurants downstairs, and offering less temptation than the close proximity of a hotel room. That was what she really wanted to do. To talk. Or at least that was what she told herself. "I read about it in one of the Vegas guides, and Sam and I were planning to go, but we never got around to it. Want to?"

She could not tell what he was thinking.
"Sure, why not?"

The Stratosphere was another hotel and casino, this
one located at the eastern end of the Strip. Its claim to
fame was a Space Needle–like tower that jutted high into
the sky, more than a thousand feet above the city. It was
reputed to be the tallest observation tower in the country, and the tallest building west of the Mississippi River.
The elevator ride to the top took thirty-five seconds.
There was a three-hundred-and-sixty-degree indoor/out-
door observation area at the top, plus a restaurant and
bar. To complete the Stratosphere experience, there were
a series of sky-high thrill rides designed to make passengers think that they actually might be flung off the tower
and down to the asphalt below.

The place was packed, even at noontime. Anna heard
several different languages being spoken, and the line for
the thrill rides was already quite long. There had been a
fortuitous break in the weather; the rain had stopped,
and the sun was fighting its way through the clouds.

Anna was standing by the glass window, looking
back toward the Strip and out at the sprawl that was
contemporary Las Vegas. Beyond that was the endless
desert. She'd seen the same view from Brock's mansion.
But what stunned her now was the huge amount of res-
idential development. This was a big city, where regular
people lived in regular houses and went to regular jobs.
She found that comforting. The glitz and the glory of

the Strip was great, even energizing. But it was nice to know that real people lived here too.

Ben slipped an arm around her waist. "What a view, huh?"

"Yeah." She leaned into him and thought about how fantastic it would be to soar out into the blue. "Dee once asked me if I'd rather be invisible or be able to fly."

"Easy. Fly." Ben smiled. "Up over all the shit. Over my parents, my school . . . Works for me."

She pressed her hands against his arms and turned her head to look at him. "Is school shit?"

"Sometimes. And sometimes it's great." He touched her hair above the nape of her neck. "Is that really what you want to do, talk about Princeton?"

No. She leaned forward and kissed him softly, right next to his mouth. Then suddenly their lips were together, and it all came rushing back—lust at thirty thousand feet with a boy she'd just met. Even now, after everything they'd shared, Anna still wasn't sure that she really knew Ben.

She pulled away, breathless.

"Let's go back to the hotel," he whispered into her hair.

"I don't . . . I'm not . . ."

"You want me to make love to you, Anna."

Very true. But that had been their mistake in the first place: too much, too fast.

"I do want you," she admitted hastily. "That's never been a problem."

"So then—"

"I don't know if we're . . . I didn't invite you here for sex."

He raised a wry eyebrow. "What, then? This view?"

"That's not what I . . . What I want is . . ."

"You want this," he insisted, and pulled her close again. When he kissed her, everything melted. Maybe that was why she'd fallen for him so hard, so fast. Because she was always so much in her head, and Ben took her someplace else entirely. But she knew that if they went back to the hotel and fell into each other's arms, they'd still have to face each other afterward. So she decided to face it all now instead and edged away from him, telling herself to be honest and let the chips fall where they might. How apt for Sin City.

"I'm confused," Anna said simply.

"By what? Me?"

"Somewhat. After you went back to Princeton, I thought it was the best thing."

"So did I, at least for a while."

"I even tried to meet some other guys. A TV producer, a surfing instructor . . ."

Ben's smile was open. "Sounds like you went for the full Los Angeles experience. Next you need to date one of the Lakers."

Anna shook her head. "I don't like guys that tall."

"What happened with all these—well, what were they? You're talking like they were experiments."

"They were, in a way," Anna told him, as a huge family in matching touristy Las Vegas T-shirts approached the window next to them, so close that she and Ben had to edge back toward the entrance. "Because in the end, it never worked out."

"Is there a reason for that?"

"I could never get you out of my head. Somehow, I knew we weren't over. At least, that's what my heart was saying." Her eyes searched his. "Does that make any sense at all?"

"Yeah."

"Your turn," Anna said, feeling incredibly unburdened. It hadn't been easy to be that honest, but it had been worth it. "What happened to you at Princeton?"

An announcement over the Stratosphere speaker system touted the newest and scariest ride, something called Insanity. Ben had to wait for the announcement to end before he could answer. "No more lies?"

"Right," she agreed. "No more lies."

He exhaled loudly. "I'm seeing someone at school."

Anna felt the blood drain from her face, surprised at how much the news hurt her. "So I guess your father was wrong, then."

"About?"

"Never mind. No. Not never mind. I'm going to tell you." She peered down at the city again, wondering if there was someone else down there who was getting the same kind of devastating news that she was getting up here, at the exact same time. It was possible. Somewhere out there in the big world, it was actually probable. "I ran into your dad at an Oscar party. He said you still cared about me. A lot. So what is it? You came to Las Vegas so that we could hook up? Cheating on—what's her name, anyway?"

Ben bristled. "Her name is Blythe, but don't jump to conclusions, Anna. I'm not in love with her. We're not some big, exclusive thing. I've only been seeing her for a little while."

Anna breathed a little easier. "Is it serious?"

"No."

"Could it get serious?" she pressed.

"Come with me," Ben instructed.

"What?"

"Just come." He took her arm and led her partway around the indoor observation deck until they reached a door that led outside. They went through it and onto a concrete platform that extended all the way around the tower. The air was fresh, the breeze fairly stiff. A high fence made the area completely safe.

"We needed a change of venue. For me to tell you that I cared about you more than I've ever cared about any girl. Don't you know that? God, Anna, I couldn't even stand the thought of not being with you. I was ready to blow off school to be with you."

A flight of pigeons suddenly took off somewhere beneath their deck. Anna watched them wheel and turn against the afternoon sky. "True. But that's not love."

"I don't think either one of us is in a position to lecture the other one on love, okay?"

She nodded. He was right. Sometimes she felt as if everything she'd learned about love had come from reading *Jane Eyre*; her personal experience was woefully lacking. Certainly her own parents were far from being role models. Evidently, so were Ben's.

"You think I liked seeing myself turn into some kind of love-struck asshole?" Ben continued. "I kept thinking, Don't be that guy. But I couldn't make myself forget you." He turned away from her, staring out at the Strip below. "It took a long time, once I got back at school, for me to even like myself again."

"I'm so sorry," she whispered.

"I'm not blaming you, Anna, I did it to myself. You have to admit, you sent me some pretty mixed messages, too."

"So . . . I guess neither of us knows anything about love."

"At last, something we can agree on." He wiped a hand across his forehead. "I do know this: It scares the shit out of me."

"Me too," Anna ventured.

"But I didn't come to Vegas to tell you that. And I didn't come just to hook up with you, either." His gaze caught hers. "We have this thing, Anna. Something." He laughed lightly. "Yeah, real articulate. What I'm saying is, I still want you."

Anna wanted to throw her arms around him. She wanted to run away as fast as she could, too.

"Geez, give me a sign here," Ben prompted. "I want us to try again. Do you?"

His right arm snaked around her slender waist, and

she leaned into him, both of them gazing out at the endless view; bright lights, infinite possibilities. She was at least as scared as he was, that was a certainty. There was Blythe back at Princeton. There were no guarantees. They were alone in a city that neither of them knew. Just him, her, this moment, the truth.

"Yes," Anna told him. "I do."